To all my fans who believed in me when I traded pictures for words.

First Published 2011

ISBN: 978-0-9871511-1-7

THE MEMORY'S WAKE TRILOGY

Book One - Memory's Wake

Book Two - Hope's Reign

Book Three - Providence Unveiled

www.memoryswake.com

Memory's Wake

BY S.A. FENECH

CHAPTER ONE

I'm falling, she thought.

Rushing air tore at her like claws and her stomach churned. She knew only darkness and the horrible, hateful wind.

She jolted into consciousness as if waking from a nightmare, one so real, so intense, it left her soul shaken. All she remembered from her dream was the noise; a furious, bellowing rumble, like the call of a hungry dragon from a dark and twisted fairytale. It turned her insides as much as the sensation of falling. Now awake, she couldn't understand why she still heard it, why she still felt like she plummeted into hell. Some other sound teased her, unidentifiable, lost in the wind.

"What's happening? Is someone calling me? Where am I?" Pain rampaged through her and the questions fell away. Her scream twisted

into a whimper.

A voice reached her. Persistent, hysterical, all static and unclear sounds.

She called out, tearing her throat raw with effort, trying to reach through the gusting void to whatever had spoken. "Can't hear. Please help, it hurts!"

The talking stopped. The wailing wind and painful rumbling continued. Her insides rattled as if her ribcage had been hollowed out and filled with marbles. She thought she might throw up.

The feeling of hands grabbing her forced out a harsh scream. Then, like slamming a door on a windy day, the tearing air stopped and the world became solid. Her skin still tingled right to her fingertips but the pain had gone, replaced by burning in her chest. Panic crawled up her back, tugging at her with icy fingers.

Stop. Look. Feel, she ordered herself, attempting slow breaths.

Her eyes stung as they opened. Dark hair hung around her face, curtaining her vision. She lay on the ground, face down. Had she fallen? Her body hurt all over, so maybe she had. Old blackened leaves spread in front of her eyes and the smell of dirt and rot added to her lingering nausea. Sharp twigs poked through her jeans. She spat soil from her mouth.

That other voice spoke again. "By the fae, what has happened? Can you hear me now?" It was a girl's voice, young, like her own. A strange accent made it curiously elegant and musical. The tremor of fear in it only made it more so.

Fighting the weakness in her body, she nodded to the voice and managed to roll over. She propped herself up on her elbows and looked out into a twilit forest of wild briars and giant trees. Beside her, another girl crouched on the ground; plump but strikingly pretty, with skin and hair so pale it was almost white against the shadowed woods.

The long hair tumbled all around the stranger, making her look like a beautiful, scared ghost.

Their breathing matched each other's; fast, labored, scared out of their minds. An intense frown of thought and calculation marred Ghost-girl's face, the look of a mind weighing options, assessing risks, looking for answers. In her own head she could feel nothing but the fractures of stress upon her sanity.

She stared at Ghost-girl, hoping for some recognition. No name came to her, but she felt a strange connection to the pale girl, almost a physical attraction. She wondered what it could mean and coughed out a giggle, hysteria rising. This didn't seem like the time to be questioning her sexuality. Her thoughts scattered in all directions, racing frantically, searching for answers to the growing crowd of questions. Every one drew a blank.

"Alward?" Ghost-girl called out into the trees. "Alward? Oh no, he didn't make it through." Wide green eyes, shadowed and full of fear, darted from the surrounding woods back onto her. "I'm not where I ought to be. Did you do this, did you bring me here? Was it magic of yours? How did you come to be caught within my Veil door?"

She could only gape at Ghost-girl. *Magic? Is that why my skin's tingling like this? But magic's not real.* She wasn't sure she could say just now what was or wasn't real, but the accusations confused and stung. She was sure she hadn't done any *bringing.* There must have been some kind of accident, she thought, feeling like the victim of something. She worked hard to find words again. "What..." She paused. So many questions, where to start? "What happened?"

Ghost-girl looked at her with a wary frown. "You don't know? Please, it is important you tell me the truth. If you are a caster of unauthorized magic, know I'm not an enemy." She made a complex hand gesture. When no response came, the girl's frown turned from

wary to scared. She gasped and spoke as though to herself. "Unless... no, you couldn't be one of Thayl's wizard hunters?"

"Whose what hunters?" Her words slurred. "Was there an accident? Shouldn't we get help?" She sat up and brushed hair from her face, wincing when she touched a tender area under her eye.

"You are hurt, but I don't know how, I don't..." Ghost-girl's voice worked up into the high pitch of panic, and she visibly swallowed it down. "I need to find out where I am." She turned away, reached down and dug her fingers into the earth, then spoke too quietly to hear. The ground trembled into a shiver, growing outwards, expanding quickly, up tree trunks, along branches, tickling the leaves at the treetops. A thousand voices whispered.

Brilliant. I'm hallucinating. She put a hand to her forehead, dizzied by the disembodied voices. *How hurt am I? Concussion? Brain damage?*

The blonde was talking nonsense again, words flying. "...too close to home. The Veil door didn't take me far enough away. They've found me, already? The hunters, they're coming this way. We have to go! Please, I don't know how you came to be here, but listen. There are people chasing me. If they find you here, they'll think that you're one of us. We have to run." She stood in a cascade of crumpled dress, face turned up toward the canopy of woven branches screening the dimming sky. "They're almost here, and their beast... their dragon..."

Everything was on fast forward. With her face half hidden behind black hair, she thought maybe she could let herself cry. It was too much, too many words, too much chaos, to still feel so empty inside. Each question seemed to tear a new hole, leaving her more hollow. She needed to pause, rewind, start finding answers, before there was nothing left to tear.

"Do I know you?" Speaking the words out loud jolted her physically. She whimpered, squeezed her eyes shut and tried to hold her head together so tightly her hair ripped. She felt the touch of Ghost-girl's hand, plump and gentle on her own. Not a ghost after all.

"I do not know you, but I can't have you caught here when they are hunting for me. Come with me. My name is Eloryn." The blonde smiled but the urgency in her features soured the expression.

"I'm... My name is..." Nothing. Nothing at all.

Her emptiness. It came into perfect, terrifying clarity. She knew nothing of who she was.

No name.

No home.

No memories.

Only a void where her life should have been.

The canopy above them shuddered as violently as her heart. An impossible creature filled her vision. It crushed through the trees, talons reaching for Eloryn. The hungry dragon from her dream. *Of course, I'm still dreaming. Ghosts, wizards, dragons, none of those are real.* But the claws were so sharp, so vivid. Squeezing Eloryn's hand tighter, she reacted, pulling Eloryn out of the way before the razor tips could strike. "Go!" she screamed, to herself, to Eloryn, or the dragon above them she didn't know, but they all began to move.

The dragon writhed, reaching for them from between the massive oaks above. Branches groaned and splintered against the beast's strength, creating a hail of sharp twigs and leaves. Strong trunks held back the black mass and it hissed in frustration, talons swiping just above the girls' heads.

"This way!" Eloryn pulled her by the hand, still holding tight. The girls crashed and stumbled through briars and over fallen logs slick with moss.

Through the grim grey trees, men in leather military jackets ran toward them. Orders were yelled, metal flashed, boots crushed ferns,

thumping the ground with heavy feet. Wings beat in the sky above, blowing about dirt and dry leaves. Talons raked at the tree line. The girls ran faster, hand in hand. The dragon roared.

Eloryn dragged her on through the woods, petticoats catching and pulling, slowing them down. In tight jeans she had more freedom to move but her legs felt weak, wobbly. She barely kept up with Eloryn. The hunters were so close.

To her left, a bear-sized man came within reach. She cried out, pushing her body to move faster. Her vision blurred, sweat running into her eyes. She cringed, expecting the feel of rough hands locking around her arm, pulling her down. Nothing came. She turned to see why. The man was gone. She tried to look for her pursuer and still watch the treacherous ground under her feet. Trees flashed past. Shadows flashed between them, toward her. Something struck another man, just to her right. A dark form dropped from the branches above, bringing him to the ground.

A cry of pain and one more hunter was gone.

The trees above cracked as the dragon plunged again. Lichen shook from the bark and fell like green snow. She ran on, begging herself to wake up. Breathing burned her chest and rattled in her throat, but a deep inner dread kept her running hard. These men, chasing her, hungry for the hunt, boiled her emotions down to pure, distilled panic.

Still dragging her onwards by a hand, she heard Eloryn struggling to breathe as well, and something else, a mumbling between each crying breath. The running became easier. Fewer branches blocked their path. Fewer brambles and thorns tore at them. The ancient trees moved, bending away from her and Eloryn, then closing back in to hinder their pursuers. She blinked but the impossible images remained.

Reaching a sudden steep incline, Eloryn let go of her hand and ran toward a rocky outcrop. "In here!" she called out and disappeared

into a dark crack in the mountain side.

Moving to follow Eloryn, the girl slowed, faint from exhaustion. Her vision dimmed and starred. Staring at that thin sliver of black, ringed by unwelcoming rocks, she shivered. Silly, she thought, to be scared of the dark, knowing what danger chased them there. She drew haggard breaths, and made her way over loose stones.

Just a step away, a creature landed in front of her, blocking the cave entrance. The shock stole her precious breath in a gasp. It also stole her balance. Scrambling backwards she fell hard onto the forest floor. No, not a beast, she saw, looking up from the ground. The figure looked back down with concerned human eyes. A young man; dirty and tattered and animal in nature, but a man. Soil darkened his skin and earth brown hair hung down bare shoulders in knotted locks. His knuckles were reddened with blood. She lay there like a deer in headlights, unable to move.

And then there were more men, pushing through the trees, growing more furious as they battled against the forest itself. Eloryn had left her, long gone into the slim crack in the mountainside. There was nowhere to go. Surrounded with the hunters behind and the beast-man blocking the way forward, she lay dumbfounded.

She wished her brain would work. Wished she'd just wake up. The beast-man reached down for her. She cowered but could see only worry in his features. Grabbing her arm, he lifted and threw her into the cave. She tumbled, barely missing Eloryn who crouched inside with her head against the stone, talking to herself.

The lost girl looked out through the cave entrance, shaking with adrenaline. The beast man stared back in. His eyes shone piercing blue even in the fading light. His shoulders shifted as though he was about to follow, but with the deep growl of a hunting cat he turned around.

The remaining men ran at the cave and the ground shook. Stones scraped against each other, tumbling and falling in a dangerous tide and the cave entrance sealed.

For the second time in the brief, harsh moments of her memory, all she knew was darkness.

CHAPTER TWO

Earlier.

Why has it become so hard just to keep my mind on a simple book? Focus, Eloryn ordered herself. Her eyes skimmed over words without absorbing any meaning. She pinched her forehead and flicked back a page, trying to find the last information she'd actually retained from *The Principles and History of Infantry Warfare.* Alward no doubt had his reasons for making this dull book part of her syllabus but she couldn't see how it would ever be much use to her, either for her teaching or in practice. If she was learning things she couldn't share with her own students, she'd prefer to be studying magic.

Learning used to be easy. As a child, Eloryn already knew everything Alward taught the farmers' children. She went to classes with them

anyway, enjoying being with the other students. They stopped coming at age ten, schooled enough for their lives tending fields. She became a teacher herself after that while her own education continued. Now at sixteen, teaching felt repetitive, and she rarely saw anyone her own age. Apart from her small clutch of young students she rarely saw anyone at all. They lived alone, just herself and Alward, here in the fortified old monastery high in the wooded hills, set apart even from the tiny rural hamlet; a place where no one might recognize Alward, or herself, for who they really were. A place they could be safe.

Eloryn brushed against the pink flowers that spilt over the garden wall where she sat. They released a syrupy fragrance and she breathed it deeply, hoping to quell the unnamed ache in her chest.

"Riddip."

Grateful for a distraction, Eloryn smiled to the speckled frog who hopped up onto her knee. "Kiss you? Why do you want me to kiss you?"

"Riddip."

Eloryn giggled. "Oh, a handsome prince under a curse, and just one kiss from a beautiful princess will set you free? I've known you since you were a tadpole, little fool." Eloryn poked him and imagined he smirked bashfully in return. But really, he always looked like that. "I shouldn't have read you that story." Eloryn sighed. Night approached, stealing away the friendly light. The high stone courtyard walls loomed over her. "I shouldn't have read me that story."

"Riddip."

"I don't know. There might be romance like that out there, and adventure and charming princes, but not here. Those things happen in places far, far away."

"Riddip."

"Shush! Really." Eloryn dropped her voice to a scandalized

whisper. "Owain only comes by to deliver produce for us. I'm sure he's taken little notice of me."

But she couldn't say she hadn't noticed him, with his feathery brown hair and strong wide shoulders. Eloryn closed her eyes and turned her face into the sun, enjoying the last few warm rays. Rather than focusing on infantry warfare, Eloryn found herself developing tactics to be the one to greet Owain on his next visit. She wondered what it would be like to hold his work-worn hands, and the heat from the sun's touch spread through her whole body.

"Eloryn!"

Eloryn jumped and a deep blush bloomed on her face.

Alward bellowed from his chamber window overlooking the courtyard. "In here. Quickly!"

The urgency in his tone made her bolt to her feet, dropping book and frog from her lap. She whispered a sorry to her friend and puffed her way up the stairwell to Alward's quarters.

Inside, Alward had shoved all the furniture aside to clear the space, knocking precious books off shelves in the process. Shards of a broken porcelain cup lay ignored in a puddle of still steaming tea, and the floor mat had been lifted and thrown over an armchair. Alward wore his normal grey suit, the top buttons now undone and sleeves rolled up. He hunched over the floor, scrawling magical symbols and words in charcoal. Eloryn recognized with excited fear what he was doing. The workings of a Veil door.

"Ellie." Alward stood up to inspect his work. Pushing his glasses back up his nose he left a line of black soot behind. His graying blond hair, tied back in its usual ponytail, frayed and escaped from its bonds. "We have to go; we've been found. I don't know how. Someone in the village perhaps recognized me. I'm sorry child. Hurry, fetch the pack."

Eloryn's mouth turned dry. She always knew they could be found,

but one thought stormed through her head, leaving her dazed. *Why now? Why have they found us now?* Her chest tightened. *Please don't let this be my fault.*

Forcing her body to move, she went to a large wooden chest and unlocked it with a spoken behest, pulling out a packed bag that had been prepared for just this day. Alward still focused on the complex spell words, so to keep busy and calm her nerves, Eloryn took a fresh loaf from Alward's desk and tucked it into the top of the leather satchel.

Alward called her to his side and she skittered to him, stepping carefully within the wide ring of soot-black words and trying to hide her shaking. She tilted her head back to look up into his face, which had begun showing the deeper lines of age. A crash of noise rattled up from the monastery entrance, making Eloryn gasp. Alward's eyes darkened and he put a hand on her shoulder.

"It will all be well, my girl. The spell is set. Stay close to me. Be brave, the experience is not pleasant." His expression held sad secrets she often saw when their eyes met. It sometimes made her wonder if he was disappointed in her, in his responsibility to care for her. Her heart leaped about and she clung to the leather pack as though it were a stuffed doll.

The charcoal words hummed and glowed when Alward began incanting in his gravelly voice. The Veil door was a long and complicated spell that most would have to read from a page, but Alward knew the ancient words well from years of study. The spell markings on the floor exploded into magical fire, and tendrils of smoke twisted around them, moving in unnatural ways. The vapor enveloped them. Eloryn watched as her own body began to take on the likeness of the smoke, shimmering into the Veil. It was wondrous, terrifying and painful.

She turned to Alward for reassurance and saw a stranger standing in the doorway.

Eloryn cried out a warning. Lost in his focus on the spell, Alward continued to chant.

The man at the doorway also called out and more men joined him, pouring into the room. One man, with a scarred face and lion's mane hair, drew a fine crossbow. He shot a splinter-sized dart that lodged itself into Alward's chest.

Alward's form became solid. Light exploded in the room, knocking back the other men. Magical fire and living smoke, no longer under control, sparked and hissed, shifting like violent shadows. Whipping mists ripped into Eloryn, still caught within the Veil, barely there.

Alward strained toward Eloryn with charcoal blackened hands. She reached back but her hand passed through his, and she was gone.

In the black of the cave, Eloryn took a moment to ease the burning in her throat and stifle the sob building in her chest. She choked. Asking the rocks to fall had seemed clever at first but now she wasn't so sure. Dust hung in the air, thick and invisible in the darkness, clogging her throat with each breath.

At least I'm safe now. Safe until Alward can find me again. Eloryn pressed her bottom lip between her teeth. Safe, maybe, but she'd already made grave mistakes. The strange girl had even seen her using unauthorized magic. Girl? She had taken her to be a boy at first, wearing what she did. Maybe it was a disguise? The girl even refused to share her name. She could be hiding something too.

Now Eloryn only needed to cast a simple behest, one of the few

authorized spells every person in Avall knew. The behest for light. "Àlaich las."

Her request granted, the wisp appeared, creating a soft glow around Eloryn's hand and illuminating the girl across the tunnel. Her strangely trimmed hair, short, ragged and roughed up at the back and long at the front, was rich black and... pink? *Could hair be pink?* She cast her gaze over the girl's face and its odd metal pins and gems, pierced through nose, lips, eyebrows, sparkling against obvious bruising. The injuries weren't from their recent chase. The yellow swelling of the girl's jaw and purple around her eye had matured a good few hours. The hand the girl pressed to her forehead had fought some battle, with grated knuckles and blood around her fingernails. She moved with stiffness and hesitation that told of other pain throughout her body.

Worry nagged at Eloryn. Just moments out of his care and she already longed for Alward's guidance. She remembered tumbling through the Veil, turning to wait for Alward to follow, and instead seeing this girl. Screaming. Shimmering in and out of existence.

How, how could she possibly have appeared there, caught in the Veil like that? None of this makes sense. How could I begin to guess her motives? Eloryn pulled her shoulders up to her ears to fight off a chilling shiver. *No, she's no older than me, just a girl, scared and lost. And it's my fault she's here. At least I won't be alone.*

Eloryn smiled at the girl and tried to keep her voice level. "We should keep moving, if you are well enough to."

The girl didn't respond. She leant against the rough stones, half bent over, chanting under her breath. Eloryn listened closer, but the girl wasn't using the language of a behest. Shaking violently, she willed herself over and over to wake up, to wake up from this horrible dream.

"Let me help you." Eloryn reached out but the girl shied away and edged farther along the rock wall.

Her head flicked up. She glared at Eloryn with oddly familiar eyes rimmed in thick black that ran down her face in dried tears. "What have you done to me? Why can't I remember anything? Not anything! Have you used some kind of... magic on me?"

Eloryn backed away. *Did you do this, did you bring me here? Was it magic of yours?* She'd made similar accusations just moments ago. Now on the receiving end, they hurt.

"It wasn't me, I, I didn't..." Eloryn said. "You don't remember anything at all?"

"No!" the girl snapped back. The sharp word echoed against the rocks around them.

A deep growl answered from the darkness, reverberating like distant thunder. With a turn of her hand Eloryn shifted the light. They stood in a twisted crack of tunnel that opened into a large cavern. The rough ceiling hung with dry and broken stalactites, the floor scattered with their fallen remains like a rocky bone yard. Deep amid the shadows and gloom, she swore she saw movement.

"We have to go," said Eloryn. "We're not safe here."

The girl made no effort to leave. She put her hands over her ears and sank further toward the ground.

"Please!" said Eloryn.

"I don't even know my name," the girl said, her words broken by a shiver.

"I'll give you a name," Eloryn promised in desperation. She'd never had anything she needed to name. Things spoke with her as she could speak with them. They already had their own names. Only one thought came to her. "Memory. Your name is Memory."

The girl looked both horrified and amused. "You're cruel."

"I'm sorry." Eloryn tried to think of an alternative, but the girl – Memory – stood up.

"No, it's... it's OK. It's better than nothing." Her voice still shook as much as her hands, which she wedged under her armpits, but the glaze of confusion had left her eyes.

Eloryn nodded to Memory, then turned and took a tentative step forward, crunching twigs that had gathered at the mouth of the cave.

The scattering of pebbles echoed back. Something crawled toward them through the dark. Eloryn mentally flicked through pages of her reference books. What lives like this? Animal or fairy-kind? What other clues did she have? She looked down and saw the sticks under her feet were in fact old, fragile bones. A slithering chatter of dark words ricocheted down the cavern walls. Eloryn realized what the creatures were before they came into view. She gasped.

"What is...?" Memory's question cut off as the monstrous shapes shambled into the light.

Flesh eaters, cave dwellers, unseelie fae. The illustrations didn't do them justice. Human in shape but larger and malformed, the creatures were long armed, with grey hanging skin that rippled underneath, as though they were made from dripping mud. Eyes like deep holes were set in their angled skulls, black and without shine. Their yellowed teeth, too big for their mouths, smelt of death. Eloryn's first sight of trolls shook her to the core.

"I'm guessing they aren't your friends either?" Memory whispered.

"They shouldn't hurt us. We should be protected by the Pact."

"*Shouldn't* doesn't really do it for me right now. Like monsters *shouldn't* be real."

Eloryn took a deep breath, also finding no comfort in her words. They were in the trolls' territory. The Pact would give them no protection here. Eloryn could hear the twisted voices of the creatures, speaking of their desire to crunch small bones. Her stomach lurched. The trolls moved closer, but circled, keeping their distance, testing

an invisible boundary. They hissed in frustration. One repeated word reached Eloryn from the mess of whispers; *Forbidden.*

"This way." Eloryn stepped between the piles of bones, edging around the side of the cavern to another tunnel.

Memory followed close behind, barely taking her wide eyes off the trolls. She picked up a large bone, holding its broken end outwards like a weapon. The trolls laughed in response; a harsh noise, like the bones crackling under their feet. They gathered at the edge of the light, coming to them from all the dark crevices of the cave, forming a wall of sharp toothed monsters.

Eloryn whispered, "When we reach that tunnel, just run. It's small. They might fit but we'll move faster."

"What if we get stuck in there? What if we can't get out?"

"Please, trust me," Eloryn said.

One ambitious troll surged forward and Memory swung the bone blade. It crumbled against the troll like chalk across a stone. She dropped the useless bone, but the troll backed away, choking laughter again. Just a few more tricky steps from the tunnel entrance and more trolls tensed to lunge.

"Run, now!" Eloryn cried, then spoke her words to the earth.

A trunk sized stalactite fell, crashing down between them and the trolls, shards and dust flying. Eloryn bolted into the tunnel. Memory tripped, stumbling into her. The tunnel floor dropped in front of them. Eloryn's knees gave way and they both fell forward, rolling down the uneven rocks and steep slope faster than they would have dared to run. Hips and elbows cracked into rocks, and hands cut as she reached out to slow her fall. The tunnel's descent smoothed and they washed up on top of a pile of broken pebbles and bones.

A blow to Eloryn's chest left her sucking breath back into flattened lungs. Fortunately she'd chosen not to wear a corset today. She

directed the glowing wisp back up the tunnel. Through the smallest gap between bends a few determined trolls could be seen making a less clumsy descent.

"Have to keep going." She got to her feet too quickly and scraped her head, the tunnel roof too low to stand fully. Wincing from the sharp sting, she was too slow to warn Memory from doing the same. The girl spat a word Eloryn didn't know. She guessed it was a curse.

They dashed over uneven ground, deeper into the mountain through the winding tunnel. Openings branched out on either side but Eloryn led on without hesitation, a clear direction whispered to her by the life in the earth. The tunnel stayed tight by their shoulders, sometimes pressing in closer and making them squeeze sideways through the narrow gaps, sometimes dropping in height, making them crawl. The sound of the trolls' pursuit faded away and the girls slowed to a tired stumble.

Eloryn's heart ached for the strange girl who blindly followed her like a lost animal almost as much as it ached for herself. Once enough stale air returned to her lungs, Eloryn gave answers to unspoken questions. She explained that the tunnel would lead them to Maerranton. The men chasing her might also head that way, it being the nearest major city, but the tunnel would be faster than travelling over the steep and heavily wooded mountain.

"Why are they chasing us?" Memory asked.

The very question Eloryn didn't want to answer. She couldn't tell the truth but it seemed wrong to lie to someone with no memory. What if that was a lie, that Memory remembered nothing? Alward often chided her for being too trusting. *Just give the simplest details,* she told herself.

"My guardian is a wanted man. Those who associate with him are also considered to be criminals. They will no doubt believe you were with us too, having seen us together. I'm sorry. Please believe that he's a good man though, that we are no harm to anyone."

"You said 'Wizard Hunters' before. Is it not allowed, being a wizard? Doing that stuff you were doing?"

Eloryn cringed, and planned her words. "All but the simplest of behests have been outlawed." Eloryn shook her head, upset at herself. "Alward, he would be furious if he knew I had been casting in front of a stranger. You wouldn't... I hope..."

"Turn you in for it? No chance." Memory looked as if she could laugh. She waved a hand toward Eloryn's wisp that lit their way. "I feel crazy even talking about magic like it's real, but I'm seeing it right now so I guess I'm crazy."

"The magic," Eloryn continued, "it could explain your memory loss. When a powerful spell goes wrong, it can often steal memories. A Veil door is a very powerful spell..."

"And it really went wrong? Ugh, just thinking about how that felt is all kinds of wrong, like the worst thing ever." Memory shuddered. "But worse."

Eloryn shook too, remembering reaching for Alward, her hand passing through his, leaving him behind. "It was interrupted. I went in and where I came out wasn't where we planned. It shouldn't have been possible, but you were there, caught part way, stuck between the world and the Veil. I helped pull you free."

"Thanks, for that. Damn lucky you didn't just leave me stuck there," Memory said.

Eloryn blushed. "It didn't occur to me to do so."

Memory did laugh this time. "It probably would have been the right decision by the sounds of things. I was a perfect escape goat for the slaughter."

Did she mean scapegoat? Eloryn's face flushed even more and she looked away. *Who would consider doing such a thing?*

"But thanks, anyway, for not," Memory added.

A loud grumble from Memory's stomach broke the awkward silence. They had been walking for what felt like hours, and Eloryn noticed her own stomach was also hollow and hurting.

"Will you share some food with me? I have enough for us both." Eloryn tried to hide the pain in her voice. It should have been her and Alward sharing this bread. She took it from where it sat upon the travelling cloaks that covered her and Alward's most precious belongings. She tore the loaf and handed half to Memory.

"God this is good. Thanks. I don't know when I last ate. Literally," Memory said with a stuffed mouth.

"I wish I knew how you appeared, that I could give you more answers. Whether you were in the forest already, or it brought you from somewhere else, or..." Eloryn let her musings fade out. She had read other explanations in Alward's research. Darker, scarier, more complicated alternatives she would keep to herself, not wanting to give more worry to her already confused companion.

"I wish even more I knew where I was before that. I mean, how am I supposed to find my way home?"

"Alward," Eloryn mumbled between nibbling on her bread. A flash fire of guilt passed through her to say his name. What would he say, when he found out it was her fault they were found? "He spent much of his life studying the Veil and doorway spells. He must know everything there is to know about them." Eloryn hesitated. She had to decide once and for all whether she would trust this girl. Her heart could find nothing to distrust, felt only warmth and sadness for her, empathy stronger than the warnings that came to her in Alward's voice. "We have another home in the south of Avall, on Rhynn island, that we were to go to if we were found here. That is where I am going and... You can come too, if you like. It is at least part my fault to have brought you into this danger, so I will help you as best I can, and am sure Alward will too."

"If you think he can help me get my memories back, help me get home, I'm Team Magic all the way."

"I'm sure he can." Even though they were separated, Alward would come for her, and if he couldn't find her he would wait for her on Rhynn. Those men couldn't catch him, couldn't hold him. He was too clever, too powerful, and she needed him. She fought back a persistent fear that tore at the fringes of her thoughts.

The two girls trudged onwards, dragging their tired bodies through the rough tunnel.

"Just one more question," Memory asked after a short silence. "Is life always like this?"

CHAPTER THREE

She had looked at him as if he were some kind of animal. Worse.
A monster. The terror in her eyes crushed his heart, as though the
rockslide that closed the cave entrance had also fallen on it.

He had waited for her for so long. He ran the moment he heard
the noise, that same gusting howl he remembered from his first night
in this world, coming from the very same spot. The night he would
never forget. Just how long had it been? The years felt longer for being
unable to count them, but shorter for his time spent with the fae.
So long, lost in that forest, doubting he'd ever see her again, that his
memories of her were even real. But here she was, looking just the
same. Same age, same hair, same clothes, even the same bruises as the
day he had lost her. He no longer doubted.

The dust from the rockslide cleared and the hunting men who had chased the girls still surrounded him. Them and the dragon. It circled above, waiting for something. To give the men their next order? He shifted his eyes upwards uneasily. He'd never seen a dragon before. They were legendary, even to the fae he knew, and scarce.

The men coughed and swore, wiping dirt from their eyes. They looked at him, wondering how he fitted into their chase, turning to their leader for guidance. He'd been mistaken as an animal by hunters before. He didn't like hunters. A growl rumbled from his throat.

If it hadn't been for him, those men would have caught her. He would not let anyone hurt her again. Not now that he was stronger. Getting out of this corner himself mightn't be so easy, but he had the advantage. This was his forest.

He sized up each of the men, picking the weakest of the herd. That bald one, who stood there puffing with a little too much weight and already winded from the chase. He sprang at the man without warning. Landing on his rounded shoulders with both feet, he pushed off, using the man's height to launch higher. He burst through a spray of leaves and wrapped a hand onto a thick branch, swinging himself up onto another. Behind him the men milled about, delayed by confusion, too busy yelling at each other over their lost prey.

Their voices grew dim behind him. He ran across branches as though they were solid ground.

His mind raced even faster. *Why didn't she recognize me? Have I changed that much?* He couldn't remember the last time he'd seen a mirror. That sort of thing lost its meaning out here in the woods, until today. Seeing her again made him think of things he hadn't thought of for half a lifetime. Things like mirrors, showers, soap.

The hunters were far behind by the time he slowed and dropped back to the forest floor. He brought his hands up in front of his face.

Black earth and muck painted his pale skin. He picked up his pace again, heading to the nearest stream.

He stopped abruptly. He wasn't thinking straight. He'd finally found her again, and lost her within the same moment. Washing could wait. He had to go after her, and he would need help.

"Mina?" He didn't call loudly. She always heard him anyway. It was up to her if she came or not. He knelt down on a patch of moss between the vast trees and lichen-covered boulders, preparing himself to wait for her arrival.

"You didn't have to call me. We're already here." She giggled behind him, her voice more familiar to him than his own.

He stood back up and turned to see Mina, accompanied by a large host of other fairies. No matter how often he saw them, he never got over the sight of the fae. It made his heart ache and beat faster just to be in their presence. He'd learned names for some of the forms of fae he had seen in his life here. Piskies, elves, sprites, fairies, gnomes, names he knew from the myths of his childhood. Mina would have been a sprite. Her true form was tiny, glowing, a dazzling flicker of sparkling light. But he knew she could take other forms, as could most of the seelie fae. Despite their names, their categories, they were each unique, changeable and perfect.

Before him now, Mina stood as tall as he did, able to look him straight in the eye. Her vibrant fiery hair lifted around her with a life of its own. She flashed a heart stopping grin at him. A dozen more sprites shimmered in the branches nearby. Watching from behind tree trunks, a few also took larger forms, some with skin tinted green or gold, some with wings, some without. He recognized Yvainne amongst them, walking – gliding – toward him, her clothes woven from strands of cobweb silk, blossoms and dew drops that drew delicate patterns across milky skin and hung in flowing waves.

"Something new has come to the forest that will affect us all." Her voice tingled in his ears.

He knew his place, and bowed. "It's her. The one I waited for."

Mina scowled.

Met with silence, he continued. "Men too, and a dragon. They chased her and another girl into the troll caves." His heart lurched. That split second decision he made could have killed her. He'd planned to follow, keep her safe, but then the cave entrance crumbled, separating him from her again.

Yvainne's eyes fluttered, irritated maybe, or bored.

"I want to find her. Can I... Could you help me?" He knelt down, bowed further, holding his breath.

"You should know she is not right. Within her there is something unnatural, something dangerous. She is not the way you remember her."

"Please."

Yvainne turned her back on him and began gliding away.

He jumped to his feet, taking a step after her. "Please!"

"We will be following her." Irritation clear in her voice, she didn't turn back to look at him. "She needs to be watched. Mina is coming with us, so I assume you will too."

She faded out of sight while her last words still rang through the air. Other sprites around her twinkled and vanished like stars disappearing at dawn.

Mina remained standing next to him. "*Her.*"

He turned around with an apology on his lips, but Mina already grinned at him, her eyes sparkling. He was used to it now, how her moods shifted so fiercely. He smiled back at her. He couldn't help it.

"They know where she is. We'll follow later," Mina said, all chimes.

He itched to leave now. After so long, he didn't want to wait a

moment when she was so close. He started to wonder what he would do when he found her again. So long... and he'd never thought of that, only thought of finding her, making sure she was safe. Could they go home? She didn't even recognize him... But those men chased her as though they knew her. And that dragon. Why?

Mina leant up against him, toying with his arm, tracing the muscles and scars with a long finger.

"Do those men follow the dragon? Is that why they chase her?" he asked.

"Her!" Anger flared in Mina's eyes and her orange hair lifted in matching flames. She let his arm drop and stalked away from him. "Those men try to leash the dragon. They give him orders. How could they? Fool men! Better to leash fire or thunder! Using that desecrated flute, that abomination. They will burn for it one day." Mina growled, and a shower of glitter dust shook from her.

"The men control the dragon?" He couldn't understand. He knew the sort of power the fae had and even to them dragons were of unimaginable might. "Tell me how, I don't understand."

"Maybe later." Something shifted in Mina's eyes and she smiled again, bringing her hands up in front of her. Luscious berries of rainbow tones spilled from them. "Come and eat with me."

His flesh shivered over his bones, his whole body pulled with desire. He had no words to describe the flavors of fairy foods, the magic they made him feel. Mina stood in front of him like a picture straight from his memory. The very first time he'd met her, she stood just the same way, holding wondrous food when he had been so, so hungry. With an almost painful effort he closed the hunger away. He tried to sound neutral when he replied. "I can catch my own food now. I'm not hungry."

Mina hissed, and threw the food on the ground. It grayed and rotted in an instant. In a flash and a blink, she was small enough to stand on the tip of a finger, and shot away into the forest like a shooting star.

"Mina, I'm sorry." No sign or sound of her returned. "Mina?" A clammy sweat crept over his skin. He had to stay on her good side, or she could - she would - leave him behind. She'd left him on his own countless times before, for days, weeks, months, as punishments for the slightest affront. He didn't mind being on his own, but now he needed her help. He looked around wildly for a sign of the fairy's trail, running after her, faster than he'd ever run in his life.

CHAPTER FOUR

"...and then the gnome said to the merchant, 'I'm sorry, I'm a bit short!'" The stall holder rumbled out the punch line. Around him, a huddle of corseted and bustled ladies giggled behind their gloved hands.

Observing as he strolled by, Roen wondered if they laughed at the man's humor or the man himself. Roen hadn't heard that joke since he was a boy and a few entrepreneurial little folk could still be seen trading on market day, bringing exotic imports and fairy goods. They rarely appeared any more and the fae had barely been importing for far longer. Funny to be joking about it now. The market suffered from their absence. One of the young ladies smiled at Roen, and he winked back, setting off another wave of giggles, quivering lace and ribbons.

Shame he couldn't stay, he thought, letting his gaze linger on them. Unfortunately, he had to get to work.

Ambling along, Roen smiled to himself. Despite his reason for being here, he enjoyed the vital chaos of the market, now in its mid-morning peak of activity. Vendors spruiked from behind makeshift carts, boisterously laid out into a rough grid of narrow aisles. Children ran underfoot. Those with money bought sweet delights to nibble on. Those that couldn't buy bullied the sweets from those that could. *Innocent thieves,* thought Roen, envious.

Maerranton markets used to be legendary throughout Avall. It had been a rich city, a wealth still evident in the tall, handsome buildings of stone and sculpted bronze which stepped down the steep cobbled streets. But these were harder times and much of the city fell into disrepair. It didn't mean much to Roen. He'd never known wealth. He did know every abandoned and derelict house, each broken and dry drainage tunnel. Hiding places. Secret routes.

Squeezing through a small gap between two men, Roen muttered polite apologies. *Decent weight, maybe some gold. I can easily do better.* He slipped the coin purse into a concealed pocket in his long coat and adjusted his cravat to cover the movement. His clothes were well suited to his career. He saw to that when they were tailored. Dark colored, neat but unremarkable, the suit had no frills or fancies such as some men wore. His sleeves and cuffs were designed to keep his hands free. The seam of his trousers hid a thin blade, the perfect tool for defeating locks, slicing straps of bags, or defending his life. Not that he'd ever let it come to that.

He wandered through the humming market, thick with the sounds and smells of people trading. A passing carriage disturbed a family of stray cats and one came closer to him, mewing for food. With a swift and casual movement, Roen lifted a strip of dried fish from a nearby

stand and flicked it across to the kitten before continuing on.

He followed a man, clearly upper class, ridiculously dressed in startling turquoise-blue tails and top hat that oozed gaudy trims. He showed off his bad taste and bulging coin pouch to a lady whose bosom overflowed from her bodice. Roen idly browsed nearby stalls' wares, waiting for the best moment to move in and take his earnings. But despite the peacock man's flippant demeanor the opportunity never arose. His hands were always too tight around his money. Roen chuckled to himself at how the busty lady fawned over the miser, doubting she would get what she was after either. He could still have the man's money. He'd just have to work a little harder.

He rolled his shoulder in its socket, still stiff and sore, and turned away. It was too risky, even without an injury slowing him down. And risks he would not, could not, take. Last week's mess, the closest he'd ever been to capture, left him wary. He needed a new mark.

Roen headed back along the crowded aisle. Nonchalantly, he scrutinized the people around him. *There. Too easy. Almost a gift.* Spotting his next target, he couldn't help but give a tiny, wry grin.

The pair showed signs of poverty, with mud and scuffs of dirt covering their hooded cloaks, but were clumsily making a deal for some food with an obscene amount of gold. Maybe thieves themselves, Roen thought, wondering who they'd rolled to get that sort of money. From their size he guessed they were younger boys, street rats, drifting through town, spending out a big take. After stumbling through the purchase of food the two moved along to a used clothing stall. They kept themselves well hidden under their travelling cloaks, but one struggled with his, his body obviously far too small for the garment. The clothing glimpsed underneath was bizarre even compared with the last man in his feathers and ruffs.

The boy in the out of place outfit fiddled with a small item of metal which flicked open into a sharp blade. He quickly fumbled it back into a pocket. Certainly fair marks, Roen decided. If anyone deserved to be victim of his crime, it was a criminal himself.

The other scamp placed his leather pack – if it even belonged to him - down on the table then turned away to trade with the merchant, picking up a plain heavy dress. Roen questioned the dress, but his mind was too fixed on the bag sitting unwatched on the table. *Surely not, could it be so easy?* Without a blink of hesitation he started into action. Strolling by he barely brushed the back of their cloaks as he passed, leaving no trace of the bag behind.

Roen kept his steady pace until he reached the end of the stalls and tucked himself into the shadow of a larger building. He might be finishing early today, after a take like that. He couldn't help but look back. He knew he should move on, away from the scene. It was poor form to remain and gloat on a take, and the large bag couldn't be hidden away like the smaller purses he took, but this intrigued him. The oddity of the pair he'd stolen from made his curiosity demand more. The inept thieves would be realizing their loss any moment now.

There.

The boy turned back to where he'd put the bag down. He froze, staring at the empty spot on the table. He looked to his companion, who shook his head under the heavy hood. They both searched around, on the ground, panic in their movements. They stepped away from the stall to continue their hunt, unthinking, still with unpaid goods in their hands.

Roen frowned. *Time to be gone.* A commotion seemed inevitable when the stallholder stepped out from his stall, raised his arms and started bellowing at the street rats. Roen turned away from the vendor's tantrum, when the large man, towering above, reached out and grabbed at the scamp, ripping back the hood of the cloak. Something caught

Roen's eye, and he looked again.

Blonde hair spilled out from under the fallen hood, and a girl's face, soft like a petal, blushed pink with distress. Roen's forehead knitted. He breathed out hard, a lump forming in his chest. No wonder it was too easy, the girl was the very image of innocence.

The girl babbled to the vendor. He started yelling for city guards, shaking her in disgust by a fistful of her cloak. *The sort of disgust with which a thief should be treated.* Guilt heated Roen's face. The stallholder kept up his hollering, building a crowd of curious market-goers around him. The girl fell out of her cloak and she and her companion ducked back into the crowd, eluding the larger man amongst the mass of people. Too busy looking behind them, the pair scampered straight toward the city guards that had come, roused by the cries of "Thieves". He looked from the girl down to the bag he'd stolen, and swore under his breath.

"Excuse me, Miss," he called out when she passed within earshot.

They both eyed him suspiciously and continued to scurry forward, clinging together. Roen snorted out a breath and swore again. He held up the bag into clear view.

That got their attention, and the still hooded figure dragged the blonde toward him. Roen stepped back further into an alley, forcing them to come to him, out of sight of the approaching guards. Two girls, he saw with surprise now they stood before him. Maybe a couple of years younger than himself, which was still more boy than man. Both were attractive despite being exhausted and worn. He'd noticed before that they were dirty but could see now they were also damaged. One black-eyed and swollen, the other, the pretty blonde one, had a scratch clear across one of her cheeks, the ruby red of it contrasting starkly against her porcelain skin. They were both shaking and on edge, eyes darting, color drained from their faces.

The guards passed by without looking their way. Roen let out a loud and exaggerated puffing noise and gave his best smile.

"Nothing like a bit of excitement to start the morning! It must be your lucky day." He continued his faux-labored breath.

The two looked at him deer eyed and remained silent. He normally had an easier time getting a smile from a girl. *Not my lucky day,* he thought, and continued the show.

"Well, I saw it all happen. Some dirty purse cutter making off with your bag. I thought I'd see if I couldn't help out."

The blonde breathed out as though she'd been holding her breath since her bag vanished. "Thank you sir, so much. Thank you. You've no idea what this means... I...."

Something about her face seemed familiar in the way that made his palms clammy. She was beautiful, even on the verge of tears, but what was yet another pretty girl to him? Roen let his act fall, becoming somber again.

"It wasn't a trouble at all. When the thief saw me chasing him, he dropped the bag and bolted."

"Just a coward after all. Bloody bully," the dark-haired girl vented.

"What more would you expect from a thief?" he asked. He flashed a grin, but could not keep all the bitterness from his tone.

The girl turned and spoke to the blonde, shooting an awkward toothy smile back toward Roen as he watched. "Come on Eloryn, we should be clearing out."

Roen walked up to the blonde girl and stood close in front of her. She blushed vividly and looked down. He smiled a little at that. It was nice to feel like the champion sometimes. *Except that I'm the villain pretending to be a champion.* His smile faded.

"Eloryn, is it? Here, so you can be on your way. Do be more wary in the future, thieves aren't always so easily beaten."

As he placed the bag down into her open hands, his fingers brushed against hers and she twitched back bashfully. They both apologized and the bag thumped down between them onto the cobblestones. A small object wrapped in fine velvet fell out and rolled around, unwinding itself from the material as if with a will to be free, drawing Roen's eyes after it. It glittered where it came to a stop. Polished and precious.

The lump of guilt in his chest began to pound and he looked from the ornate amulet to the girl again. Her mouth just slightly open, she grabbed for the intricate medallion as he picked up her bag. Her effort to remain casual was ruined by her quivering lips. He could see her trying to judge his reaction, if he recognized the heirloom, if he made the connection.

He did.

A noise from the marketplace turned his attention the other way. The city guards returned, searching this time in a begrudging manner that made them all the more surly and determined. The vendor had certainly scolded them straight to work. The guards walked right toward the alley he and the girls openly stood in. Any moment now the lawmen would see the girls they were searching for, and him standing with them. *Not good.*

Roen broke into movement, kicking in an old door. Grabbing the girls around their small shoulders, he pushed them through, both too surprised to stop him. All three fell down broken stairs into thick, pungent mud. The two girls landed flat on their backs, stunned and winded.

Roen spun around and pushed the door back into place. Her dress pinned under his knees, Eloryn tried to wriggle free. The other girl swore liberally at him. He turned back and dropped his body down on top of them, hoping the dark shade of his coat would hide them. He slapped a mud covered hand onto the swearing girl's mouth and gave a vehement shushing gesture to them both, pointing back through the holes in the door at the passing feet of the patrolmen.

The girls stilled. *Thank the fae.* Roen breathed out a silent sigh of relief. Another wriggle or scream would mean all sorts of difficult explaining to be done on his part and likely much worse for them.

The guards poked around in the alley way, making the appearance of a hunt. The dark haired girl glared at Roen. He removed his hand from her mouth and she wiped dirt from it angrily. Despite the buildup of rotting refuse, run off from the markets, this ancient, half-buried basement had been a hiding place for him on more than one occasion. Ignored by most people in the sprawling city, it even held an entrance to the city's large underground tunnel system through a half crumbled wall.

After he thought the guards had passed, Roen waited a few moments longer, just to be sure. Only then did he realize he pinned Eloryn's body down full length with his own. He could feel her pounding heart through the clothes between their chests. She stared at him with worried eyes in a haunting shade of green, probably planning how to get away from him. *What a way to make an introduction of this importance.*

Roen rose to his feet with steady movements in an attempt to not panic the girls further. The odd dark haired girl stood up next to him. She looked down at her freshly muddied clothes and swore again.

Roen reached down and helped Eloryn to her feet with as much care as he could offer. They kept their eyes on each other, waiting for the other to make a move. He knew he had to offer a sign of his allegiance.

Roen dropped down onto one knee in front of the girl, bowing low toward the unpleasant ground. "Princess, forgive me."

CHAPTER FIVE

Roen swallowed away the lump in his throat and waited for Eloryn's reaction.

Her mouth opened a little then closed again. She turned to her friend as though Roen weren't even there. "Memory, can you see, is our way clear? We have to leave now."

Memory blinked as if she'd missed something. "Huh? But he...? What did he mean?"

"She doesn't know?" Roen had assumed the princess to be in the care of this other girl. He hoped his assumption would not be the cause of more trouble to her.

"Know what?" Memory said.

"Nothing, I am not," Eloryn insisted to them both, flustered.

Roen pushed back to his feet, took hold of Eloryn's arm and moved her away from Memory. He placed Eloryn with her back to the furthest wall and bent down to whisper to her.

"Hey, let go of her!" Memory moved after them, but Roen gave her a warning look, stopping her in her tracks. He turned back to Eloryn who stared in alarm at where he held her. He pulled back his grasping hand and clenched his teeth. This was all going very wrong. For a moment that he, his parents and so many others had dreamt of for so long, to find this person of such importance, and here he was, throwing the princess into rubbish and manhandling her.

"Please," Roen beseeched her. "Trust I am no enemy. Tell me it's so, that you are the heir. You're the right age. You're in possession of our late Queen's medallion," he swallowed, skin tingling with goose bumps, "and her appearance."

She looked from him to Memory with fear in her eyes. Roen dropped his voice to an even lower whisper. "This girl, Memory, who is she? Is she a threat? If she's a danger to you in any way, I can help."

"She's not, I'm not, she's..." Eloryn panted out the words then her knees gave way and she fell in a faint. Roen blinked in disbelief, just managing to catch the falling girl. Memory dashed across the room and took Eloryn's weight out of his arms, the two girls sinking to the floor together.

"What did you do to her?" she demanded. "What was that interrogation about?"

Roen stood above them, hand hovering near his mouth. *Could I be entirely wrong about this? No. Everything adds up to the same answer. She has to be.*

"You really don't know who this is?" he asked Memory.

"I just met her yesterday," she snapped at him. Eloryn's eyes fluttered back open and Memory loosened her bear hug hold of her.

"We haven't slept. We've just... just been running."

The girls gave him matching glares. He didn't blame them. He couldn't believe in his desperation to know the truth he'd driven Eloryn - already injured, terrified and exhausted - to collapse. He felt sick to his stomach. Even if she wasn't who he believed her to be, he'd acted poorly. If she was, it was unforgivable.

"I'm sorry. Please forgive my behavior. Whoever you are, and it doesn't matter who that is, I can assume you've been running from someone, or something, terrible?" He dropped down next to them. Eloryn now kneeled unsupported, but swayed as she stared warily at him. Memory hesitated, then nodded for the both of them.

"You don't have to tell me what it is. Just let me help you. I can sneak you from the city, past anyone who might be watching, to somewhere safe. I give my word you will be safe."

No answer came. Roen bowed his head, unruly hair dropping over his face. "Forgive me, I only want to help," he whispered.

"You promise?" Memory asked with a pout, sounding very much like a child.

He nodded with all the sincerity he could show.

"Will there... be food? And beds?"

Hope tweaked the corner of his mouth into a small smile. He stood and stretched a hand to her, which, after one false start, she took gingerly. He then offered a hand to Eloryn.

Looking defeated, Eloryn brought herself up to her feet with the wall as her aid, ignoring Roen's hand. "Memory, I don't... I don't want to go with him."

Roen put on his most charming, pleading look for Memory, who at least acknowledged his presence. He didn't know how she fitted into this situation, but if she could help persuade Eloryn to come with him, that was what mattered right now. No girl he'd ever known had been able to say no to that look.

"We need rest. We're a mess, Lory. I don't think either of us knows what we're doing. We might as well have had flashing lights on our heads out there. If he can help us get away from here then I vote we go with him." Memory's voice became a little kinder. "If he was going to rat us out, he had his chance before. He's helped us twice already. That has to count for something."

Eloryn gave the faintest nod.

Roen dug Eloryn's bag out of the debris pile where it had fallen and walked back to her.

"My name is Roen. Here." He did not pass the bag to her this time. Instead, he draped the large satchel by its strap over her shoulder and across her torso. His hand brushed her waist while he adjusted the strap and pressed the bag to her side. "Wear it like this. Keep it always close to your body." Letting the bag go, he stood the barest space away from her. "You should take more care of your belongings, and try not to be so tempting with thieves about."

"Oh, come on," said Memory. "You're going to make her faint again."

Memory walked beside Eloryn, following more than a few steps behind Roen. He led them through a system of tunnels under the town. Tunnels and caves were almost all Memory knew of life so far. Maybe that was why she didn't feel the discomfort that being down here seemed to bring out in the other two. Maybe she was just too tired. No, she was definitely too tired. She felt like a visitor in her own body. It kept moving along of its own accord. She barely felt the ache anymore.

Earlier while they walked around the market, Memory had fished through all her pockets, trying to find out something about herself. Lots of things came to her naturally – words, actions, general knowledge - but still not a single memory of herself or her past had come back. She felt like she was learning everything from scratch again. *I don't even know what I look like.*

Her heart had sunk when she found a crumbled mess of multi-colored metal and plastic in her back pocket. She guessed it might have been a phone, before it was crushed some time during their hazardous journey the night before. Maybe earlier. When she asked Eloryn if she had a phone she could use, Eloryn looked at her as if she spoke a foreign language. Not that she knew any numbers or names of people to call anyway. But still, everything felt so strange. Magic. No phones. The fancy clothing everyone wore. Maybe she'd gotten lost at a LARP convention. Maybe she was just more messed up in the head than she thought.

That is *entirely likely,* she thought, glumly. She second guessed the reality of everything she'd seen so far. Dragons, moving trees and trolls were hard to believe after all. Even that beast man in the forest. She'd thought at first he was just another of the scary chasing men, but when he took hold of her, he threw her to safety, relatively anyway. She thought she saw recognition of some kind in his wild blue eyes, but in the riot of confusion that formed her first moments of consciousness she couldn't be sure of anything, not even his existence. How could she ever find him again anyway? She somehow doubted he'd have a phone number, even if she still had a working phone.

The only other things she found in her pockets were a piece of cherry gum and a knife. One look at the knife told her it wasn't the kind you take camping, it was the kind you threatened people with. *Is that who I am, the kind of person that threatens people?* She decided to keep the knife to herself. Eloryn already looked at her sometimes as if she was dangerous, and maybe she was, but that wasn't the sort of thing she wanted to find out about herself. Besides, she wasn't the only one keeping secrets and Eloryn's seemed much bigger than a knife in the back pocket.

Memory wiped her hands on her jeans, but gave up when it only made them dirtier. Resigned to eating even more dirt than she had already, she unwrapped the gum and popped it in her mouth. The candy cherry flavor rushed across her tongue, unfamiliar. She turned to Eloryn. "So, *Princess,* what was that all about?" Memory realized that she hadn't even known Avall was a monarchy. Then again, she only knew the name of the place because Eloryn told her.

"It meant nothing." Eloryn kept her eyes averted.

"It didn't look like nothing." The way Roen had grabbed Eloryn, moving her against her will, left Memory with a strange, ill feeling inside. She discarded it, filed away with all her other confusing emotions, and tried to judge Roen anew. She hated how handsome she found him, how she just wanted to touch that soft caramel hair, and how when he smiled, she couldn't help but like him. It made it hard to say no to him, and left her wondering if she'd made the choice to go with him for the right reasons. Why was everyone she'd met so far so damn *pretty!* Amnesia or not, Memory knew pretty people lied too. *Everyone lies,* her heart told her.

Wow, learned something new about myself. Turns out I'm a cynic. Surprise. She looked at Roen walking ahead of them. Not very tall, lightly built; Memory kept telling herself the two of them could overpower him if they needed to, but the way he moved revealed a casual, confident strength that made her worry.

"Really, I just felt faint, from exhaustion. That was all." Eloryn blushed so earnestly Memory had to suppress a giggle.

"I heard what he said, Lory. He said Princess. And with the kneeling and all."

Eloryn's eyes shifted as though looking for a way out of a trap.

Memory sighed. "Look, I'm working with nothing here, know nothing except what you tell me. Why the hell would you leave out a detail like being a princess? Seriously, if it's for reals it's kind of cool, right?"

"We're nearly there," Roen called back to them before Eloryn could give an answer.

So intent on needling Eloryn, Memory hadn't noticed the rich orange cast of light falling into the tunnel up ahead. They were at the tunnel's end, and it opened out onto an untended set of terraced fields. The sun had just begun to brush the sky with color as it fell toward night, and lit the dried crops to a burnished copper.

Eloryn and Memory caught up to him where he waited at the exit, haloed by the golden light. He pointed through the rambling reeds to a small rundown cottage.

"That's where we are going." He gave a small cough and Memory thought he almost seemed embarrassed.

"My parents and I live out of town because, in a way, we are also running from something." He began walking forward again, but slowly this time, not letting them hang behind. He directed them straight through the web of unharvested corn stalks and twisting weeds, bending them out of the way. Dry stalks crunched satisfyingly under their feet, releasing wafts of musty mud fragrance.

"My parents, you see, are Grand Duke Brannon and Grand Duchess Isabeth Faerbaird. You may have heard of them?"

Despite Eloryn's studied indifference, her voice held an edge of

suspicion. "I have. But if you were their son, you would be a prince, then?"

Memory swallowed her gum, coughing. "What, seriously?" She couldn't hide her surprise, but Roen didn't seem to care. He continued to watch Eloryn intently. Princes and princesses everywhere. She felt left out.

"I'm no kind of prince. If my parents were still ruling, then I may have had that title. But my parents were close friends of Queen Loredanna's, and our family loyal to the Maellan bloodline. When Thayl Vaircarn killed her and the King, my parents lost their titles, land and more, fighting him. It is his fault my parents have been forced to live poorly for so long."

"These are dangerous words," Eloryn said, her lips tight and stubborn.

"I believe I've already made my allegiances clear. If I'm endangered by that, can it be worse to explain why they are so?"

"Explaining is good," Memory said. "I like it when people explain things."

"Well," Roen continued, rewarding her with a lopsided smile, "I've plenty of stories to tell. My parents always believed Loredanna's newborn survived Thayl's slaughter. They and my brothers fought to remove Thayl, to find the lost heir, or at least assign a more worthy leader. Obviously to no avail. We went into hiding after that. We've still got a friend or two in the nobility who make sure we remain overlooked when needed. It's been hard for my parents, so I look after them now. They miss royal life, and it's risky even for them to be seen in town. So I work, and try and bring them things of value when I stumble across them."

"Things of value...?" *Like a missing princess?* Memory looked sidelong at Eloryn. Could it be true? And if it was, what would it mean? She had no idea. She didn't get politics, and didn't know the first bit of this history.

Roen shrugged and grinned. "Although, most of my stories aren't nearly as exciting as the time I saved a couple of pretty girls from a thief and got to take them home. That one's my favorite."

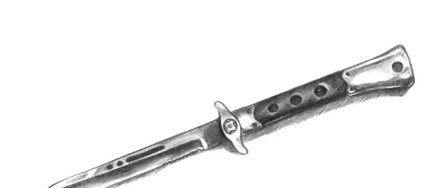

CHAPTER SIX

They pushed through a thicket of weeds into a small clearing. A neat garden of herbs, lettuce and pumpkins surrounded the cottage, hidden by the overgrown fields. Apart from the smoke that escaped the chimney, the house looked abandoned. Shutters hung off hinges. Windows were closed up with grayed, splintering planks. Grass and daisies grew from the roof. Memory dreaded going inside, in case the rickety structure fell on her.

Roen stepped forward, a small frown denting his forehead. He seemed to hesitate for a moment, then knocked. "Mother, Father, it's me."

A heavy bolt slid behind the door which squealed in protest as it swung open.

"I didn't expect you home 'til tomorrow." A graceful white-haired woman met Roen with a loving smile. The elaborate high-necked gown she wore contrasted starkly with the derelict cottage. Her smile fled the moment she saw Roen had brought guests.

"Who are they?"

"They were in need of help, and I offered it." Roen stepped aside, tilting his head to the girls.

Isabeth looked them over with her lips pursed. She placed her hand over her heart when she saw Eloryn and it rose up to her mouth when she looked at what Memory wore. Memory hated how different she looked to everyone else. They all wore long flowing gowns and there she was in a t-shirt and torn jeans. She felt even dirtier than before, bloody, bruised, and unsteady on her feet. Eloryn wasn't much more presentable. She folded her arms into herself, and gave a closed-lipped, nervous smile.

Isabeth turned to the side, talking into the house instead of out toward her son. "Well. Well they are here now. I'll not be known for denying aid." She moved in, beckoning them after her.

Inside, only thin shafts of the setting sunlight broke through the blocked windows. Memory stepped in after Roen and Eloryn, seeing only gloom while her eyes adjusted to the darkness.

The door slammed behind them like a crack of thunder, shaking the cottage walls. Memory spun around and stepped backwards, running into Eloryn. Shadows shifted near the closed door and a figure loomed toward them.

"Mem, we shouldn't have come," Eloryn whispered over her shoulder. She clung to the back of Memory's shirt as though she stuck there when they bumped together.

Thanks for the told-you-so but we can't go anywhere now. Isabeth and Roen stood behind them in the small room. The man blocked the doorway,

the dark silhouette of his features starting to clear in Memory's eyes. He stared down at the girls. Memory tensed. A shiver of terrified nausea crept up her back, and her hand moved itself toward her back pocket.

"What do you think you're doing?" He strode past them, straight at Roen, anger growling in his voice. He shook Roen by the shoulder with an outstretched arm. His only arm. Memory gasped. His right arm was missing from the elbow down, hidden by a rolled and pinned sleeve. Memory forced her mouth shut, trying to look anywhere but at his missing limb. Her eyes were inevitably drawn back.

Roen spoke calmly and looked the man in the eye. "Father, please, can we talk?"

"Brannon, love, they're just children," Isabeth said.

"No, they aren't. Look at the state of them. They... are trouble." Brannon kept a grip on Roen as though he would throw him back out of the house. He turned and glared at the girls. Memory cringed.

"We'll go. Let us go, please?" Eloryn's clutch on Memory's shirt tightened and her pitch rose.

"No," Roen cried, then his volume dropped again. "I mean, please stay, you are welcome here."

"You know they aren't. Get rid of them before their trouble follows them here."

"Father, please, they can't go. They still need help."

"Why would you bring them here? You should know better. You're free to come and go as you please. No one knows who you are. Has that made you forget what it's like for your mother and me? The danger we're in? You know what will happen if we're found."

Roen's composure cracked and his volume rose to meet his father's. "We weren't followed. They won't-"

"Do you even know what trouble they are in? Bringing a couple

of strays home without any idea of the risk? What have you told them about us?"

Roen frowned, opening his mouth but not speaking.

Memory found words rushing out of her own mouth instead. "He really didn't tell us much – anything – nothing at all. We just needed some help."

Brannon scowled at her, the deep wrinkles in his face twisting around a grey-streaked beard. He pushed Roen out of his grasp. "I want them gone." He stormed across the room to a curtained off doorframe, and disappeared through it. A second later another door slammed.

Roen rolled the shoulder his father had grabbed. He turned to Eloryn and Memory with a strained smile and a shrug. "You don't have to go anywhere, really. Mother?" He gave Isabeth a pleading look and hurried through the same doorway as his father. The smell of bread wafted out, teasingly, and Memory glimpsed signs of a kitchen before the curtain fell closed again. Her stomach gurgled from the combination of hunger and stress.

Eloryn tugged at Memory's shirt and whispered, "We should go now."

Close behind them, Isabeth tutted. "I don't see the harm in letting you get cleaned up and fed. Don't mind my husband, he just worries."

Memory breathed in the scent of fresh bread again and closed her eyes. Whatever Eloryn's reasons to go, the lure of 'cleaned up and fed' overwhelmed Memory. She hoped Roen wouldn't be in more trouble if they stayed just a little longer.

Memory turned around to face Eloryn, who eyed the front door. "Roen promised we'll be safe. Let's just rest a little, then go."

Eloryn's lips pulled thin, but she gave a tiny nod.

"Take a seat and I'll see what I can find for you both," Isabeth

muttered. "So dark in here. Àlaich las." A warm glow magically lit the room. Isabeth walked out to the kitchen without looking back, as though it were the simplest thing to create light with her words. With the gloom cleared, the room suddenly seemed a lot more solid, even pretty. Furniture was sparse, but elegant and well cared for. Memory took a seat at a small dining table of carved dark wood. A thick curtain sectioned off the end of the room. Partly open, it showed behind it a simple single bed and a store of shelved belongings; books, clothing, and tools that she didn't think she'd know the uses for even if she did have any memories. Two curtains were draped across doorframes leading out, but Memory guessed there couldn't be much more to the cottage beyond them.

Eloryn sat beside her, head tilted, hiding behind her hair. Memory sighed and chipped black polish from her fingernails as her frustration rose. Her second day in the world for all she could remember, and she was left to make all the small talk. At least Eloryn wasn't making them run any more. It was nice to sit. So nice. Memory thought sitting might be her new favorite pastime.

Isabeth returned, carrying a tray of food, drink, and some small cloths. A steaming bowl of water balanced in the middle. The clatter of the crockery as she put the tray down on the table didn't cover the sound of Brannon yelling again from outside.

Isabeth dipped two cloths together into the water bowl and squeezed them out. She handed the girls one each. "Trouble indeed."

"Thank you, for letting us come in. And helping us. And stuff," Memory said. Her words became progressively more awkward but she kept tacking them onto her failed attempt at being polite. Roen and Brannon's voices hammering through the thin cottage walls didn't help her train of thought. She focused on wiping her hands clean.

The back door slammed again, and Brannon walked in. Roen

followed, head low and jaw clenched.

Isabeth clicked her tongue. "These won't do." She picked the already muddied cloths out of the girls' hands. "Roen, fill the tub."

He went back into the kitchen without a word, emerging again a moment later with a large pot of water which he took into the other room. Brannon moved up and sat across from the girls at the table, staring at Eloryn who shyly looked down and away.

Isabeth lifted the pot of blackened water and rags off the table and took it away. "It may not be much, but please go ahead and eat. No formalities tonight, considering," she said and left the room again.

Memory mumbled thanks and looked nervously from the food to Brannon, not sure what formalities would have been anyway. Brannon reached out and tore off some crusty bread. He pushed the rest closer to them without a word. Her smile in return was ignored, so she took a filled ceramic cup and slunk back into her chair. Finding that the cup contained wine surprised her, but no one suggested she shouldn't drink it. The rich taste made her eyes droop and it added to the warmth that already burned in her chest. Had she been running on nothing but shock and adrenaline since she woke up? She was so tired she couldn't think straight, and now her body no longer moved, it was giving up any fight to stay awake. *Yes. Sitting. Good.*

Brannon fortunately had calmed down and had little to say to her. He tried to start conversations with Eloryn a couple of times. They led nowhere. Memory tried to chew on some food but her mouth refused to function. She watched Roen take pot after pot of water from kitchen to bedroom.

She didn't realize she'd fallen asleep in her chair until Isabeth came and shook her. "Dear, I hate to be waking you, but the bath is drawn, best to get cleaned up now."

Memory looked up and saw Eloryn gone. She couldn't see Roen

or Brannon either. Somewhere deep inside panic burbled, but her body wouldn't respond. Isabeth steered her like a sleepwalker into the bedroom. A polished brass bath tub stood in a corner, half behind a dressing screen.

Memory noticed Eloryn lying on a bed canopied with red velvet. She was clean and asleep, a towel tucked under her still damp hair. The undercurrent of anxiety in Memory eased seeing Eloryn safe and still with her. If she knew Roen wasn't somewhere being bawled out by Brannon again it would be even better.

Isabeth moved as though to help Memory undress for her bath, looked her up and down and backed away. Memory sighed in relief when Isabeth left the room; she would have felt even more self conscious without privacy. Stepping behind the screen she pulled two t-shirts, worn short over long, off as one piece. She winced when she lifted her arms over her head, and looked down at a spot that had been hurting her. A multi-colored bruise covered half of her ribcage. Even worse, an old, large and twisted scar marked the middle of her chest. *Nasty,* she thought, wondering how she got it. *Do you even know what trouble they are in?* Brannon's words bothered her. *I don't even know myself. Could whoever did this to me follow me here?* Pulling down her pants, she forgot her shoes and wobbled about trying to extract them from the tight jeans. Peeling off a striped sock, she discovered blood around her toes. *Well, that could have happened anytime,* she thought, considering their chase through forest, cave and tunnel and the many hazards to toes they held.

Feeling cold and exposed in the open room, she quickly stripped off her underwear and stepped into the tub. The warm water came up to her shoulders when she sat down. It smelled of milk and honey, and soap suds made it almost opaque white. Memory breathed the syrupy steam and let the warmth seep into her. Finding a cloth hanging over

one side, she washed it over her skin, soaking away the filth. She began seeking and removing clips from her hair. Feeling mud caked on the back of her head, she leaned back and dunked her hair into the water, massaging her fingers through. She closed her eyes and smiled.

This was the most content she'd ever felt, she thought wryly. She lay back in the warm water, letting the aches and tiredness seep out of her. She felt she could just sit in there for hours, until she remembered she wasn't alone in the room. She was in a house full of strangers where she wasn't welcome. She sighed and lifted her head back out of the water.

Her lazily opening eyes snapped wide with horror. Simple confusion blurred with possible nightmare. The white bath water had turned a sickening black. She screamed, she couldn't help herself. Eloryn woke with a start. Memory splashed about, trying to pull herself from the tub. She managed to slip over the side and fall onto the floor behind the bath just before Roen, Isabeth and Brannon ran into the room.

She cowered behind the bath while they stared at the water and then at her. Isabeth rushed across and draped a blanket over her.

Memory stuttered, "The water, it just turned black. I don't know what happened."

Isabeth wiped some dripping water from Memory's shoulder and showed her the color. "Your hair has a dye in it, that's all. It's washed out in the tub."

Memory couldn't help but feel ashamed at the tone in which Isabeth told her this, as if she was a simple child. Her panic felt laughable. "I didn't know. I didn't know it was dyed."

"You two, out!" Isabeth snapped at her husband and son. Roen, who had been averting his eyes, moved quickly to hide a spreading grin. Brannon followed along at a slower pace, a war of glances shared between him and his wife.

Isabeth started drying Memory off, and she was too taken aback to protest. "How could you not know, child? It's your own hair."

Memory started to talk, but Eloryn shook her head at her. This wasn't missed by Isabeth, who briskly finished drying Memory and dropped a billowing chemise down over Memory's head, leaving her to find her own way through the expanse of fabric into the arm holes.

"I know it's not a noble thing to pry but I got barely a word out of this one," she said, sticking her chin out toward Eloryn. She rested fists on her thin hips, her voice scolding. "Roen told us who he thinks you are. True or not we could trust you both more and help you more if you would talk to us."

Eloryn didn't lift her eyes to meet Isabeth's as she asked, "And what do you think of what Roen believes?"

Isabeth softened a little, the slightest tilt to her head. "I think you are two hurt, frightened girls who need our help. It would be my greatest wish to see a child of Loredanna's alive and well. I've hoped it for the longest time but was never so foolish to imagine the heir would just walk through my door."

Eloryn choked on a tiny sob, her eyes still downcast. "I have."

CHAPTER SEVEN

Isabeth's hands rose to her mouth.

Tears flowed down Eloryn's cheeks, and she slumped forward where she sat on the edge of the bed. "I'm sorry. I'm sorry for sitting here silent while you've given us all your help. I couldn't even give you the honors of your rank. Grand Duchess, I've been so rude. You must know that I can't, I shouldn't tell anyone. Even my being here is putting you at risk, but I just don't know what to do. I don't know what to do on my own."

"Oh, child!" Isabeth wrapped her arms around Eloryn and held her as she sobbed.

The details fell into place in Memory's head. No joke, Eloryn really was a princess. A real goddamned princess on the run. Daughter of

a King and Queen who were killed for their throne by some bad man who makes people poor and cuts their arms off. *Blah blah wars, blah blah Thayl, hunters, hiding and terror.* Had Eloryn lied to her about why those men chased them? What else had she lied about?

I don't know what to do on my own. Eloryn's words made her face burn. She didn't matter at all. The girl with no memories and no use to anyone. In competition with a princess, why would any of them help her?

Isabeth called out to Brannon and Roen. She nodded to them over Eloryn's head, stroking her hair.

"Hush child." Isabeth rocked Eloryn ever so slightly. "You are doing fine. By the fae, you are alive! That's a greater thing than many even dared hope for."

"But how?" Brannon moved in closer, crouching on the floor in front of them.

"Wizard Councilor Alward saved me, raised me." Eloryn's sobbing slowed and she worked at wiping her face dry. "He was known before as Pellaine."

Isabeth and her husband nodded in comprehension. "We saw… Well, never mind what we saw just now. But we had reason to hope Pellaine had escaped, that Loredanna's baby had been saved."

Memory's nose wrinkled. She watched Isabeth fussing over the princess. Her heart ached, imagining a mother of her own out there somewhere, worrying about where she was and wanting to hold her while she bawled her eyes out like that. *I have to find my way back to my mother, my family, my home.*

No one flocked to help or console her. Why would they with a princess in the room? *Whatever, deal with her problems. I'll be fine on my own.* Like a ghost, she drifted out the doorway, through the kitchen, unbolted the small back door and walked out.

What the hell am I supposed to do now? She breathed deeply through a bout of panic, staring into the night. A forest backed the cottage, dark and imposing as though the house had been built in the open and the forest had marched right up to it like an army. A bitter vanilla fragrance wafted to her from a vine curling up around the back door, its white flowers still open at night.

A crisp cold settled on her skin. *Too cold to be sulking and smelling the flowers.* She swore at the pettiness that drove her out there alone, not even knowing where she'd go next. She pulled the chemise back up onto her shoulders where it didn't like staying, and hugged her arms around her chest. The cold bit at her and she considered going and sulking in the kitchen near the hearth.

Something moved high in the dark branches of the trees in front of her, catching her eye. Humming stars hovered still then zipped from place to place. She could see no detail, only beautiful, mesmerizing points of light. Each one glowed in vivid hues that shifted through a rainbow of color, blue into green, yellow into orange, red into purple. She took a step closer and they jumped away from her, a startled school of fish shimmering in the trees.

A voice shocked Memory, jolting her focus away from the lights.

"There must be something special about you."

She turned to see Roen had joined her outside. How long had he been there? She hadn't heard him come out.

"Making friends with a Princess and attracting sprites." He stepped up next to her, pointing into the trees. "They're so rare to see these days. It's like they've come here for you."

Memory snorted. "More like they came for Eloryn. She's the special one, right?"

Roen laughed an honest, easy laugh. "And you just met her yesterday! Had you ever imagined just stumbling upon the Maellan

Princess?"

Memory sobered up quickly. He caught her mood and his laughing stopped.

"So nothing's been said then, about me?"

Roen frowned and shook his head.

"Not that I'd expect it, what with everything. I guess my problems aren't exactly the priority."

"No, not really," Roen said. She was about to tell him where to stick his priorities when he continued. "But you can tell me anyway."

Memory gaped, lost on where to start. "I can't... remember anything." She felt stupid now saying it out loud. "Before yesterday. Before waking up and meeting Eloryn and just running ever since, I have no memories."

Roen said nothing, only stared, his forehead furrowed crookedly. The intensity of his gaze brought an uncomfortable feeling rushing up through her chest. She kept talking to suppress the heat rising in her face. "Eloryn said it might be caused by this weird magic thing that happened. She said she'd help me, so I just went with her, but she never told me who she was..."

"And now you don't think she will help you?"

"Why would she? Why would any of you? I just need to find some way to get my memories back so I can go home."

Roen stood silent for a while, then said, "If I were you, right now, I'd stick close to the person who has offered you their help, despite their own troubles, whether they can help you or not."

"Are you talking about her, or you?"

Roen grinned.

"Thanks for that, by the way. I didn't realize it would be such a big deal with your parents. I hope you're not in too much trouble."

"Trouble? I just brought home the missing Maellan heir. They've

got nothing to complain about. Even just to know she's alive has given them so much hope. If we can get the news to the resistance, it might be what they need to make some real change, get back some of what's been lost."

"There's a resistance?"

"Oh, sorry. I'll need to explain everything won't I?" He laughed.

Memory opened her mouth wide and punched her fists onto her hips in exaggerated insult. "You can start by explaining why you're out here bugging me instead of your beloved princess."

Roen dropped his head. His caramel brown hair fell over matching tawny eyes. The colors in combination made him look like a statue made of gold. A sense of loneliness crept into his expression, hidden under the glossy facade.

Why would he be lonely? He has a home, a family. Memory's heart jittered, worried he might actually go back inside. She searched for something to say that would stop him from leaving her on her own again.

"You said about brothers before. They don't live here too?"

"None of them still live. The five eldest died in the wars, and the sixth, well, he's dead to us either way," Roen said through half his mouth.

"Oh god, why is everything so horrible? Every single thing that's happened."

"Except meeting me, right? That isn't turning out too bad," Roen looked back up, smiling again in a way that creased his eyes. "Don't worry for me, I barely knew my brothers. I was youngest of the lot by more than a few years. I don't even know what it's like to be a noble, except from what Mother and Father tell me." Roen leant toward her and whispered as though sharing a secret. "When I was younger, Mother used to train me in noble manners. One day she just stopped. I guess she gave up thinking I would ever be a prince."

Memory tried to smile in return, but her lips kept falling downwards.

Roen cleared his throat. "Enough about my family. I hope one day you can tell me about yours."

"Do you think… my memories could just come back on their own?"

"They might. But better to stay amongst friends all the same." Shaking his head, Roen leant on the wall near her and chuckled. "At least now I understand your odd name. Still don't understand what you were wearing before."

Memory turned away from him, staring at the strange magic of the tiny fairy creatures glowing in the trees. *How could they even be real? How could any of this?* Loss and confusion flooded over her. A sob shuddered up through her body and she caught it in her throat, swallowing it. She tensed to stop the tears that tried to escape.

"Hey, look here, what is that?" Roen stepped up in front of her. He stared at her ear, his face twisted in a strange half smile.

"What? What is what?" Memory released a worried giggle.

"Here, let me." Roen reached toward her and pulled a large white flower from behind her ear.

Memory's mouth opened wide again, this time in honest amazement. "How did you do that? How did that get there? Was that magic?"

Roen laughed so heartily it took a moment before he could talk again. "I can't believe that worked! You really have no memory at all?" He wiped his eyes. "I'm sorry, normally that only works on children."

His laughter was so good natured she couldn't begrudge him for it, but put on her best pout, and asked, "Show me how to do it?"

"All right. But only because you need something to fill that head of yours. It's simple really. Not magic at all. Just a bit of a distraction and a flick of the wrist." He showed her the flower tucked behind his

fingers then pulled a funny face, pointing at it with his other hand. "That's the distraction."

"Oh," said Memory. "No wonder it only works on kids. Still, can I try?"

She picked a star shaped leaf from the ground and tucked it into her hand, trying the same movements he had used, reaching her hand up to his ear.

"Not bad. If I didn't already know what was happening."

"Yeah, yeah, be a smart ass. How about this?" Memory moved her arm again, fumbling the leaf. It slipped from her grasp and fell to the ground. Roen ducked down to pick it up for her at the same time that she did and they collided midway. They stood back up together and he held the leaf out for her.

"Poor." His mocking came gently with a smile.

"Really?" Memory said, raising an eyebrow. She giggled when he looked down and saw another large leaf poking from a buttonhole in his waistcoat.

He picked it out and looked at it, and then her, in amazement. "See I was right, you are special."

"Who would have thought?" Memory smiled and shrugged. The chemise slid off her shoulder again, revealing another dark bruise. She glared at it. *I'm going to have to start naming you blue bastards to keep track of you all.* Roen frowned at it as well. He looked from the bruise on her shoulder to the one under her eye.

She suddenly became aware of just how close together they stood.

"You've been attacked. So many bruises on you..."

His eyes darkened and a muscle twitched in his cheek. The look of concern only made his pretty face more charming. She could feel his warm breath on her, making the hair on her neck stand on end.

Her heart drummed and she began to understand how Eloryn had fainted so easily.

"Oh, no. I mean, yes, we were attacked, or chased, yesterday. But we got away OK. I don't know where these came from. You know, the whole not remembering thing." She pulled the chemise back onto her shoulder, covering the bruise.

"Still, I do hope it was nothing too terrible." He brushed a finger across the purple under her eye. She flinched under his touch, even though it was too gentle to hurt.

A deep growl rumbled from the trees above them. Roen stepped in front of Memory, putting her between him and the flower-covered wall. She looked past his arm but saw nothing except the continued movement of sprites shimmering about, undisturbed by the noise.

"Just some wild animal in the woods. We should head back inside. It's too cold to be out anyway." Roen extended an arm, inviting her into the house in front of him.

The warmth of the kitchen made Memory's chilled skin tingle. She looked back past Roen for one final glimpse of the magical fairy lights. In the dark trees, a silhouetted figure moved amongst the twinkling, living stars. Moving into the kitchen she arched her neck for a better view and yelped when she walked straight into Brannon while looking the other way. Roen closed the door.

"Son, a word." He stepped back and opened the curtain to the main room, ushering them both through. Isabeth lay on Roen's thin bed, and another blanket had been laid out on the floor next to it.

Brannon led Roen across to the front door before looking back to Memory. "Eloryn is already asleep. You will be sharing the bed with her," he said.

Pulling back the curtain to the bedroom doorway, Memory lingered to watch, to make sure Roen really wasn't in any more trouble. Brannon talked to Roen in a whisper then slapped his hand on Roen's shoulder, giving it a small squeeze. Roen replied then turned and nodded a goodnight to Memory where she stood watching. His eyes drifted to her side and a smile tugged the corner of his mouth. Memory turned to follow his gaze and saw Eloryn sleeping on the bed, her hair draped like ivory silk over her small shoulders. The sound of the front door closing turned Memory back to find Roen gone. Only Brannon remained, watching her thoughtfully. She let the curtain fall

closed between them.

Buried in a bundle of thick down quilt, Eloryn heard soft footsteps approaching the bed. Having just shared the biggest secret of her life, one she and Alward had kept for sixteen years, her insides churned under her skin. She feigned sleep to stop the eager questions and looks of Roen's parents. But when she lay down, despite her utter exhaustion, her mind would not quiet and let her get the rest she needed so dearly.

"All tuckered out from being a princess I suppose. Must be hard," Memory's whispering voice muttered from beside the bed. Her strange words made little sense. Eloryn hoped Memory would understand her words in return.

Eloryn sat up and looked to see they were alone. The double bed felt vast around her small form. Memory stared back for a second, her eyes red rimmed, making the green more vibrant in contrast. Then she turned away from Eloryn and sat on the other side of the bed.

"I'm sorry," Eloryn said to Memory's back.

She didn't respond.

"I'm sorry I didn't tell you, but you have to understand how important it was to remain secret." Eloryn gripped the quilt, wringing it in her hands.

"I get it OK," Memory said. "It's just on a serious level of suck. I don't even know what the hell is going on and you got me all caught up in it."

"I promised I would help you, and I will. We will still try to find Alward, find out what happened with the Veil door, and help you get home. My heritage changes nothing there."

"My ass it doesn't."

"You don't understand. You don't know-"

Memory turned and glared at her and her words cut off. *Of course she doesn't know. How could I have said that to her?* Her effort to apologize turned wrong rapidly. She hardly knew how to talk to someone her own age, even without the communication gap Memory suffered. She'd never been able to make friends, even when she was allowed to mix with children her age in class. Always too shy, too different. The weight of her secret always added an extra boundary.

With a look of exhaustion, Memory turned her back on Eloryn again. She pulled back the covers and wedged herself between them, as far to the edge of her side as she could.

I have to try again. Eloryn knew her title meant a lot more to everyone else but she only wanted simpler things, to be safe and happy with people she cared about. "I know I made things worse by hiding who I was from you. But maybe I can help you understand. I was raised by Alward, the man who saved me when my parents were killed." Goosebumps prickled her all over. How she'd dared to feel dissatisfied with her life before made guilt simmer inside. Their life together was good, comfortable, and safe. Alward did everything he could for her, to keep her safe and make her happy. He treated her as his daughter

even though she wasn't, and she knew it meant he never had a chance to have his own children, his own life. If anything happened to him, it would be her fault. "It was hard, growing up, to understand why we lived how we did, the terrible things that had happened. Alward used to tell me a bedtime story..."

Memory made no movement, and Eloryn thought maybe she'd fallen asleep. Still, Eloryn pulled her knees up and put her chin on them, and spoke the words of the fairytale she knew by heart.

"Once upon a time in a beautiful land, surrounded by seas, man and fae lived side by side, peacefully, under the Pact. The Queen of this land was beautiful and young, and time came for her to take a King. Many tried for the place but only one could be chosen for her. One man, Thayl, became obsessed with the Queen. He swore vengeance on the Wizards' Council when they picked another man to be the Queen's husband. Then he disappeared, vanished without trace. The Queen married and grew large with her first child. The time came when the Queen went into labor, and on that night, Thayl returned."

Memory turned over and propped herself up on one elbow, wide eyed and enthralled like the children in Eloryn's classes.

"Thayl stormed Caermaellan and slew all between himself and the Queen as he had vowed. The King, the council of wizards, the castle guard, all fell before him as he unleashed a terrifying new magic. One wizard escaped and ran to save the queen. Too weak from her labor, she ordered the wizard to take her newborn and flee, to only and most importantly keep her child safe. He did, and the Queen was left to her fate. Thayl took control of the kingdom, forever still hunting the few wizards that escaped him and seeking the heir he knew survived that night. Some tried to fight, but none could stand against him and his new powers.

"The wizard went into hiding and raised the Queen's daughter, caring for her and teaching her, and keeping her safe from all those he knew would be hunting her." Eloryn finished, and Alward's voice echoed in her head, the words he would speak each night before kissing her forehead and dousing the lights, *Always, always, keeping the princess safe.*

Memory stared unmoving for a long moment after Eloryn finished her tale. When nothing else came, Memory blustered, "But! What? He couldn't have her, so he killed her? That's crazy person logic! What kind of story was that?"

Eloryn cringed and wiped away a tear. "I thought it would help you to understand, to know what happened."

"He killed all those people? And this guy is still looking for you? Bloody hell." Memory put a hand over her mouth. "You were right, I didn't know. There's a lot that I don't know. But, it's a little bit less now."

Eloryn slid back under the covers, hiding her face and the tears that refused to stop. *Alward, where are you?* As her consciousness faded away into sleep, Memory whispered, "I hope your fairytale gets a happy ending one day."

CHAPTER EIGHT

She stood in an alley way. All grey.

Impossibly tall buildings, sharp and slick, bent over and watched.

She looked up, not into them but into a hand.

It glowed. It hurt her. It belonged to a man.

The hand, the man, the buildings spun.

She was losing herself.

Then found a young boy.

He yelled, punched, pushed the man and made him disappear.

One, two, three. They all fell into nothing.

An eternity of darkness.

They dissolved and swirled. Ran through trees.

Brambles tearing.

Talons and scales. Thundering, hungry roars.
She held his hand, he held hers back.
Their wrists matched.
They couldn't hold on.
She screamed.

She screamed. Strong hands held her down. She thrashed, clawed, bucked. Sweat and tears drenched her skin. Her eyelids felt glued. She tore them open.

Heart thundering and chest burning, Memory's eyes darted, trying to refocus in the morning light.

Where am I? How did I get here? I can't remember, I can't…

Oh… right. That amnesia thing.

Roen knelt on the bed next to her, holding her still by her shoulders. The feeling of his hands pushing her down kept her panic racing, and she pulled away, backing up against the carved headboard. The red velvet of the bed's canopy shook like blood dripping down from the ceiling.

Across the room, Isabeth had her arms wrapped protectively around Eloryn. Both had wide eyes and tangled hair, just awoken. A bathtub of black, cold water stood in the corner. Brannon watched from the foot of the bed.

"Sorry." Memory's voice cracked, sore from the screaming she'd done. "Nightmare."

She felt an awful disappointment that she hadn't woken up somewhere she recognized, with people she knew and memories of who she was. She wished that the few things she could remember were the nightmare that she could wake from.

Roen gave her a kind smile. "As long as you're all right." He looked tired and grim, and wore the same clothes he did yesterday. He got back up off the bed and seemed to be trying to catch his father's eye.

Brannon looked at Eloryn. "Are you sure she remembers nothing?"

"No, *she* doesn't," Memory cut in.

She wished she hadn't when Brannon turned on her, a hard line across his forehead. "Memories or not, you have to understand how strange you are, how risky it is for all of us to trust you here."

Roen choked. He apologized with his eyes before dropping his head away.

"I'd leave if I knew where to go!" Memory winced at the shrill tone in her voice and tried to calm it. "But I don't. I don't remember anything. I just want to go home and will as soon as I know where that is."

Tears from her nightmare still wet her face and she wiped it furiously. She felt like a two year old, sitting in bed crying while everyone stared at her. She wished she had somewhere else to go so she could leave right now.

Eloryn sat down on the bed next to her. "What did you dream? It might tell us something about where you're from, so we can help you get home."

Memory looked up just in time to see Isabeth and Brannon glance at each other with matching disapproval.

"There was a man. I think he did something...?" Acid rose in Memory's throat, startling her and stinging her eyes to tears. She paused, breathing deeply. *The hand, the man, the buildings spun.* Her head hurt. The images from her dream faded out of her grasp. "It was a mess of stuff, confusing. I don't know."

"It was probably just a dream, nothing real." Isabeth set her mouth rigidly. "One look at you says you've probably just had a knock on the head and gotten lost."

Memory pulled back the sleeve of her chemise and twisted her arm around to see the inside of her wrist. Obscured by a yet another bruise was a small tattoo in rough, dark ink. Like a symbol for eternity with a swirl through the middle. *Their wrists matched.*

Brannon turned his attention to his son. "Roen, all done?"

"I just got back when I heard screaming and came straight in here. I have news for you. I will tell you in a moment, needn't do it here." He gave a single nod to his father, and their eyes locked.

Eloryn stood back up. "News-?"

Isabeth spoke straight over the top of her. "Come then. Let's have you both dressed and fed. Then we can talk more." She flicked her head at Roen and Brannon, who turned to leave. On his way out, Roen gave Memory an apologetic smile. He started to smile at Eloryn, but then bowed shortly to her instead, making the rose in her cheeks turn bright.

"Have you any clean clothing?" said Isabeth.

"No, but I can clean what we wore." Eloryn continued to speak a string of musical nonsense. Their muddy clothes strewn around the tub wriggled to life. Dirt and filth shivered off them, shed onto the floor as though the fabric repelled it away. Torn holes in Eloryn's dress drew closed, threads weaving themselves back together.

"You couldn't have done that yesterday? We looked like we'd just left a mud wrestling tournament," Memory said.

"I didn't want anyone to see what I could do. I'm sorry."

"Right to be careful too," Isabeth said. "Few people could cast a behest that complex, and those are just the people Thayl is trying to find. My, you're good with your words though, just like your mother. But we'll still need a dress for Memory."

"I can't wear my own clothes?" Memory was dismayed. Her jeans and t-shirt felt way more comfortable than the tent she wore now.

Slipping into her dress, Eloryn looked at her with pity. "They stand out too much; we already talked about this. But we'll keep them,

of course."

Memory watched how natural Eloryn looked in her dress, with her long flowing hair and pretty rounded shape. She guessed that was what a princess should look like. She imagined herself in a dress - bony, bruised, boy haired - and shuddered. She grabbed a bristle brush from a side table and made an effort to smooth her teased hair.

Isabeth dug through an inlaid wood chest filled with clothing. "I may have something that will fit. Roen brings such lovely dresses for me, but not always just the right size. Still, it's the thought that's sweet. He's done so well to afford to look after us how he does, considering. Maybe... No that won't fit, scrap of a thing you are."

"I can just wear this," Memory offered, motioning to the gown she had on without enthusiasm.

Isabeth rolled her eyes, muttering in exasperation under her breath. "That is an under dress, dear. No, here, this is what I was looking for. We should be able to lace it down enough to fit you."

She pulled a simple rust-red dress from the depths, dusted it down and instructed that it should go *over* the *under* dress.

Grumbling to herself, Memory took the dress and struggled to make sense of the laces, layers and yards of fabric. While Isabeth was distracted brushing Eloryn's hair, Memory slipped the flick knife out of her jeans. She tucked it up into the binding sleeve of her dress, then stuffed her clothes into Eloryn's bag. She pulled on her skater shoes, glad the long skirt covered them, and stood back up.

Memory flinched, thinking there was a stranger in the room. It took a moment to realize she saw herself in the reflection of a gold framed mirror. There were things she'd gathered about her appearance, just from living within her body for the last couple of days, but seeing herself now struck her greatly. She was so little, slim-nearing-skeletal, smaller even than how she'd felt. She knew she was about the same

height as Eloryn, but if Eloryn had an hourglass figure, she'd be a minute glass. She wished she had managed to eat something last night.

She frowned, seeing the fading black and pink color of her hair clearly for the first time. Of course it was dyed! And then there were the bruises. Despite having a pretty dress on, she still felt far from fairest of them all. She wondered if Isabeth had any eye liner then found herself thinking about Roen's eyes.

"Was Roen out all night?"

Working at braiding Eloryn's hair, Isabeth tutted. "Well, there was hardly enough room here for all of us. He often stays in town when he works late. Did he tell you he is assistant to one of the most successful businessmen in Maerranton? He's always been lucky, in his way. An unexpected gift he was, when we didn't intend to..." Isabeth cleared her throat. She shifted on her feet, pausing awkwardly. "You know, Roen was just a toddler when we heard Loredanna was with child. We had hoped it would be a girl for him to play with and look after. But then, well… Then we hoped there'd be a child alive at all."

Apart from her very first answer, Isabeth directed everything she said to the princess. *I might as well be invisible. She's been setting them up since before Eloryn was even born.*

"You said before, you had reason to believe I lived. Please tell me how?" asked Eloryn.

"It's not a pleasant story, love."

"I would still like to know, please."

Isabeth tugged at her thin fingers then sat down on the corner of the bed. "After Thayl struck Caermaellan castle, we had our wizard send us through a Veil door to your mother's estate, to warn her."

Eloryn slipped down onto the edge of the bed beside Isabeth, shaking her head. "Estate?"

"Lady Loredanna stayed at her country home, just across the

mountains here, during the last months of her pregnancy. I don't know how much you know, but your mother wasn't happy after her marriage. She lived there as much as she could, isolated from the court, her husband, even her closest friends."

"I don't think Alward knew my mother much at all, not in person. But he said... are you sure she hadn't gone back to the castle?"

Isabeth's skin wrinkled around her face into a frown and her hand covered her mouth. "Oh, love. We found her at the estate. We were too late. She was already dead, surrounded by the bodies of every other man and woman from her staff. They must have tried to protect her. I don't know what happened. They were all out in the forest... But Loredanna was no longer with child and there was no baby among the dead. We knew there had been a younger member of the Wizards' Council at the estate, Pellaine - yes, Alward - who also couldn't be found. That is all we knew. That was enough to let us hope he got you away to safety."

Eloryn squinted as if she'd been slapped. "I know of the estate you mean. The children from the village called it a ghost house. It was close to where we lived, within walking distance, but Alward never said... I thought she was with my father when..."

Memory watched silently. *Turns out I'm not the only one who didn't know everything.* Something seemed to pull from the inside of her chest like a magnet, as though she should do something - hug Eloryn, say some comforting words - but nothing she could think of seemed natural.

Isabeth patted Eloryn's hand consolingly. It looked as awkward as Memory felt. "I wish you could have known your mother. You are so much of her! In Faerbaird castle we had a portrait of Lady Loredanna from her coronation, when she wasn't much older than you are now. She wore the crested medallion in that portrait, the one you dropped in front of Roen. Mind you take better care of it from now on."

Eloryn moved her mouth, and it took a moment for her voice to find its way out. "Do you still have her portrait? I'd like to see my mother."

"I'm so sorry. There have been times we've had to run, and it was lost. Still it served its purpose." Isabeth gave her a knowing half smile. "Had Roen not grown up besotted with the lady in the painting, he might not have spotted the medallion so easily."

A clatter of plates brought their attention to the door. Roen's cheeks were noticeably red when he pushed through.

He brought in a silver tray laid out with bread and dry fruit and placed it on the dresser next to Memory. He seemed on edge and didn't even look at her.

Roen walked over and whispered to Isabeth, then bowed to Eloryn and backed out of the room. *Even if helping me isn't important to them, at least they're feeding me.* Without a thought to politeness, Memory grabbed a bread roll, stuffing large chunks in her mouth. Her stomach was a roaring pit of hunger. The absence of coffee dismayed her. She could really do with some coffee.

Isabeth excused herself and followed Roen.

"Are you going to eat any of this?" Memory asked Eloryn. There wasn't a lot of food, and while her stomach hurt less, she could easily keep eating. She eyed the entire platter with a lusting hunger.

"Please, quiet," Eloryn whispered. She stared intently at the curtain screen between the rooms. Over her chewing, Memory hadn't noticed the hushed, serious tones of the conversation coming from the living area.

"Are you eavesdropping?" Memory whispered back around a mouthful of bread. "What are they saying? They aren't going to make me go, are they?"

Eloryn paled.

They are. They're going to kick me out. Memory couldn't make out any clear words, only quiet mumbling. It couldn't be worse than what she imagined they were saying. Looking at the green tint to Eloryn's skin, Memory bit her lip. *Nope, worse, and not even about me. When has anyone been that worried about me?*

"No," Eloryn gasped and bolted out into the living area. Memory followed on her heels, grabbing the last bread roll on the way past.

CHAPTER NINE

Roen's body shivered in an ongoing tremble he couldn't control. He was exhausted, but he often worked all night and it never left him like this. *Why am I so anxious?* His father looked grave, but smiled at Roen and patted him on the shoulder.

After the entire night spent listening in, seeking gossip and spying, Roen explained to his parents what he saw in town during the dark hours of morning. He'd finally managed to bring his parents something of such value it could change their hard lives. Pride mixed with bitter anxiety at the news he now delivered.

The princess burst through the curtain from the bedroom with a look on her face that made Roen shake harder. He gripped his hands together to still them.

Isabeth tried to herd the girls back into the bedroom. Eloryn ducked past her, straight to where Roen and his father were sitting at the table. They cut off their conversation.

"It's not true. He couldn't be," Eloryn insisted.

Roen turned to his father, not sure how to respond. Brannon shook his head in the smallest of movements.

Eloryn came to a stop in the middle of the room, her chest rising and falling from sharp breaths. "No secrets, please. I know what you said, but you must be wrong. They couldn't have caught him. Couldn't have!"

"Princess, I'm sorry. I saw him myself." Roen's muscles still ached from the strain of moving unseen and unheard to get as close as he could to Alward's cell. But all he could do was watch, blocked by too many guards and gates locked by magic instead of mechanisms that would click open for his fingers.

"He is nearby? I have to go to him." Eloryn headed toward the front door.

With two huge steps Brannon moved in front of her. He held his only hand out in a calming gesture. "It is your safety that is most important, you know this."

Eloryn shook her head in a way that made her blonde hair shiver around her.

Roen forced his words out, wishing there were some other messenger for this news. "Alward is alive, but they have poisons that block his magic and he is heavily guarded. The wizard hunters also had a good view of you both," he said, looking from Eloryn to Memory. "They're already heading back out to continue searching for you. Fifteen of them, some heading back into the forest, others onto the roadways. The rest have begun searching houses and farms around Maerranton."

Isabeth dropped into a nearby seat as though her legs had been cut out from under her. "They won't be safe here, will they?"

Brannon shook his head. "We need to get Eloryn away from here, as fast as possible."

"And yourselves," Roen added. "They are Thayl's men. You can't risk them recognizing you if they come this way."

"No." Eloryn eyed the door, hysteria in her eyes. "No, I can't leave Alward."

Brannon stood as a barrier between her and the exit. "There's no doubt Thayl will come to see Alward himself, to be sure who it is. Once he is sure, he'll do everything he can to find you. Did Alward have somewhere else for you to go, to someone else he trusted?"

"He considered at times going to others from the Wizards' Council-"

"There are others still alive?"

"But we never did. I don't know where to find them on my own. We were meant to go to our other home on Rhynn together, to be safe there. What must I do to get him back? I have to do something to free him."

"Lory, that doesn't sound like a good idea. Not if that Thayl guy might be coming. Remember the part about him being a crazy person?" Memory mumbled from the back of the room.

Brannon's voice flooded over Memory's. "It's not what Alward would want, nor will we let you try. You're too precious to be lost taking such a risk."

Doubt and denial showed clear on Eloryn's face.

Brannon rubbed his eyebrows for a moment then spoke again, his voice smooth and comforting. "We will do everything we can to have Alward freed. There are local resistance fighters we can call on. They will be better fitted for the job, readier for such a task. Leave this to us."

Roen raised his eyebrows at his father's words. They hadn't been in contact with the resistance since the warring ended and they went into hiding, over a decade ago. "And what of Eloryn?"

"We'll send her to Lanval." Brannon nodded to his son, and Roen recognized the look of warning on his face. "If any of the Wizards' Council still survives, he'll be the best chance of finding them." Brannon turned to Eloryn, bending down to look her straight in the eye. "Duke Lanval is an old friend. He is trusted and well connected. It is wisest that you go to him now, understand?"

She nodded obediently, a tear dropping to the floor with the tilting of her head. Roen found himself on his feet, one hand wrapped tight around the backrest of the chair. His father had the sort of tone it was hard to say no to, the tone of a duke, last remnant of his lost nobility. To see it used on the Princess in this way lit a rebellious fire within Roen. He breathed deeply to cool it down. *After all, Father is right. We can't let Eloryn go after Alward. Who am I to judge his lies?* There was nothing they could do.

Brannon straightened back up. "Then you leave right away."

Eloryn turned so quickly to Memory it made her jump. "You'll come with me?"

"Err, yeah, of course," Memory muttered. Being included in the conversation left her looking dumbfounded.

"Can't we go with them?" said Isabeth.

"Too many of the wrong people in the Duke's court still know our faces," Brannon said.

"But the Princess..." Isabeth looked stricken.

"Roen visits the Duke often, he knows the way. He'll do his best to get her there safely." Brannon gave his decision without a look to his son for confirmation. His tone sounded more disappointed than trusting.

Roen cleared his throat, worried the tightness in it would taint his voice. He handed his father a piece of paper. "You and Mother must leave as soon as possible too. Go to the inn at this address. Ask for Scarlett, she'll make sure you aren't found."

Brannon took the address and everyone began to move. Roen let out a lungful of air. He hadn't really expected a thank you. He was happy at least that Brannon had the grace not to ask who Scarlett was. Of all the sons in the family, he knew he wouldn't have been their choice to be the only one they had left. It was the simple fact of *what* he was that meant he could never be enough. *What they would think of me if they also knew what I did to make a living...*

Eloryn sniffled and drifted back into the bedroom. Memory hovered while Brannon and Isabeth rushed about preparing to leave. Roen threw a pack over his arm, stuffed it with a change of clothing and considered what else he might need. Still in his work clothes from the day before, he had most necessary items on him already and had few other belongings worth taking. It wouldn't take long to escort the Princess to Duke Lanval's. Once he got her there they would find someone fitter for the task of protecting the Maellan heir. Heading to the kitchen for food, he met his mother, who pressed a small jar of ointment into his hands.

He smiled at her from below pinched eyebrows. "Mother, my shoulder's fine now."

"You know you've got no healing behests to sort it out if it acts up on you again. Take it." Isabeth pushed it into his hands. "Look after her well. One day, maybe she'll be Queen, and remember the help we've given her." For a moment she looked over her son's face, her expression split between a frown and a smile. She left to join Eloryn and Brannon in the living room.

Ready to leave, Eloryn wore her satchel with the strap diagonally across her chest, tucked tight under one arm as he had shown her. Roen's lips twitched.

Shuffling out of the way, Memory backed into the kitchen and bumped into Roen. They both watched Isabeth wrap her arms around Eloryn in a strong embrace.

Memory tilted her head. "Don't you get one too?"

Roen whispered into Memory's ear. "I think we all know who is most important here."

Her eyes narrowed shiftily. "Me, right? Is it me? Yep. Definitely me." Memory lifted one corner of her lips into a cheeky smile which he returned.

His parents took their lightly packed bags and they all headed out the back doorway of the cottage. They knew how to pack for this risk, taking only essentials and a few identifying heirlooms and leaving their home so it didn't appear to have been fled in a hurry. With luck, the hunters would not come this way. Or if they did, they would find nothing suspicious and move on, and he could find his parents and bring them home in just a few days. *And return to...?* The question made his chest ache and he shook it off.

Brannon took Roen's hand and held it firmly. "Get her to the Duke's quickly. Don't let us down, son."

Isabeth fussed, brushing back Eloryn's hair from her face. "Be safe, and watch out for fairy rings."

Roen nodded a goodbye to his parents, and they headed separate ways.

Following Roen, Memory put on her best impersonation of hope. Lanval sounded like someone powerful, someone with connections who knew other wizards, so maybe he would be able to help her as well. *Because everyone's been falling over themselves to help me so far.*

Roen led them along a dirt track through the tall, untended crops. He turned his head continually, watching all around them.

Memory's legs ached and moved like rusty robotics, unhappy from their overuse. Beside her, Eloryn seemed to be struggling just as much with hers. She chewed on her bottom lip. Also failing at being hopeful, perhaps.

Memory nudged her with an elbow. "You 'K?"

"Sorry?"

"Don't worry. They'll sort things out, with Alward. Maybe the resistance guys will free him and he'll meet us at this Duke's place?"

Eloryn nodded and looked away.

"How far is it anyway?" Memory asked Roen.

"Normally, just a short trip through the city. His palace is actually that way." He pointed, and to Memory it looked as if he pointed back the way they came. "But it will be safer to travel out into the forest, avoiding the city and roadways, and coming back into the palace from the other side."

"Not safer for my legs," Memory whined.

"You won't have to walk far. Just down the hill from here is the Draper's farm. Good folk, lots of daughters. I know them well enough that they might lend us some horses."

Memory raised her hand. "Um, I don't know how to ride, I think."

"You seem like a fast learner to me." Roen winked at her.

Memory found herself blushing, and turned her focus toward the forest that followed the edge of the fields. She stared high into the red and yellow tapestry of leaves, hoping to see the little fairies she'd

seen last night. In the morning sunlight she saw nothing but birds and insects humming through the treetops.

"Look forward to being well treated when we arrive at the palace. Duke Lanval is quite fond of me. He knew my parents well, and while he cannot safely host them, he lets me visit often. He has no children of his own, so I think he enjoys the company." Roen continued walking ahead, talking to them over his shoulder. The flow of his words seemed nervous. Eloryn had clammed up again and Memory had nothing much to say either, so she let him talk.

"Most think the Duke is loyal to Thayl, but the truth is more a loyalty to his wife. After my family and others refused to accept him as king, Thayl needed someone influential on his side. He tortured Lanval's wife to secure his compliance. Lanval won't risk his wife's safety again, but has no love for Thayl. He takes no action against Thayl himself, but has contacts in the resistance, whom he also funds. You can trust him, by my life."

Coming around a bend, the field ended and the path wound down a terraced slope. They were met with a view of a pretty farmstead at the bottom, and a scream that pierced through the air.

Roen pushed them back into the cornfield they'd just stepped out of. Down the hill, spooked horses jittered near a stable. From one of the buildings came the sound of someone yelling and a door slamming. A man stepped into view around the corner of the stables, dragging a young woman by her blonde hair. He threw her to the ground, and more men appeared from the other buildings, two younger girls in tow.

Roen grunted and stepped forward.

"They're looking for me, aren't they?" Eloryn whispered.

Roen clenched his fists, but didn't move any farther. The wizard hunters lined up the three girls. Kneeling in the mud, the sisters squirmed in confusion and the men pointed, stared and argued. One

man ran his hands over the youngest girl's face, the one closest in age
to Eloryn. He pushed her chin up, tilting her face for closer inspection
and stroking his hand down her neck. A tangy taste filled Memory's
mouth, and she realized she'd bitten into her tongue. Her feet were
backing her away into the corn, but her gaze remained fixed on the
farm below.

A man ran through the field toward the girls, their dad, Memory
guessed. The hunters drew swords, and the man stopped. He held the
hoe he carried up in front of him. The yelling between them echoed in
the small valley, their sharp words barking back and forth. The farmer
lunged and Memory shrieked. The daughters did the same, covering
the sound. Their father slumped. The hunter he attacked stepped
backwards, revealing a bloodied sword. The farmer fell face down.

Memory ran. Terror pumped her feet and she bolted back through
the crisp dried corn stalks, out of the field, into the forest.

"Mem." Roen raced up behind her. He grabbed her arm, pulling
her to a stop. Eloryn caught up.

Memory wrenched her arm away, stumbling against a tree. "He
just stabbed that man." Memory's stomach cramped and she bent
forward, sucking in deep breaths. "If they catch us, Lory, what's going
to happen? Are they going to kill us? What are they going to do to
me?"

Eloryn winced, looking green. "I don't know."

Roen glanced over his shoulder, fists still clenched. "It will be all
right. I'll get you both to the Duke's safely. It'll just take longer."

Eloryn whimpered, tugging at the ends of her hair. "They were
looking for me. I have to... I could help the farmer, heal him if he is
still..."

Roen grabbed her shoulders, turning her to him, away from the
direction of the farm. "It's not your fault. You didn't make the farmer

challenge the hunters, and you didn't make the hunter use his sword. But yes, they're after you, and they'll catch you too if you go back there."

"He could die," said Eloryn.

"And so could we," said Memory. "We need to get gone. Now."

"If he's still alive his family will see to him. Memory's right, we have to go; we're already slowed for having to walk," said Roen.

Eloryn fumbled her words, starting three times before anything made sense. "I can get us some horses. I can ask with a behest and they will come to us here."

"Come to us? Can't you just abracadabra and make them appear? Instant horse?" Memory paced, chewing on her nails. She couldn't stand the idea of waiting.

"Magic can only make requests from what is there, whether it's horses, the mud on our clothes, or the energies of nature. The farmer left the back field open. I don't think anyone will see the horses leave from there."

Roen looked over his shoulder again and nodded. "Bring them, but only if you're sure there's no risk. The faster we can be gone, the better."

Eloryn nodded and spoke another language into the surrounding woods, the lyrical words clipped between panted breaths. She stopped, and a short moment passed in silence. "They're coming; it won't be long."

"So, it's just pretty please, but in fancy magic words? How did they even hear you?" The whole concept seemed flimsy to Memory. Even having seen magic in use, the idea of relying on something she felt skeptical about when those hunters were so close left her stomach turning.

"The ancient words give the meaning, but it's the spark of

connection that lets us communicate our behests. The internal connection to magic that you feel, in here," Eloryn put her hand to the centre of her chest. "The Pact has meant all people of Avall have the spark of connection within. Don't you feel it?"

Memory turned the concept around in her mind, wondering if she could connect to magic in any way. She looked down at her chest, feeling the warmth within her she'd known these last few days. She thought it was just panic-induced heartburn.

Three sleek horses trotted through the thin woods, crunching leaves under their hooves. One horse walked up to each of them, sniffing them in a friendly manner. Memory patted the brown horse beside her with a stiff and timid hand. She wanted to get away from here as fast as possible, but felt tiny next to the huge beast. What was she supposed to do with it?

Eloryn whispered to the dappled horse that nuzzled her. The horse knelt before her, allowing her to climb upon its bare back. "You don't need to know how to ride. They will look after us." Eloryn still looked nervous when the horse rose to its feet.

Memory patted her horse on the nose again and mumbled, "You're not going to do that for me are you? At least don't let me fall off and add to my bruise collection, OK?"

The horse whinnied. Memory took it as an affirmative, if a mischievous one.

"Quickly now, and keep your voices down," Roen said, and offered her a boost. She wanted to mount her horse gracefully, but in the end was happy just to drag herself on top of it. She clutched its mane with hesitation, afraid to either fall or annoy her ride.

Roen scanned the forest again and hopped up onto his pale tan steed with ease. *Well, he doesn't have a dress to contend with. I miss my jeans. I could run faster in jeans.*

The desire to run re-ignited the fire that burned in her chest since her first moments of memory when that demon dragon thing attacked them. *It must be somewhere, nearby, if the wizard hunters are here.* Her skin crawled as vivid flashes of the beast pulsed in her mind. She worried they would need something a lot faster than horses.

"So, you can't just want something and say, "bring me something to ride" unless you know… the… magic…?" Memory's chest flared hot like coals under bellows. Her mouth tasted of blood and the air around her bent in a way that made her seasick. She blinked, trying to shake the sense of vertigo that hit her, as though being up on the horse were suddenly higher than she could bear.

Eloryn gaped, her face twisted in confusion.

A hideous cry broke through the forest.

Darkness gathered around them. Living patches of ebony formed within snaking mist. A sucking wind and swirls of shadows met in a ball of heaving black.

The noise. The mist. The wind. Memory felt sick.

Something moved within the solid shadows, a shape, folding and emerging.

The huge form writhed and twisted. A jungle of powerful limbs lashed and tangled with smoky vines. Scales like black jewels sparkled dangerously on the flicking tail. With a final, louder cry, it tore from the tormenting mist, pushing itself through, still caught half way within.

It roared again. Angry. Hungry.

The dragon.

CHAPTER TEN

The dragon thrashed, trying to free itself. It screamed, vicious and guttural like murder and grief combined, clawing at the grey cobwebs of smoke that held it back like chains.

"No." Memory shuddered. The impossible creature matched her, shaking against the grip of the malformed Veil door. The very same torment she had experienced, the first horrors of her memory, the winds she thought would tear her apart. The magical gale gushed outwards, spinning leaves and dirt into the air. A high pitched hum filled Memory's ears and her eyes watered.

Closest to the beast, Eloryn cried out. Her horse wheeled on the spot. Its eyes rolled and froth dripped from its mouth.

Eloryn hugged it around the neck, and it steadied, pawing at the

ground. She faced the dragon.

"Cuirdhùnadh fanhl," she called and waited, as though expecting something. The dragon's head swung to her words, flesh sliding back from its mouth. It hissed and twisted toward her in confused wrath.

"Princess, tell me you can make it leave." Roen grunted, pulling his skittish horse toward Eloryn by handfuls of mane. It whinnied and turned him back away.

"Fanhl," Eloryn cried again, her voice cracking.

"Lory, get away from it," Memory begged. Empty, wrung out, she sagged over her horse's neck. She couldn't think. Her mind had become chaos and body felt burnt out and charred.

Eloryn shot a look at Memory. Terrified, angry confusion twisted her lips back from her teeth. "You did this. How did you do this? How can I make it go?"

I did...? Memory gaped at the creature, the immense, inconceivable mass of muscle, talon and black diamond scales. Her thoughts split and twirled like a kaleidoscope. *Magic can only make requests from what is there.* She only wanted to run, a faster way to run. *Bring me something to ride.* Did saying the words make the request? A request that brought her the very thing she wanted to run from? *It's impossible, impossible...*

The dragon contorted, as though in pain. An armored claw burst free of the Veil. Eloryn's horse bucked in panic, throwing her off its bare back. She hit the ground hard and the dragon's talons lashed out, stripping skin from the horse's neck.

The horse cried a horrific scream, sounding too human, the scream of a child or woman more than that of a beast. Eloryn matched it. The horse crumpled and fell a fraction away from crushing Eloryn beneath its weight.

"Eloryn!" Roen struggled on his wild horse, close to being thrown off himself.

Memory's horse remained eerily still beneath her. She was just as petrified, fixated on the stream of blood running from the fallen animal's torn neck, and its motionless, turned back eyes. Roen yelled at her, trying to tell her something. It came through her ringing ears as crackling static. The dragon flailed, crying through an army of sharp teeth. Its ruby red claws flashed as it slashed away its misty bonds.

Roen's voice broke through. "Memory, ride, go!"

Memory squeezed her eyes closed. She was going to be ripped apart by this creature that had come for her, called by her. A demon she couldn't control. She opened her eyes and the nightmarish dragon was still there, glaring with thin slit cat eyes, judging her. It pushed another claw free of the Veil, its bonds dispersing into vapor.

Roen kicked his horse into movement. He tugged it by the mane to where Eloryn wobbled on her feet and scooped her up. Cradling her in his lap, he rode the horse back toward Memory.

"Hya!" he hollered, slapping her horse on the rump, startling it into movement. It jerked into a gallop and he herded it roughly ahead of him. Memory held on finger-achingly tight and they rode hard.

The dragon bellowed behind them. The sound of it thrashing and tearing itself free chased them through the forest.

Held in Roen's arms, her frightened face splattered with the horse's blood, Eloryn stared at Memory. Memory turned away, bent down close to her horse's neck and begged it to run faster.

Roen led them on a zigzagging chase across the landscape, across rocky crests and through sparse copses, out into untended fields, across roadways and back into forests again. Trees swam in Memory's eyes as they sped through them. On the verge of vomiting or passing out, she breathed deeply to avoid either.

Time blurred and night turned the world blue-grey. At times they stopped, stilled the horses and hid in the dark from the beating of

vast wings in the sky above. Everyone kept utterly silent, as though a single word could bring the dragon to them. From their shared horse, Roen and Eloryn peered at Memory in a way that turned her stomach. The dragon could have torn them all open like that horse and they thought she summoned it. Her head and heart both pounded with painful ferocity. *How could I do that? Who am I?*

Finally they came within sight of a grand palace, standing at the edge of the other side of the city they had left when it was still morning.

Memory clung senselessly to her horse, her fingers chilled and knees locked. The neckline of her dress was soaked in tears and sweat. Uncontrollable shudders railroaded through her.

Riding up to a stone wall, Roen pulled up his horse, lowered Eloryn down and then dismounted. He pulled Memory's horse to a stop and calmed it, then pried Memory off, catching her as she slid to the ground.

Eloryn thanked the horses and consoled them for the loss of one of their herd. Memory watched the survivors gallop off. A pang of guilt started her tears flowing again.

Roen looked into the clear dark sky, scanning the horizon. He took her shivering hand, pulling her after him, Eloryn at his other side. They moved along the wall, ducked down, cut across through an arched gate, ran through an orchard and up to a small servants' door at the base of ancient stone walls.

Roen let go of her hand abruptly. He gave the door a push, tried to force it, lift it, but nothing moved. He grunted and hit the door with a fist. Pausing, he took a deep breath, then knocked loudly.

"Wipe your tears," he hissed at Memory. "And smile."

She did her best to obey, blotting at her face with her sleeves, wiping her nose. Just as she coughed her throat clear and put a shaky smile onto her face, a peephole in the door slid open and a pair of

clouded eyes peered out.

"Roen, boy? Is that you?" The peephole closed, latches clicked in sequence and the door opened. A short but straight-backed old man met Roen with a wrinkled smile.

"Uther, thank the fae," Roen breathed out, smiling.

"Wherefore are you knocking here so late, hrm?" The way he spoke sounded as though he already knew the answer. He squinted past Roen at Memory and Eloryn.

Roen grinned and leant across the threshold, whispering to the old man. He tilted his head back, indicating the two girls. "Please, Uther, my man. You've not denied me before."

Uther winked and stepped clear of the doorway. He turned his head, pretending not to witness Roen and his ladies entering in the night.

Roen patted his friend on the back when he passed. He took both girls by the hand and led them at a brisk pace through the laundry room. The old man saw to re-barring the heavy door, chuckling behind them.

Roen pulled them around a few corners in a maze of narrow halls then stopped. He turned toward Memory so forcefully she backed up against a wall.

"What was that, back there?"

"I don't know, I don't," Memory stammered, unable to look at them.

Eloryn's voice came as a plea. "But it was you. I felt the power come from you. You brought a dragon, unwilling, through the Veil. That magic was... It shouldn't be possible."

"It wasn't me. I couldn't." Memory turned her face toward the wall, gripping her aching head in her hands. Her world, her small, short, confusing world fell apart with every step she took. She felt nauseous, the fire inside melting her away. She slumped and Roen grabbed her waist, supporting her.

"Is she going to be all right? Could she be damaged from what she did, by the magic?" Roen's voice blurred in her ears. Angry or concerned, Memory couldn't tell.

A silence, then Eloryn's voice came out trembling. "I don't know. This is... contrary to everything I... Even if she had the right words, what she did would be dangerous magic. She summoned *a dragon.*"

Memory flinched, bringing her hands up in front of her face as though the words struck her physically.

Roen spoke again, this time more softly. "We'll work it out later. We need to get her to a room. Let her calm down. Make sure she's all right."

Someone had Memory's hand again, gently pulling her forward, off the wall and down the corridor. She didn't know who. She stumbled after them, blinded by tears. *Damaged? Nothing feels right in me already, and I might have just messed myself up even more.* The words, the desire, the flame that rushed through her like a blazing tornado... it was her. She'd brought the dragon. Magic, impossible magic. *Who am I?* Moving forward made everything blur into streaks. She pulled her hand free, to stand still and ease her pounding head, only to have her legs crumble away. Roen caught her just before she hit the hard, stone floor.

Roen carried Memory through the servant corridors and up into the more ornate halls of the castle. Still unconscious, she shivered in his arms. He wondered at how fragile and light she felt. *It's surprising*

she made it this far.

Beside him, Eloryn trotted to keep up with his longer stride. He took them through the not-so-secret passageways to avoid servants and guards going about their night time duties. Designed for fast escape in case of a siege, they were used more often for romantic meetings and the staff gave them a wide berth at night. Roen had hoped to get inside without anyone seeing Eloryn, but if he could keep it to just Uther, that would have to do. Uther could barely see anyway.

Roen tried the sapphire suite, across the hall from his normal guest room. Marian had just finished redecorating and his guess it would be vacant paid off. Finding the door unlocked, he went inside and laid Memory onto a bed.

Eloryn hovered next to him. "What she did, I..."

Roen shook his head. "We have to go and tell Lanval what happened, now, in case we can't stay."

"Should we be waking him?"

"With this sort of news he needs to know right away. We'll be back to check on Memory soon."

Roen hurried Eloryn to the Duke's chambers, marked by a doorway inlaid in gold with a design of a lion's face. He knocked gently. Putting his ear to the door, he listened then took a small step back to wait. Mumbling and shuffling soon turned into the creak of the door. It swung open wide, and a generously built man filled the frame, staring at them with sleep bleary eyes. He wore long rich bed robes, in a deep maroon that lit his whiskey colored beard from beneath.

"What is it, what is it? Roen, son? Why visiting so late?" Lanval held Roen's hands and patted them. He took a quick, second look at Eloryn's blood spattered face. "What's happened? Don't be bringing me bad news now."

"Good news, my Lord, great news. Maybe a little bad as well. I'm sorry it's so late, but we really must talk now." Roen bent forward in a shallow bow. Lanval put a finger to his lips and stepped out. The doorway through to the bedchamber stood open, and by the warm glow of dying embers, Roen saw Marian, tossing in her sleep on a massive, pillow-strewn bed. He frowned. *She still has nightmares.*

Lanval rubbed his eyes. "Never mind, I was awake. Come down the hall, we can talk there without disturbing Marian." He directed them to another room, a small meeting chamber with walls encrusted in carved flourishes that shone with gold leaf. It held a single elegant table, velvet padded chairs, and a woven tapestry of a captured unicorn.

Lanval took the largest chair at the end of the table, gesturing for the others to sit either side of him. Roen and Eloryn remained standing.

"Introductions, and then you can explain, what is this good news, great news, with a little bad, that is enough to drag me from my bed? News of a betrothal? That would fit the announcement." Lanval lifted an eyebrow.

"My lord, the news is in the form of an introduction. I fret my upbringing has not left me equipped for such an honor as this meeting. But still. Duke Lanval de Montredeur, this is Eloryn, daughter of Queen Loredanna and King Edmund. We have found the Maellan heir." Roen bowed his introduction with a small flourish to Eloryn.

Lanval blanched around his beard. He looked at Eloryn for a long moment, his face stern. "Found at last. Well met, Your Highness. It's good to see that Thayl wasn't able to destroy all things."

Eloryn curtseyed. "It is my honor to meet with you, Duke de Montredeur. I'm sorry for the late intrusion."

"Polite and lovely. Brought up well I see, wherever you've been hiding. Seems you've had some trouble finding your way here?"

Roen and Eloryn glanced at each other and Roen spoke again.

"We have. Before anything else, we must know our trail has not been found leading here to you."

"There is a risk?"

Roen nodded.

Lanval stood and marched to the doorway, bellowing down the corridor. He turned back to Roen. "What else?"

"Wizard Councilor Pellaine, now by the name Alward. He has been captured and imprisoned here in your city. We hope for news of his escape, or chance for his release."

Lanval's fingers drummed against the door. "I've had no news. I'm to be informed when any wizard is captured within my borders. This is not well. What of your parents, Roen, are they safe?"

"Last I saw them." Roen swallowed.

Footsteps hurried up the corridor. Lanval stepped out, closing the door behind him so the small group wouldn't be seen. Orders were rushed out, the footsteps fled again and Lanval re-entered the room.

"Gawain, one of my trusted. He will look into these matters and let us know quickly if we've cause to worry." Lanval returned to the table. Grumbling out a breath he lowered himself into his seat. "Until then, sit. You make me weary just seeing you stand."

Roen pulled out a seat for Eloryn then sat down himself.

"So, how?" Lanval stared at Eloryn, rubbing his beard. "No, never mind that. Why, why come to me? I'm happy you're alive, no doubt, but I won't be able to shelter you. If you're not too proud to accept like Roen here, I can provide whatever money you need to find safety elsewhere. But I won't risk Marian's safety further than that. Not for anyone."

Eloryn hesitated, and Roen answered for her. "I would never ask of you what would risk you or the Duchess's safety."

"Then ask boy, what do you need?"

"We hope to know if you have contact with any remaining Wizards' Councilors, or with any who know how to reach them. We feel that until the Princess is able to rule again, she is best safe in their care."

"You believe so, do you?" Lanval bent forward on the table. It groaned under his weight. "They are hard to find, and for good reason. They're not only hunted by Thayl. I've heard the unseelie fae seek them as well. I don't know why. The fae have been causing more trouble all over Avall since Thayl has been in power. Would you find safety for your Princess with the most hunted people of this land?"

Lanval leant back in his chair again, gesturing to Eloryn. "And what of the Princess's wishes, how do her plans meet with yours and your parents, for returning her to the throne? Does she want that, considering she has done naught but hide these last sixteen years?"

"I do not," Eloryn said in a rush, then dropped her voice, embarrassed. "I only want to find Alward again, to be safe with him. I have no wish to rule, or way to remove Thayl so I could. Even if he were gone, I cannot say I would be the right choice to rule."

"Ah, a lady of little ambition, after my own heart," Lanval said with a fond smile.

Roen's shoulders tensed and he stared at the table. "A Maellan heir is the one hope the people of Avall have held onto during these hard times. We all have paths in our lives we don't want to take, but we must if it can help others. Your path could help the whole land, you cannot deny that."

"You speak well, son. And you, dear Princess, best heed him. The people want the Maellan line returned. So will the Wizards' Council, should you find them. Is this still where you wish to go?"

Eloryn, head bowed and silent, couldn't have looked more unsure.

Roen nodded firmly. "I still believe it is our best hope for the Princess. If they have managed to remain hidden so long with so many

seeking them, then they will be able to keep her safe."

"Very well. I'll make inquiries." Lanval rose out of his chair and shuffled to the door. "Now, it is more morning than night, and for all your youth, you clearly need sleep even more than myself. I'll send word the moment I hear anything. Pray we don't hear the worst."

CHAPTER ELEVEN

"You... very good at that, you know. Should be... professional damsel catcher," Memory muttered, coming back to consciousness.

Warm, padded and covered, she opened her eyes and found herself alone and folded, not neatly, under sky blue covers of a single bed. Still fully clothed, less her shoes. A waft of sweat reached her nose, tainted by fear and turned pungent. She hoped she hadn't smelt like this last night. Roen and Eloryn were kind even to have removed her shoes.

The previous day came back to her and shame came with it, swallowed by outrage at the feeling. Why should she feel ashamed? She hadn't known what she was doing. It was an accident if anything. Apart from that poor horse, they were all OK. Or at least she hoped. Eloryn said she could have damaged herself somehow with the magic,

but she felt fine, in fact, even better than she remembered. Although she still didn't remember much.

Memory stumbled out of bed. The sun burned bright lines around the edges of blue velvet drapes. Shades of blue and silver covered every surface of the room, in brocade designs across the walls and a trompe l'oeil ceiling of a cloudy sky. A mirror above a cornflower colored dressing table showed all her scrapes and swelling gone. She poked at the bruising on her ribs through layered clothing, but felt no pain. Her hair, however, was painful even to look at.

"Huh," she said aloud, wondering where Bill, Ben, Bob and Barry the Bruises had gone. The room echoed. Three doors stood in walls around the room, and Memory had no idea where any led. Door Number One already stood open, revealing an adjoining chamber – just as blue – with another bed, empty and unmade. She really was all alone. Memory stood in the middle of the vast blue room at a loss for what to do next. A latch clicked, making her jump. Roen peeked in through Door Number Two, and seeing her awake, strode in followed by Eloryn. They were both neat and clean, Roen dressed in a fresh white shirt, worn loosely, and Eloryn in her same grey and ivory lace dress that always managed to look perfect. Her hair was no less perfect. *Ambushed by the pretty people. Not fair damn it.*

Memory mumbled a curse and made a casual attempt to finger comb her hair, keeping her armpits wedged closed. "Um, morning guys. I just woke up."

"We were starting to wonder when you would. It's well into the day," Roen said, a line of worry across his forehead.

"Guess I needed the sleep. I feel much better though, in a few ways." Memory pointed to where she'd had a black eye the day before.

"After you fainted, I tried to heal you." Eloryn looked at her sheepishly. "Your surface injuries healed but there must be trust and

consent for a stronger healing, and... I could not reach deeper and wake you. We were so worried for you. Still, I hoped if maybe the cause of your amnesia was more mundane that the healing magic might return some memories to you?"

"No change, but I think I'm OK, apart from desperately needing a shower."

"The bathroom is just through there," Roen said, indicating Door Number Three. He propped himself against a wall and raised an eyebrow. "Are you sure you haven't been here before?"

Memory shook her head and glared pure irony at Roen.

"Only that you would ask for a shower is curious. Castle de Montredeur is one of the few places in Avall that has such a luxury, thanks to the underground water system that supplies the estate. Still, if you were from around here, I'm sure I would remember you. You're not the type to go unnoticed," Roen said with a smirk.

"Not smelling like this anyway-"

A distant knocking made Roen interrupt her. "That sounds like my room." He opened the door again and leaned out. "Uther! Here, my man."

"Still not in your room, young sir?" The old servant spoke with laughter in his voice.

"Not the worst place you've found me now, is it? You've a message for me?" Roen asked.

"The Duke sends word that he requests your presence at the feast and ball this afternoon. That of yourself, and your two lady friends. A formal invitation." Uther handed Roen a wax sealed envelope.

"I'm not sure my companions have the energy for a social event. Not after last night," said Roen. Memory swore she saw him wink very unsubtly.

"The Duke thought that may be the case, but instructed that I

assure you the ball is a masque, so you may all hide your faces, if you're feeling a little under the weather," Uther said, his battle to keep a straight face lost quickly.

"Is that so?" Roen clapped Uther on the shoulder with a returned laugh.

"He is sending the Duchess's very own handmaidens to see to the dressing of the ladies shortly." Uther, still grinning, bowed and whispered before he left, "Careful or you may find some competition for these two beauties."

When Roen closed the door and turned around, both Memory and Eloryn stared at him open mouthed.

"My deepest apologies Princess. It is only an act," Roen said, walking back into the room. Passing Memory he whispered just within her hearing, "As if there'd be any competition." With a hint of smile still on his lips, he took a seat at the end of the bed and cracked the seal of the envelope.

Memory, stunned, wondered more about who the two beauties were. Trying to be nonchalant she glanced at the mirror. Hair and clothes were as crumpled as each other; even a few visible wrinkles from her mummy-wrapped slumber still marked her skin.

Maybe being this disheveled would make the Duke more sympathetic to her when they met. She'd take her bruises back if it would mean he'd help her. "Are we going to see the Duke soon?"

Roen shook his head, looking over the letter. "We spoke to him already, last night."

"Oh, of course you did." *I bet I wasn't even mentioned.*

Roen read the note from Lanval aloud.

"Your arrival was well timed to match our grand Autumn Masque, which a well connected man within my trust will also attend. I believe him to be the source of the information you seek. Best he also meets

the subject of the required information, that he has strong enough reason to trust in sharing it." Roen closed his eyes for a short moment then smiled. "This is good news, Princess. You'll be in safe hands soon."

"Should we really be going out? If Lory looks so much like her mum, what if someone else recognizes her?"

Roen shook his head. "We're lucky the masque is tonight. I doubt we'll spend long at the ball, but it gives us freedom to move around the castle without anyone seeing either of your faces. The Duchess's handmaidens will have you not even recognizing yourselves. Clarice, Saoirse and Lily are the best."

"It says no more within the letter? No news of Alward?" Eloryn's voice lifted an octave.

"None, I regret. It also shares no bad news which is our luck, either of Alward or of us being tracked here after what happened yesterday."

And there it is again. I guess it was too much to hope they'd just let that whole summoning a dragon thing slip, Memory thought.

"So, whoever you are, Memory, you've got some talent in magic," Roen said. Memory thought he seemed too grateful to turn the topic away from Alward and shot him a glare telling him so.

Eloryn shook her head. She had never seemed more scared of Memory than she did now. "It's not only that. No one should be able to connect with magic in that way without the use of the magical language. There's only one other person ever known to be able to do that."

Roen and Eloryn looked at each other, drawing silent.

"Oh come on, who?" Memory asked, not sure why she needed to know another name that meant nothing to her.

"King Thayl Vaircarn."

Damn. She did know that name.

"That's probably not good, is it?" Memory asked, shaken. The few clues she had about herself kept leading to unwanted places.

"It's hard to say what it means, except that you need to be careful. Careful in what you say and how you say it," Eloryn told her. "When you cast that spell yesterday, at the same time you spoke, did you feel the connection to magic within you?"

Memory nodded, feeling her chest still toasting away.

"That is what you need to avoid. Better you try not to cast anything at all until we know what has happened to you," Eloryn said, her gaze turned away from Memory.

"But maybe it's better I try and learn what I'm doing, so I know how to control it?" Memory said, her voice husky, nearly breaking. "I mean, I did that yesterday completely by accident. I don't want to have another accident."

Eloryn frowned, shaking her head slightly.

"Please. It really scared me," Memory whispered.

"Perhaps just try something simple with her," Roen said.

Eloryn bit her bottom lip, but nodded. "Something simple then."

"The verbal light switch looks handy," Memory suggested.

"Very well, the behest for it is Àlaich las. First, just practice the words. Then focus on what you want to happen. The behest brings to you a wisp, a type of fae made of light, alive, but more a pure energy than a conscious being. Feel the spark of connection within you, and then say the words again," Eloryn instructed.

"Àlaich las." Nothing happened. *Fair enough, first try, and the pronunciation is a bit crazy*, Memory thought. She breathed in, trying to stoke the fires in her chest, to feel them burning this time. "OK. Àlaich las." Nothing again. "Àlaich las?" she whined. Still nothing.

"I suck," Memory said.

"Maybe something more physical that she can focus on," Roen suggested.

"Do you wish to demonstrate perhaps?" Eloryn asked.

"I'm sorry, please continue. You'll be a much better teacher for this than I." Roen got back to his feet and took a few steps away as if he'd been scolded to the corner by a teacher.

Eloryn took his place at the foot of the bed, and called Memory over next to her. "This is not as simple, and not authorized either, so be wary, if you learn it, not to use it where seen. But it is more *physical* in nature."

Roen cleared his throat. "Mind, what the Princess can do is somewhat more powerful than normal, and almost always less authorized."

Eloryn blushed in her usual, annoyingly cute way. "Not powerful, only, well, different. More complicated behests require more words, and it's more important that those words are correctly used. It's like speaking a contract. Alward taught me so much of the magical language and I can use it to ask what I need, without learning structured and proven behests. It is the talent of the Maellan line."

"So, if I pick this stuff up, how do I know what's authorized?"

Roen sniffed. "Nothing but fewer than a dozen household spells. Light, Branding, warming water, some very basic healing. Metal workers, couriers and doctors can get permits for more but it's watched carefully and all very arbitrary. Most people realize the law is only there to flush out true wizards. It's made life harder, and generally better to use no magic at all."

"Well, if I can't pick this one up, using no magic at all will be my next choice. So what do we do, Lory?"

"See the hair brush on the dressing table there? Beirsinn fair nalldomh." Eloryn reached out a hand, and the hair brush flew into it.

Memory swore. "That's cool. Yeah, I wanna learn that one."

Eloryn replaced the brush on the dresser, and walked back to Memory, facing her where she sat on the edge of the bed. "You heard the words- beirsinn fair nalldomh. You should be able to easily focus on what you want here. Wisps can be contrary at times. Remember, work on feeling the connection to magic within you as you speak the words."

Memory repeated the words, again and then again, trying to find some connection inside her. Nothing happened, not a twitch, and she felt frustrated and foolish. "Oh just come here!" she snapped, reaching her arm forward in one last attempt.

Movement. The brush moved, but so did the dressing table. The wooden feet of the dresser cried as it scraped across the stone floor, speeding toward her and Eloryn. Memory pulled her legs up away from it. The dresser slammed into the foot of the bed. It spewed its drawers out onto the covers, wood splintering against the bed frame. Eloryn moved too slowly, saved only by Roen's speed, the professional damsel catcher in action. He grabbed and spun her out of its way.

As the dresser rocked on its feet, Roen held Eloryn in his arms a moment longer before he seemed willing to let her go. Memory could see a battle of color in her face, paling in fear, blushing in embarrassment.

Memory swore again. "Sorry."

"It's all right. She's safe," Roen said, only looking at Eloryn.

CHAPTER TWELVE

Three matching slim, raven-haired handmaidens arrived, introducing themselves with a row of curtseys.

Memory puffed a breath into her hair, thankful for the interruption. No one had been eager to speculate on her attempt at magic, and an awkward silence had grown long. Roen grinned at the ladies, and Saoirse and Lily chased him from the room with a spree of flirtatious giggling.

The handmaidens turned straight to fawning over Eloryn and Memory took the chance to slip into the bathroom.

It practically glowed blue. Above an aquamarine tub a brass showerhead shone like a small sun with two decorative taps like stars beneath. Memory glared at it, wondering what exactly was so amazing

about a shower.

Memory struggled out of her dress and left it in a pile in the corner, tucking her knife out of sight underneath for safe keeping. Stepping gingerly across the cold tiles and into the tub, Memory spun the hot tap and a stream of steaming water soon sprayed down on her. It was a blessed relief to wash away the stink of the previous day. Showers were a luxury after all.

With a deep sigh and forced physical effort, Memory turned the shower off. As the sound of running water echoed away down the drain, she heard faint knocking from beyond. Not the bathroom door; the entrance door perhaps. No other sounds came from the main room, and the knocking persisted.

She wrapped a towel around her dripping torso, her hair still running dye-tinted streams down her back. Peeking out the bathroom door she saw the main room empty. Not sure what should be done, she tiptoed across the room and opened the entrance door just a crack.

Roen greeted her with a markedly amused expression. "I only wonder how you would have appeared had I knocked a moment earlier."

Memory dripped water into the carpet and tried to hide her embarrassment. "No one else was around to answer the door."

"I do hope this is what you're intending to wear to the ball. It's quite striking."

Memory smiled, hating that she couldn't hold it back. "You're not entirely dressed up yourself."

He wore the same simple shirt as before, its fine, nearly translucent silk overlaid with a plain and elegant satin coat in embroidered silver. It made his unkempt hair even more golden.

"Well, it'd be a crime to hide this face." He leant close to where she stood in the partly opened doorway.

"Is this how you talk to all girls?" *Except Eloryn,* she thought.

Roen looked both ashamed and audacious as he smiled back.

"And, it works for you?" Memory made herself sound so unimpressed that Roen actually looked hurt for a moment before she couldn't help but smile at him again. But by the time she did, Roen's eyes were elsewhere.

Memory turned to see Eloryn had emerged from the side chamber, fully dressed and done up. She looked like a porcelain doll, hair curled and pinned up on top of her head in ringlets of shining ivory. A silken gold dress clung around her bust and dropped in simple, shimmering waves.

Memory slumped. *I hope the mask that goes with that covers a lot of her face. Although I doubt any man will be looking at her face.*

"Does it not suit me?" Eloryn sounded nervous. Memory realized both she and Roen had been gawking at her since she walked in, albeit probably thinking different things.

Roen, dumbstruck for the first time Memory had seen, detached himself from the doorframe and straightened up as though about to speak, but said nothing.

"You look fine," Memory said, as kindly as she could manage.

Eloryn picked up the matching mask. It was quite large, after all – a butterfly design of filigree silver and gold that would cover most of her face.

The handmaidens buzzed back into the room and clucked when they saw Memory standing at the door with Roen, wet and wearing only a towel. Clarice, eldest of the three with a beauty mark that Memory didn't believe was real, walked right up to her and stared at her face judgmentally.

"There was no one else to answer the door!" Memory blurted.

"The jewels in your face; it will be easier when we begin your

make up if you can remove them. Also, you may want to leave them out." Surely she meant it as kind fashion advice, but it still sounded just a little catty.

Roen winked at Clarice, stepped in and closed the door behind him. Shrugging, she smirked back and nudged Memory across to the dresser next to where Eloryn had been seated again for final touches.

Memory nodded thankfully to Clarice and started removing the piercings. What did she know about fashion anyway? She felt like an ugly duckling, even damp enough to be one. At this point, she would do whatever she could to fit in.

Sharing the short upholstered stool in front of the dressing table mirror, Memory and Eloryn were flanked by handmaidens. Lily cooed over their shoulder, "What handsome sisters you are, so much alike."

Memory snorted. The only thing they had in common was the color of their eyes, and even that Eloryn used to better advantage. But still, sitting together in front of a mirror, she could almost see what Lily meant. Both the same height, and without her black eye and swollen jaw line, her face looked a lot more delicate, like Eloryn's. It was... eerie.

Eloryn's skin had paled more than usual. She didn't seem pleased by the comparison. In fact, she looked downright skittish. Memory bit her lip. Even with her fading dye job and bony figure, was it really that insulting a comparison? Maybe Memory did have a sister out there somewhere. She had to find her real family, one way or another.

Memory turned back to Roen, on edge again. "So why were you knocking the door down anyway?"

Roen had taken a seat on the bed. "Duke Lanval wishes to introduce us to his friend who has arrived. They are waiting for us."

"The young lady is certainly not going anywhere until we have her dressed," Clarice muttered.

Roen lowered his gaze, shifting it between Eloryn and Memory. "Truth is, Lady Memory is not invited to this meeting. I am to escort Lady Eloryn only."

Memory paused half way into unscrewing her labret. She wasn't sure why the news surprised her, or hurt, but it did both. She couldn't even think of a valid reason to argue why she should be allowed to go. It had only been a matter of time before she was left behind. She looked to Eloryn, whose face showed a battle of emotions. When Eloryn saw Memory watching her she turned quickly away. Memory dragged out her last piercing and faux pouted at Roen. "I guess I'll have to entertain myself then."

"There will be plenty of entertainment at the feast. Some fun will do you well, and perhaps you will recognize someone? I'll even owe you a dance," Roen said, half smiling apologetically.

Saoirse finished tying Eloryn's mask into place around her elaborate hair-do and the three handmaidens turned their full attention to Memory. She shot Roen a look of terror as they backed her into the side room. He laughed in response and the door closed between them.

A range of ball gowns and accessories had been laid out to choose from. Despite her natural aversion to dresses, Memory actually got excited when she saw one, all black, amongst the pile of colorful gowns on offer. She picked it without hesitation.

The maids gossiped about people Memory didn't know while they approached her with the mounds of black fabric. Memory stood shivering, and just closed her eyes and tried not to wince as they went about their work lacing, tucking and stitching the dress into form. When they were done, Memory had to admit she felt a little bit kick ass. The dress was hot. Bodice all black lace over black satin, tight and low cut, only just high enough to cover the scar in the centre of her chest. The multi layered skirts combined both rolling ruffles and

translucent gauze. Maybe in this, even next to Eloryn, she could be considered a beauty.

Directed back into the main room, Memory found Roen and Eloryn were gone. *They didn't even say goodbye before going to their fancy nobles-only meeting.* Memory coughed a short, insulted laugh. She wondered what part Roen had there, other than being there for the Princess. Who would be there for her in this big, unfamiliar castle?

Memory sat in front of the previously mobile dressing table. The handmaidens stood back discussing options with pinched mouths then got to work. For all that there were only three of them, at times Memory felt like there were a dozen hands on her, poking and primping. They managed to pull her hair up into an ornate design that made it look like she had twice the hair she did. Her face was pinched and painted. She tried, between bursts of powder, to tell them to keep the make-up simple, worried about receiving stray beauty marks. Clarice tsked, but followed her wishes. When they were done, Memory looked at herself a moment then smiled an approval to them. As they turned away to gather up the unselected dresses, Memory grabbed a remaining kohl brush and added more black around her eyes.

"My lady, some guests are already gathering in the northern grounds. If you're happy with your presentation, we will take our leave. We'll have your clothes taken to the laundry so they will be fresh for you tomorrow."

Memory nodded thanks to them all, relieved that they were done with her before she remembered something. "Oh, just a moment!" Memory said, dashing into the bathroom. She grabbed her knife from under the pile of filthy dresses and slipped it down the secure front of her corset. No matter what it was for, the knife somehow made her feel better. She wanted to keep it close. She smiled at Lily who followed her in, and returned to the main chamber to find the others gone.

The remaining gowns and accessories had been taken and only a pair of crystal encrusted slippers remained.

Memory looked longingly for a moment at her sneakers, then grabbed the sparkling shoes and tugged them on. At least they weren't heels. Her stomach rolled with a tide of hunger and she focused on one word. Feast. If there was food out there somewhere, that is where she would go, even alone.

Memory picked up the mask that matched her dress, hurriedly tying its ribbons behind her head. She stepped out the entrance door and through the thin eyes of her mask the hallway seemed to stretch endlessly in either direction.

Lily caught up to her, laundry tied in a neat bundle on one hip. "Do you not know the way?"

Memory winced a no.

"Just down the hall that way. A left, down two floors, a right at the Duke's portrait, then out past the water channels, through the archway and into the grounds. You'll have no trouble." She bobbed a short curtsey and headed the other way up the hall.

Memory stood still a moment longer, repeating the instructions in her head while they were still fresh. She headed off at a brisk pace, mouth already watering at the idea of long missed sustenance.

A left, a right, oh hell. Left or right again? Memory quickly got lost. She wandered down long corridors, stopping to ask directions at every person she passed. Finding what she assumed to be the Duke's portrait, she smiled, glad to be heading the right way. *Jolly looking fellow, would have been nice to meet you.* Finally she saw an archway ahead through a large entry hall. The corridor ran straight through it, becoming a bridge bordered by knee-high stone walls carved with flowers. Rectangular pools of water ran the length of the hall on either side, burbling with

deep undercurrents. She slowed, exhausted from the shallow breaths the corset forced her to take.

Out through the archway, the path led Memory into an emerald green paradise. Tall, well-trimmed hedges looped around the grounds, separating small and large areas full of flowers, statues and fruit trees. Running water sounded from everywhere. She could see, some way down the path, a large marquee posted amongst climbing roses and pine trees where people milled about. Looking back at the castle itself, Memory blew out a low whistle. *The place had goddamned towers.* The sun still shone, but dipped low. It had taken them some time to get ready, but she really must have slept most of the day for it to be this late. She had breakfast, lunch and dinner to make up for.

Part way down the path she froze, sure she had heard Eloryn's voice. Looking around, she couldn't see anyone down the long path to the grand tent. To both her sides, hedges stood tall and thick. But then there was Roen's voice too. She walked soft-footed, trying to trace them.

Soon she stood with her ear up against a hedge. They were on the other side of it, talking in hushed voices. What were they doing out here? They were supposed to be at their exclusive meeting. Had they lied to her? Betrayal burned in Memory, and she stilled herself to listen in.

"...your concern. It was right of you to mention this in private," Roen was saying.

"You see it too, the resemblance between us? I don't want to think it, but it explains too much." Eloryn sounded scared.

"I know she is strange in ways, but she hardly seems malevolent."

Memory sucked in her breath. *They're talking about me.*

"I've told you how she appeared, caught within the Veil door. What if she did not come from Avall?"

"There is no human land beyond the Veil anymore. There is only Avall, and the land of the fae. You don't think she is some type of fae?"

Feet shuffled. "A fairy changeling? I wondered so when we first met, but I shared bread with her and fae won't abide bread."

"But you still don't believe her to be human?"

"How she appeared, through the Veil as she did, how she looks so like me, how she has no memory or life of her own... Alward's research told of the hell beyond the Veil. He believed demons from there could find their way through. Doppelgangers that could cling to a traveler through a broken Veil door, taking their appearance so they can appear human..." Eloryn's voice faded out, distressed.

Ice shivered under the surface of Memory's skin.

They thought she was a *demon*.

CHAPTER THIRTEEN

Memory backed away from the hedge. She couldn't stand to hear any more.

A demon?

She sleep-walked along the path and into the grand tent. She'd thought she was just lost, confused, maybe even brain damaged. But she'd only been asking who she was, never *what* she was.

Memory passed by people in the tent. Some tried to speak to her, but she walked on. Wide gowns filled her vision with color, men dressed as admirals and highwaymen, women as peacocks and angels. Some of the guests hardly seemed human, in shape or sheer beauty. Their revelry only made the bitterness in Memory rise. The weight of betrayal dragged her down. She took the nearest seat, and

glared through heavy eyes into the growing crowd. Other guests in the marquee stared back at her, gossiping behind lace gloved hands and enameled masks.

Fury burned Memory's eyelids and she huffed cooling air at them, refusing to let herself cry. Emotions did battle within her, taking all her energy and blocking out the surrounding festivities. It took her a while to realize she was being spoken to.

"Huh?" She turned to see a young man with shining black hair smiling at her. He wore no mask, just a well tailored black suit and a felt hat which he held in one hand against his chest.

"Perceval. My name. And if I might have the honor of knowing yours?" He smiled.

Memory hesitated. "Mem... Just Mem."

"It is a pleasure, Lady Mem."

He took her hand. She twitched, confused, but he kissed it gently, and returned it to her lap. She tried to smile at him and failed.

"You aren't enjoying yourself? It is a fine feast the Duke has put on this evening."

"Sorry, I'm just not..." *Human?* Memory swallowed bile. She was being ridiculous. She felt human, didn't she? She set her teeth against each other so firmly they hurt. *How dare Eloryn say I'm not human?*

"I haven't seen you before, have I?" Perceval didn't wait for her to answer. "You must be new to court. Everyone here has their eyes on you."

Like she needed the reminder. "I wish they wouldn't. I feel bad enough already."

"Bad? They only look at you either in desire or in jealousy. You're the most splendid lady here this eve."

Memory lost what she had been thinking and blushed in a way that would challenge Eloryn. She shook her head, unable to reply in any other way.

With her gaze locked on Perceval, she was startled by someone clearing their throat to her side. Roen had appeared out of the crowd in front of her.

"There you are. My Lady, the dress transforms you. Not that your previous attire didn't flatter as well."

Memory turned her face away from both men, her lips pulling into a sneer. She steeled herself then met Roen's eyes. He smiled but it didn't hide an expression too serious to be seen against the backdrop of giddy revelers.

When the silence dragged on, Roen frowned over his tawny eyes. "Have you eaten today? There is plenty of food about."

"Why aren't you with Eloryn?" Memory muttered.

A flash of hurt marred Roen's face then passed. "I was only to escort her to her meeting. I'm now free to enjoy myself."

"Right."

"And I do owe you that dance." Roen offered a hand to Memory and smiled again in a way that looked fake.

"Can't. Won't." Memory turned her back to him, unwilling to keep up any guise of conversation.

"You aren't being troubled here at all?" Roen eyed Perceval.

"Not by him." Memory smiled at Perceval, who gave Roen a victorious look that satisfied her.

"Well then, I wish you a pleasant evening." Roen walked away into the crowd, one final look over his shoulder which Memory pretended to ignore. He quickly found a flock of fawning ladies, and broke off into a dance with one wearing a devil mask.

Memory narrowed her eyes. "God, I could do with a drink."

Perceval eagerly signaled to a servant who brought filled goblets to them in an instant.

Memory laughed aloud, and lifted her cup to Perceval in appreciation. "Good service here."

"Indeed, a fine gathering. So I must ask, what could have made the heart of the most lovely lady here so shadowed?" Perceval clicked his goblet against hers and took a sip, his black-brown eyes never leaving her face.

Memory wasn't sure she liked the way he looked at her. It was nice to be the focus of attention, but it left an odd ill feeling in her gut. Still, she liked having someone to talk to who didn't care about the Princess, or whether she was human or not.

She took a large mouthful of mead from her goblet, enjoying the sweetness of it.

"I just want to go home," Memory said, staring into the honey liquid.

Perceval's shoulders dropped. "So early? Could nothing persuade you to stay?"

"No, I mean, I'm not going anywhere right now. But I sort of, can't get home. I'm kind of lost."

"Lost? Lucky then that I found you. I may be of assistance."

"You'd help me? I don't see any shining armor."

Perceval twisted his eyebrows at her comment, but smiled over his clear confusion. "In truth, I would help. See, you've not yet allowed me to tell you to whom I serve." Perceval flourished his hand. "For serving is what I do, and I do it very well indeed. If I am unable to help you, then he, of all people, is sure to have the power to help in any way needed."

Memory warmed to him. Or maybe it was the mead. She gave him a wry smile.

"It's really nice of you, but I'm not entirely sure anymore that anyone can help with the full scope of problems I have."

"Not even the King himself?" Perceval revealed under his breath. "Indeed. I am in his personal escort, and he has come here tonight on an urgent matter."

Memory froze mid sip. The King... Thayl? Thayl who was chasing Eloryn, who killed her parents for the throne. Thayl, the only other person ever known to use magic like she did. The most powerful man around, both in magic and in title. Her mind sped through her index on this man, Thayl, until it caught up with her emotions. Thayl, who for all she knew, might not be all that bad, who might treat her like a human being. She had to find her family, people who really cared about her. The only person who had offered to help her so far also called her a demon. *If Eloryn thinks I'm a demon, how true can the rest of what she says be? Thayl's probably no more evil than me.*

"King Thayl, he's here, at the ball somewhere?"

"Hush now, his attendance is yet unannounced," Perceval said, looking pleased with himself. "He partakes in some business before coming to the feast."

"He's not meeting with anyone up in the palace just now, is he?" A small shiver of worry for Eloryn came to Memory unbidden. She searched her gaze over the crowd but couldn't see Roen. Both he and his buxom dance partner had vanished.

Her mood flipped back to dark. Why should she worry about them? She was obviously nothing to them, at best, and at worst she was a demon. The only thing Eloryn had done for her so far was give her something she could negotiate with to get help from Thayl.

She chewed her lip, considering her options.

"No, he is through the grounds here. I'd just passed a message of his arrival along to the Duke's staff when I saw you here, inexplicably alone, and was more than thankful my duties for the evening had ended." Perceval smiled at her with dark, half closed eyes. "And at

the end of duties comes drinking," he raised his goblet to hers, "and dancing, if you…"

Memory interrupted him. "I want to meet him. I want to meet the King."

Roen excused himself to his dance partner as soon as he politely could. She turned away with a cute pout and flick of perfect ringlets. She could have been an amusing distraction, but Roen found himself in no mood to dance. He couldn't think why. He should be celebrating. He had brought the Princess here safely, and soon she'd be escorted to the Wizards' Council and under their protection. *It's for the best. She deserves better guardians. It's a good thing.* Roen repeated the words again in his mind, but he had to keep forcing the smile onto his face. After doing it all day, that smile wore thin.

Memory's hard tone lingered in his head, adding to his mood. She was normally so good humored her sudden coldness made him wonder if he'd stepped too far with his own words. He spoke so openly to her only because her wit matched his own. He enjoyed that.

Catching a glimpse of Memory laughing with the dark-haired man, Roen wondered again where he had seen him before. Roen skirted the feast, pacing through the crowd in a short lived attempt to kill time then found himself wandering back up into the castle, toward the private meeting room they had used with Lanval the night before.

He knew he wasn't welcome. Lanval made it clear his contact would see only the heir, no one else. Roen felt himself drawn back that way regardless.

He should at least find out when they planned to have Eloryn leave, to make sure he could see her on her way. He tried to play out the farewell in his mind. Should he have a gift of some kind for her? What did one do in a situation like this? Nothing seemed appropriate.

Even the thought of parting ways felt wrong.

Reaching the top of the stairs, he stuck his hands into the familiar pockets of his pants; his normal, plain but neat fitted trousers with concealed pockets for the tools of his trade. Maybe he should have dressed up more. Not that it mattered. He would be back to his normal life soon.

Coming around the corner into the corridor which held the meeting room, Roen almost ran straight into Duke Lanval. He came barreling past with a look of grim concern. He didn't slow down, but called back as he sped away. "Get her out of here Roen, just take her away!"

A message boy stood trembling at the open doorway to the meeting room. Roen increased his pace, and Eloryn met him in the hall. She looked as pale as the time she had fainted on him.

Before he could stop himself, he put his hands around her shoulders, holding her gently. "What happened? Are you all right?"

Eloryn seemed frozen for a moment, then jerked back to awareness. She stepped out of his hold and ran down the hall.

Roen looked at the quivering messenger and snapped louder at him than he meant. "What message did you deliver?"

"That King Thayl has arrived."

Roen bolted after Eloryn, catching up to her quickly. "That's not the right way. We have to get you out of the castle, keep you hidden."

She kept running. She shook her head and her voice came out as a panicked whisper. "She's out there all on her own."

S.A. FENECH

Perceval's mouth hung open at Memory's request. "I'm not sure I can…"

"Oh please?" Memory pouted, rolling her shoulders back, allowing the corset to squeeze up what little cleavage she had. "You said you would help me. Maybe you can just walk me to him?" Memory wasn't sure if casually meeting the King was a done thing, but it was worth a try.

Perceval grinned as though sharing a secret and extended an arm to her. He hooked his elbow around hers and walked her away from the marquee, pulling her close beside him. Perceval continued his inane small talk and boasting and she tried to hide how uncomfortable she felt on his arm.

He led her around hedges formed like a maze, through smaller gardens, past larger trees to another part of the grounds, getting her thoroughly lost in the process. They emerged into a stone paved courtyard where a group of men in a range of armor and uniforms stood about in serious discussion. Perceval placed her against a hedge, winking at one of his friends who looked their way. Memory tried not to feel like a groupie.

"Which one is he?" She hoped she sounded innocently naïve. Her nerves jangled. She tried to calm them, but an odd sensation grew within her.

Perceval leant in and whispered into her ear, "Dark hair and dark purple coat."

Memory found him quickly. His hair was indeed dark, a tumbling shoulder length mass contrasted with a small and well trimmed beard.

He wasn't as old as Memory expected, maybe thirty-five years, and she was shocked again to find he was actually gorgeous. All except for his eyes, which were dark and tired.

More surprising still, Memory felt as though she recognized him from somewhere.

The uneasy feeling within her swelled. *But I don't know anyone.* She took in his features, trying to trace the fragments of familiarity within her barren brain. He seemed to share her discomfort. He shook his shoulders in an abrupt shiver, and reached up a gloved hand, stretching and clenching it before his face.

Memory's legs turned to chalk, ready to crumble. He was the man; the man with the hand. The glowing hand from her dream. She turned her face away from him.

"We should go. I don't want to interrupt him." Her voice wavered. *How could it be him? It was just a dream, wasn't it?*

"I'm sure I can make your introduction to King Thayl, Lady Mem. You no longer wish it?"

Right. Now *you're sure.* Memory shook her head, urgency panicking her. "No, let's go. Now. Let's go somewhere else. Private," she said, with a small smile and wink. A wide grin from Perceval told her she'd succeeded in speeding him up.

They turned to go.

"Do I know you?" A deep, smooth voice interrupted them. It had the tone of someone not interested in formalities, and not having need of them.

Thayl stood by her side, looking down at her. Memory reached up to touch her mask, comforting herself with its presence. "No, Your Highness." Was that even the correct way to address a king? Memory didn't know. She tried to force a blush to her chilled skin, tried to curtsey in the way she'd seen Eloryn do, low and formally. She

wobbled, inelegantly righting herself. "No, I don't believe so."

"Remove your mask, girl," Thayl said.

Perceval's look told her to take this request seriously. She untied it with shaking fingers. The bow caught and pulled loose strands of hair, bringing tears to her eyes. With the mask off her face, Thayl's expression didn't change, showing indifferent confusion only.

"Your name, where are you from?" Thayl asked. "There is something about you…"

"This is Lady Mem, Your Majesty." Perceval took over for her when she hesitated too long. "I met her just moments afore. She requested to see you."

"You did? And why would you…" Thayl's face twisted with discomfort again. He tugged the glove off his right hand. Memory gaped at the mass of scars it held. Shapes and lines covered it to the wrist, carved into the skin long ago and turned to puckered flesh by time. A faint glow built around it.

Thayl looked from his hand to her. His expression was still confused, but no longer indifferent. It was fierce, frightened. "You? How can it be? You've not even aged. Devil, how did you get here from that Hell?"

Thayl grabbed Memory with both hands. His fingers dug into her, wrapping fully around her slight arms with bruising strength.

Memory's heart stopped. His grasp made panic burn inside her. A blinding light burst around them, joining the glow from Thayl's hand. Her heart started again, thunder against the weakness of her body. Her vision back-flipped.

She stood in an alley. She looked down upon herself, mesmerized by the glow of light.

The life escaped from the other her, no longer wanting to be trapped within. It flowed into her outstretched hand, making her stronger.

She watched herself scream.

She blinked, back in the green castle grounds. She stumbled backwards in shock, free to stumble, with Thayl's hands no longer holding her. He stepped back too. She tripped on her own foot, her slipper left behind.

"Your Majesty." A booming voice broke through. "My apologies that I couldn't attend you sooner. Your presence tonight wasn't anticipated."

Thayl turned around in a stupor. Duke Lanval marched toward them with an entourage. Memory stood still, shell shocked. Rough hands grabbed her from behind. One forceful tug pulled her back into the scratching leaves of the hedge.

She tried to wriggle free, but strong arms pinned her against a body of firm muscles and furs. Dragged through the dense foliage, she closed her eyes to the twigs that rushed by. In a burst of leaves, she and her abductor emerged from the hedge. She looked up into blue eyes. Blue like the sea, they even made her feel sea-sick looking into them. Eyes she remembered from the forest.

She must have looked as though she would scream, because the young man put a finger across his lips. He grabbed her arm and pulled her forward. She drew a rough breath, unable to get enough air into her corseted chest. She wheezed and floundered. The savage man lifted her, threw her not too gently over a shoulder, and ran.

The savage's pace did not slow as he carried her through hedges and corners of the gardens shadowed by the coming night. The delicate fabric of her sleeves tore and the fine work of the handmaidens on her hair was lost to passing branches.

The mad dash ended before she could decide whether to cling on or try to get free and he pushed her out onto an open pathway. She fell to her knees. *It's like he knew I needed saving even before I did, as if he*

knew Thayl would hurt me. Me, a king, a savage; how could we all know each other? When she spun around, nothing but the rustle of hedge leaves remained of the man. She saw a familiar archway in the distance, and two familiar figures emerging from it. One ran to her.

"Memory, by the fae, what's happened?" Roen knelt beside her.

Memory couldn't force words out, her lungs still out of shape from being knocked against the beast man's shoulder. She coughed out a leaf.

"Was it that man from the ball? What did he do?" Roen's voice was slow and intense.

Memory shook her head. "Ran through bushes. Had to tell you. Have to go."

"Mem, are you all right?" Eloryn caught up to them, looking no less concerned.

Memory frowned. "Thayl. He's here."

"We know. We came to find you so we could leave," Roen said, helping her up.

Came to find me? If they knew Thayl was here, why didn't they just leave without me? They thought she was a demon, but here they were, looking at her with all the sympathy of someone on her deathbed. Memory's heart jittered.

A group of men led by Perceval, clutching the slipper she'd left behind, rounded the other end of the pathway. Perceval pointed, and the men ran for them.

Roen took both girls by a hand and ran back toward the palace. Gowns too long, corsets too tight, neither could move fast, but they had a head start against Thayl's men down the long garden pathway.

"We'll lose them in the secret passageways once we're in the castle." Roen sounded confident, but Memory felt his anxiety in the way his arm strained to pull her faster.

They passed through the archway. Across the pathway that bridged the pools of water, a tall man with lion's hair and a scarred face stopped in his tracks. He glared with wide eyed intensity.

Eloryn gasped a scream, stopping so suddenly she tore from Roen's grasp. "He is the one who captured Alward."

Roen turned from the imposing man to the approaching group. They stood in the middle of the pathway bridge, blocked at both ends. Water rushed in deep channels to either side.

Memory looked to Eloryn. "Can you cast something? Help us get away?"

Eloryn rushed out words in the magical tongue, hesitated, shook her head, started again. Memory had no idea what she asked of what. The wizard hunter drew his crossbow and shot a tiny dart. It hit Eloryn's neck, and she fell, tumbling over the low wall. Roen reached an arm for her, this time too slowly. With a splash she disappeared beneath the churning water. One final glimpse of gold like a fish in the depths and she was gone.

"Princess?" he whispered. She did not resurface. "Eloryn!"

Roen dived into the deep channel without a second breath.

Left alone on the bridge, Memory looked from the dark water to the approaching men, terrified of both.

"Capture the demon," Perceval called out.

Memory took as deep a breath as her clothing allowed. She stepped over the wall and plunged into the water.

CHAPTER FOURTEEN

The ice of the water's touch burned Memory's skin. She could feel no bottom, no sides, just a rush of water pulling her down. The channel ran deep and fast. The fabric of her skirts tangled and lifted about, tying her limbs. She sank, breathless, reached the distant bottom then pushed up. Her cheek scraped against the rocky ceiling. She gasped air in the smallest pocket of space before being pulled under again. The channel narrowed around her, knocking her against rocks, finally expelling her into a great expanse of water.

Her chest ached and her mind lost focus. Ribbons of reeds twisted up from the ground, and she floated, still and suspended in the blue-green night. In the distance, Eloryn and Roen danced in the air. More figures joined them, lifting them into the sky; small, slender

women with white skin and ridiculously long hair. Some flew around her, keeping their distance. She reached for them, wanting to touch these beautiful, flying angels. They scowled with large black eyes. The surreal moment ended and she realized they didn't fly. She was still underwater. They swam, and she could not breathe. Her lungs exploded and the last of her air burst out in bubbles around her. Her vision darkened at the edges.

Large hands pulled at her. Reaching the surface she filled her cracking lungs. The savage broke through the water next to her, droplets forming in his dark tangle of hair. Supporting her fabric-weighted mass with one arm, he made a slow journey across to the edge of the lake, dragging her with him. They were alone on the bank where the savage crawled out of the water. She lay at its edge, unable to lift the waterlogged skirts any farther. He collapsed face down, gulping breaths.

Memory coughed out a stream of water, aching as though she'd been wrung out and wishing she was at least that dry. She wiped clinging hair from her eyes, trying to get a clear view of the strange man, wanting to be sure he was real. He still looked more like an animal than a man. He had a lean build with wide shoulders, every inch of bare skin muscled. She could just see the profile of his face, showing high cheekbones and long dark lashes that dripped water. He wasn't familiar to her in the slightest.

"Who are you?" Memory said.

Lying on his stomach, he lifted himself up onto his elbows and looked at her as though she'd just slapped him. His pale eyes flashed like lightning under heavy black brows.

In the distance, Roen called Memory's name.

"I'm here!" she yelled through a hurting throat.

The beast man's body tensed, and he stared in the direction of

Roen's voice. When he turned back to her, his harsh expression caught her off guard. Anger, fear, accusation? She couldn't quite tell. He shifted to his knees, pulling himself up with a harsh breath.

"Don't go, they're my friends, they won't-" she begged, but he vanished in a rustle of leaves.

"Thank you," she whispered to the empty space he left.

Dragging the heavy gown from the water, she just managed to stand when Roen and Eloryn found her. Wet and bedraggled, Roen had Eloryn under one arm, supporting her protectively.

There were grim expressions all around, not helped by the lingering scent of swamp.

Memory couldn't meet their eyes. "I didn't know Thayl was there, I didn't know who he was until he spoke to me." The lies caught in her throat but she couldn't tell them the truth.

"He spoke to you? What did he say?" Eloryn asked.

"Nothing. Just an introduction." Over Eloryn's shoulder Memory saw the silhouette of the savage through the trees, watching her lie. The weight in her dress and her heart made her want to crumple to the ground. Thayl's words still rang in her ears. *Devil, how did you get here from that Hell?* Eloryn was right. She was some kind of demon.

Eloryn shivered. She'd never been so cold. Her home with Alward had always been warm and comfortable. Her teeth chattered and she tried to still her shivering, which just made her rattle harder. Roen must have noticed because he pulled her closer to him. His body felt warm against hers. He'd lost his silver coat in the lake somewhere, and she

tried not to look where the translucent silk of his shirt clung to his skin.

"They will come straight to the lake to find us," Roen said. "The estate's water channels all flow down to here. Princess, is there any way you can make a behest to cover our path, so they can't track us? Let them believe we drowned."

"The dart was poisoned somehow. It's closed my connection to magic. I have nothing I can do. I'm sorry." *This is what they did to Alward, how they were able to catch him,* she thought. He would have felt just as useless, and he was all alone. She took a deep breath to hold off tears.

Roen let her go. He turned, eyes seeking landmarks on the lake shore. His hair sprinkled droplets of water over his face. "You two, head along the lake's edge this way. You'll soon come to a small inlet stream. Follow it. Stay in the water, leave no footprints. First bridge you come to, take the low road. It will lead you to an inn, Elders Bridge. Don't go in. Just wait and hide. Do you understand?"

"You're not coming with us?" Eloryn tried not to sound hurt. She could still feel the warmth where he'd held her, but it faded.

Roen looked at her with hooded eyes. "I will head away from the lake here. There's a main road not far through these woods. I will leave enough of a path for three people, then disappear when I reach the road. They may think we caught a passing wagon. I only hope it will be enough. I wish I could do this and also remain with you. But I will be at Elders Bridge, Princess, I promise you. Be safe."

Roen bowed to her and smiled to Memory as he always did. His departure left Eloryn with an ache inside. She didn't think he'd ever smiled at her.

"We should go quickly then, so his plan works," Memory said. She wrung water from her skirts, hitched them up, and began wobbling along the lake shore in ankle deep water. Eloryn thought she seemed agitated.

When she and Roen had taken the chance to discuss Memory in private, the one thing they agreed was that her loss and confusion seemed nothing but honest. *Even suffering that pain, she's only tried to help me. No matter what she may be, or how frightening her magic, she's been a friend. And I still haven't been able to give any help in return.*

Sometimes Memory looked so much like her it chilled her bones. More often, she was so different – from her angular build to her blunt words – it seemed ridiculous trying to make comparisons. Eloryn wondered what Alward would have said. Had she over-reacted? She missed his guidance dearly. Still, despite Memory's sometimes ill temperament, Eloryn felt better having her nearby. *A friend.*

Travel was slow, and Memory wasn't talking. The night became thick around them, only a clouded moon lighting their way. The slippery rocks around the lake and up the small stream slowed them even more as they picked between them. Both girls fell into the water more than a few times and had to drag out and wring the heavy dresses before walking again.

The fifth time Memory fell in she actually laughed out loud, surprising Eloryn.

"Are you all right?" she asked, helping Memory out of the black water.

"I'm fine. I just lost my other bloody shoe." She sighed out the last of her laughter.

Eloryn didn't understand why this improved Memory's mood, but was glad for it. Memory continued to cling to Eloryn, and she clung back, unwilling to let go of the barest comforting warmth shared between them. By walking close together they also managed to avoid falling into the water again. Each time one slipped, the other held her up.

They were chilled through and aching by the time they reached a bridge. They hoped it was the right one, hoped they'd picked the right road, and hoped the inn wouldn't be far. Before long they were rewarded with a sign posting "Elders Bridge Inn" and a wide two storey building with a couple of smaller buildings close behind. The road continued along the front and thick forest surrounded every side. Golden light shone from the windows, radiating warmth. It looked so inviting it made Eloryn shiver harder.

"Sure we can't go in?" Memory whispered between knocking teeth.

"We were told to wait." Eloryn turned away from the light regretfully. They trudged a little farther behind some trees where undergrowth and darkness would hide them but they could still see the brightly lit inn.

The girls bundled up together in the embrace of a large buttressed tree root.

Memory glanced over her shoulder into the trees behind them, then whispered, "How's your magic going? Any better yet?"

Eloryn shook her head, unsure if Memory saw in the darkness, but unable to answer aloud. She felt miserable. She could not dry them, could not warm them. They had no other clothes. Everything Eloryn still owned in the world, even her mother's amulet, was left behind.

"I could maybe try something? Anything is better than freezing to death, right?" Memory said.

Eloryn hesitated, needing a moment to compose herself. Memory started muttering random words and phrases to do with heat and warmth. Eloryn turned to give her warning, but a flame already sparked in front of them, lighting the dry leaves at their feet on fire. Memory swore and smothered it with the wet bulk of her dress.

"OK, burning to death? Not better. Point taken."

Eloryn looked to the inn. There was no sign that they had been seen. People came and went, but not Roen. Before they were interrupted, Duke Lanval's contact had given her information and a token with which to contact the Wizards' Council. When she fumbled and dropped it in their flight from the castle, Roen took the token, keeping it safe, keeping her safe. *He should have been here by now. He could be captured as well.* Sudden tears filled her eyes and she winced to hold them in. Thayl had appeared at Duke Lanval's estate in such a rush. There could only be one reason for it: Alward. Thayl had him now, and she knew what became of any wizard Thayl captured.

The thought made her ache. That these people would risk so much for her, suffer so much hardship, just for a title she owned only in name. *No wonder Roen never smiles at me.*

Memory looked over her shoulder again.

"What are you looking at?" Eloryn asked, following her gaze, hoping to see Roen arriving.

"Nothing. I mean I can't see anything, but I was looking for something." Memory paused, then turned seriously to Eloryn. "OK, I don't want you to freak out, but there's this guy. I think he's following me, or us. I saw him in the forest when we ran into that troll cave. He helped me then. And again at the castle, well, he saved me in the lake I mean."

Eloryn blinked. "You think he helps you? Could he know you?"

"Don't know. It's weird. He's all Tarzan and stuff, like some sort of guardian-angel-cross-savage. I haven't even heard him talk, if he can. I can't think how I'd possibly know him."

"He sounds like a foundling child. There are lots of stories about them, children who become lost in the woods at a young age and are raised by animals or the fae themselves."

"He sure looks like an animal. You haven't seen him? At all? Maybe

I've just really lost it."

"If you say he's out there then I believe you. There must be a reason he's following you. Alward says nothing is ever truly lost, everything goes somewhere…" Eloryn's voice faded out.

"Alward, he's like your family, isn't he?" Memory said. "We're going to meet a whole group of wizards, right? I'm sure they'll be able to rescue him. Maybe he's already free. Brannon said someone would try."

Eloryn just nodded. Saving Alward is what she should be doing, if only she could, if she only knew what to do. Instead, it was left in the hands of more capable strangers, still more people put in danger on her behalf. "I hope they will be able to help you too, to find out who you are and where you're from."

Memory shifted, hiding her face in shadow. "Yeah. Me too."

Eloryn turned back to the inn. The door opened, spilling warm light and a pair of bodies out into the night. "Is that Roen?"

Memory perked up.

Across at the inn, Roen stumbled down the steps, a pint glass in one hand and a red-headed barmaid tucked under his other arm. She stroked long fingers over his belt buckle, working it loose.

"If it is him, I may just need to kill him," Memory muttered through blue lips.

Roen whispered in the busty barmaid's ear, a huge grin on his face. He indicated with his hands. *You, me, two more.* The slap she gave him echoed out across the quiet night.

Roen laughed and rubbed his cheek. The red-head stormed back inside. As soon as the door closed, he sobered up, put the glass down on the stairs and pulled a key from his pocket. He scanned the area. Memory threw a rock at him, glancing off his shoulder. He winced and looked their way.

"Maybe not the best way to get his attention, but satisfying," she told Eloryn before he reached them.

When he did, Memory's voice became shrill. "Have you been in there the whole time? While we've been freezing our tits off?"

Eloryn stared between the two, confused and muted from overwhelming emotions- relief, shock at Memory's behavior and a strange cold pain in her chest.

Roen spoke urgently with his jaw set. "Hush. I'll explain it all. But let's get you both warm first. I got us a private room at the back. There's some food that will still be hot too, if we hurry to it." He ushered them through shadows to a door in one of the back buildings, unlocking it for them. He let them in, waiting outside.

"Strip your wet dresses, before you are ill from it. The fire is lit so you'll be warm inside. Knock for me when you're decent, then I promise I will explain everything."

Roen closed the door on them.

CHAPTER FIFTEEN

Inside the musty room at Elders Bridge Inn, Eloryn looked from the closed door to Memory, confused. Memory shrugged and skittered straight to the roaring fire.

"Oh. My. God. This is so good, you have to get over here." Memory tore her wet dress off and stepped out of it so all she wore was a scant black shift and petticoat. She turned herself around in front of the flames.

Eloryn fumbled to undo the clasps of her dress with cold, numb fingers, and soon dropped it to the floor. She tried to not feel self conscious so undressed. Her attire matched Memory's, only in ivory.

She looked around the small room for a space to hang the dresses so the fire would dry them. A modest sized bed with age-faded

blankets filled one end of the room. A covered bowl on a table let out a small, tantalizing waft of steam, fragrant with thyme and pepper. It was surrounded by a stack of smaller pottery bowls, cups and a large flagon. Nothing to wear anywhere.

Memory peeled the top blanket off the bed and wrapped it around her shoulders. She tugged the next layer free and handed it to Eloryn when she joined her near the fire.

"Togas it is. Are we decent enough yet to let Roen in, or should we leave him waiting a bit longer?"

"I'm sure he had good reason to keep us waiting as he did." Eloryn muttered, remembering the way he had grinned when he pulled the barmaid close to him, putting his face into her hair. "But maybe, maybe just a little longer." She felt wicked, but Memory gave an encouraging grin. She smiled back, and they jiggled the cold out in front of the fire, a haze of steam lifting from them as their petticoats dried.

Eloryn felt well and truly thawed before they invited Roen back inside. He made no comment at the time it had taken them, just took a seat by the food and served some creamy broth into bowls. He took none for himself. Memory and Eloryn sat on the bed, soup bowls cradled in their laps, looking at Roen with wry expectation. As his eyes passed over her, Eloryn shifted and pulling her sheet tightly closed.

"Princess, I am sorry you suffered so much waiting for me."

Memory cleared her throat.

"My apologies to you too, Memory. Once I'd entered the inn, there was reason I had to stay so long," Roen said, his voice low. "It is not what you think. I went in to book lodgings, and overheard men at the bar bragging. They said they were Thayl's men, hunters, who controlled a mighty dragon that does their bidding."

Fear stabbed at Eloryn, a feeling she hadn't grown used to no matter how often she'd felt it since leaving her safe home. "Could they have tracked us here already?"

"I worried the same thing. Having overheard them, I thought it wouldn't be wise to leave again too quickly. I didn't want to lead them to you, or appear more suspicious than I already did." Roen indicated to his torn and muddied clothing. "There were but three I saw at the bar. I didn't recognize them, nor they me. So I stayed, made pretence of being social and tried to find out what I could while I was there."

"And what information did Miss Frisky Fingers have for you?" Memory pouted through a mouth full of soup.

"She was nothing but my excuse to leave." A muscle jumped in Roen's jaw and he looked at the floor. "I'm sorry you had to see that. I spent my time inside listening in on the hunters and drinking with an older man, a traveler from Farwall in the north, who knew some lore about dragons."

"The dragon isn't here, is it?" Memory paused from eating for just a moment.

"I don't believe so, but the man from Farwall had opinion on how the hunters are able to give orders to the beast," Roen told them. "He said they use a magic flute. With it, even if the beast is far away they can call it."

Eloryn swallowed. The very men who knew her appearance and her connection to Alward, the men who were hunting for her, were right here, and could call the dragon to them at any moment. "Shouldn't we leave, be away from here before they find us?"

Roen put a hand out in a calming gesture. He met her eyes until she stilled, then looked away. "I think it better we stay. To flee a paid room at this hour would only arouse suspicions. It could put you in more danger. They know what you both look like, so we will keep you hidden in here until they have moved on. No one at the inn has seen you. I will keep you safe and keep watch on them."

"I don't know. Even if we are safe, any time we spend here lessens our chances to rescue Alward. Shouldn't we travel on to the Wizards' Council right away?" Eloryn tried to keep her voice steady.

Memory looked at her with an exaggerated frown. "But I just warmed up again! Also, no clothes."

"At least one night, Princess, so that we can recover and make better time travelling tomorrow," Roen said.

"It'll be OK." Memory bumped her shoulder against Eloryn's and wiped the last of the soup from her bowl with a finger. Eloryn looked down into hers and realized she hadn't even touched it. She put it back on the table. She didn't have the stomach for it. Memory grabbed the abandoned bowl and kept eating.

"If you think it's best, then we'll stay," Eloryn said.

Roen nodded grimly. He lifted the flagon and poured three cupfuls. "Here, I thought there might be some nerves that would need calming tonight."

"Understatement," said Memory, reaching for a cup.

"You know, sometimes what you say makes barely any sense. The rest of the time it makes none at all." Roen half smiled and tipped his cup to her.

Eloryn took a sip, her stomach still uneasy, and coughed when the first mouthful went down. "What is this?"

"What it is, is just what we need," Memory wheezed and passed her cup back for more. "Come on Lory, don't pretend you've got no worries to drink away."

Roen raised an eyebrow, tilting the flagon to her to see if she accepted Memory's challenge.

Between Roen, whom she believed knew a good many worldly things, and Memory, who couldn't remember anything of the world, Eloryn wondered how, with all she'd learned, she always felt the one who knew the least. She downed the charring liquid and held out her empty cup with a restrained grimace.

Roen gave her a respectful nod, and poured more for them both.

Even the first cupful had Eloryn feeling dull and distracted. She wanted to ask why Roen wasn't finishing his, as he poured for them again, and then again. But she couldn't do it. Memory could have; she'd say anything, and frequently did. She was currently exchanging scar stories with Roen. Roen seemed to have some interesting anecdotes about his. They wafted in and out to her while the alcohol took effect. All of Memory's sounded the same-

"Check this one out, how do you reckon I got that?" Memory leaned forward, pulling her slip down and showing Roen right down the front of her chest. Eloryn turned away in shock.

Roen blew a low whistle, shook his head and chuckled. He leaned in conspiratorially to Memory. "A flagon to share, two girls in naught but shifts and sheets... any other night and this would have been interesting indeed."

Eloryn barely heard him, but even his tone made her blush pink. She wished she wasn't so prone to that, that she could keep her face under better control. She didn't feel she could control anything just now. Time seemed to be skipping forward in small jumps. Roen talked on with Memory but Eloryn kept catching him look toward her, small looks, so small she probably imagined them. She stared as the fire consumed logs greedily. Her mind drifted around, exploring dark places where she imagined Alward was held, hurt, or worse. Had he been saved? Was he now looking for her? Had he been tortured? Did he even still live? Was it all really her fault? She'd never meant to use her magic in front of the children, but she couldn't let them be hurt. Images jolted into her head of the heavy shelf toppling forward, books spinning and re-arranging themselves in mid-air, the wide eyed awe

from the children caught underneath, unharmed in a protective space built by ancient tomes. *Lucky chance,* she had told her young students, *back to work and don't speak of it again.* She should have told Alward what happened, but was too scared of disappointing him. Barely more than a week later, the hunters came for them. A feeling of sickness blocked her throat.

Roen's laughter drew her attention. "Just devilish, you are!"

A cheeky smile on Memory's face disappeared. Her mouth clamped shut, bottom jaw sticking out. "I need some air," she said and wobbled for the door.

"You can't go out, someone may see you," Roen warned.

"What's wrong?" Eloryn stood up.

Memory waved limp-wristed at them. "I just, I… bah. My trains of thought are leaving the station too quickly," she slurred and pushed her way outside.

Eloryn took a step after her, but found herself going down instead of forwards. The world slipped around inside her skull. She awaited the ground's impact with numb clarity, but instead felt the hold of Roen's arms around her, lifting her back to her feet. Her sheet slipped down off her shoulders, and he reached to pull it back up. Her bare skin ached pleasantly where he brushed it. She'd never had this much to drink before, and wondered if it always had this effect.

"Careful there," Roen said. She continued to sway and he held her steady, just the barest space between them. He smelled of cloves and mossy stones, a scent that intoxicated her as much as the alcohol. She felt queasy with guilt. What had she been thinking about before? She couldn't remember.

"You've had well enough to drink, delicate thing you are. Time to rest. I need to bring Mem back in," Roen said, something worrying his expression.

"You do not enjoy my company." The words escaped Eloryn's mouth before she could make the distinction between speech and thought.

"That's not true." Roen's voice was gruff, as though caught off guard and choking out a lie. It hurt Eloryn more than logic could account for.

"I know I'm a cause of trouble for you. Is this why you don't like me? I see how you can be such easy friends with Memory, and it seems to me you enjoy the company of women, and yet I cannot even bring a smile to you." Eloryn's heart beat too hard, pushing all her blood up into her face. She dropped her head and let her hair fall to hide the shameful color.

Roen inhaled deeply. Eloryn didn't want to look, sure he'd be frowning at her again. One of his hands dropped to the side and curled into a tight fist. She felt every muscle in his other hand tense where it held her steady.

"I'm sorry if I've made you think that. All I can say to explain my behavior is that there are times when I feel no great value in myself. It is... easy for me to be with women, and take comfort in the value they have of me. Memory, she is special, I must admit. But you, El," he breathed. The way he said her name made her shiver. "You are a princess."

Eloryn shook her head, confusion coming out in words. "I am hardly a princess. I've grown up in a small house by woods and never known a throne or kingdom, and that kingdom which was to be mine is not, even if I had want-"

Roen gently interrupted her rambling. "It's no matter. You are everything a princess should be: kind, clever, brave, beautiful. If I behave differently for you, it's only because whatever I was, whatever I am, I need to be better for you."

Eloryn lost her ability to breathe. A racing dizziness overwhelmed her. Her head bowed, she stared at his clenched fist. She wanted to say something in return, but had no words left in her.

Gently, she unwrapped his hand and held it with shaking fingers, lifting her head to give him a timid smile. Roen's eyes met hers, frowning and questioning. His mouth was set and troubled and a soft noise like a moan escaped from his throat.

Then the small distance between them vanished and he kissed her. His mouth closed around her bottom lip, firm and soft in the same moment. Her heart rushed and her eyes snapped wide open. Her hand squeezed around his and he kissed her harder.

One of his hands slid up her shoulder to the base of her neck, fingers twined into her hair. His other hand broke free of hers and moved behind her waist, pulling her body into his.

She brought both hands up and placed them against his flat stomach, some polite voice inside telling her she should push him away. Once there, feeling his smooth muscles beneath the thin silk fabric, she ached to think of the touch breaking.

She gasped breathlessly, lips parting, and he pulled her body up toward his with a strength that lifted her off her feet.

Memory sat on the steps of their room, staring out into the endless twisting trees around them. They swayed in her half closed eyes.

She tried to remember why she'd gotten angry. Her brain played over recent memories like a faulty video, all slow motion, slurring voices and skipping frames. *Devilish*, that was it. Why did he have to say something like that? They were all getting along so well, she'd almost forgotten she was probably a spawn of Hell.

The air was icy, but the alcohol provided enough fuel to keep her warm. Everything smelled of earthy wood smoke. Somewhere inside her she knew there was something she ought to be aware of, frightened of. She ignored the feeling, mentally filing it into her "Everything So Far" folder, and let her eyes glaze over.

"Don't try to use him," a hesitant voice said from nearby.

Memory turned around so quickly she slipped off the step down to the next with a bump.

A dark shape sat hunched on the small roof above the doorway.

A flickering sprite hovered around, casting just enough light to show a body covered in animal furs.

"Ah, he speaks. Doesn't make much sense though," Memory slurred.

No reply.

The sprite had vanished and only the shadow of a hunched figure remained. Memory squinted to see if it really was her savage guardian, and shook off a wave of nausea. "Ugh, is this real life?"

"The dragon." His voice sounded real, real enough to sound frustrated. "He's under a man's control. He can't do what he wants."

"If it catches and kills us, it doesn't matter to me if it wanted to do it or not," Memory said. "Were you eavesdropping?"

The savage's voice took a hard edge. "It's a living thing, not a weapon. The men use a flute-"

"Knew that."

"-made from bone of the dragon's soul mate, that they killed. You have to understand." The wild man's voice dropped back to a whisper. "They make him belong to them."

"That's..." Memory drew quiet, the smug smile falling off her face, "really sad."

The cold crept into Memory's skin. She watched the curling mist match the frost on the air that she breathed. With each breath, her frown deepened.

"Why do you keep helping me?" she asked after a while.

Nothing, again.

He was gone.

She stood up quickly, a little too quickly. She felt as if she left her head behind her, too heavy to follow that fast. She could only remember every second thing. Swearing, she fumbled her way back inside, swiftly plummeting into a woozy black sleep.

The sound of scratching at the door latch froze Roen and Eloryn in place, his nose still pressed against hers and uneven breath brushing over her lips.

"Pray pardon. It was wrong of me," Roen said. The frown had never left his face. He backed away from her and turned around as Memory stumbled inside.

Eloryn's legs conspired to collapse beneath her. She dropped in slow motion and found herself on the edge of the bed. Eyes closed in a slow blink and she filled her breathless lungs. She shook her head from the alcohol and emotions but could not clear it.

"Why the hell did I go outside? It's cold out there. You 'k Lory?" Memory flopped belly first onto the bed.

Eloryn put a palm to her forehead, blinking through her shock. "I don't… don't know."

Memory said something that was muffled by her face in the bed.

"Sleep well. I'll see you in the morning, hopefully with good news." Roen took the flagon and left the room without looking back.

Eloryn fell onto the bed next to Memory. Her heart beat hard enough to shake her whole body.

CHAPTER SIXTEEN

His knuckles split as he hit the rough bark of the tree. Leaves above rustled in protest.

A giggle rang out like the sound of chimes in a soft wind. "My sweet pet, come here, let me make it better for you."

"She was drunk," he growled low.

Mina appeared behind him. Her fingers stroked around his neck and she spun herself in a pirouette to his front. She bent into his chest with a smile. "Of course she was, blind drunk. Why else do you think I let you prattle on how you did?" Her voice lowered as she spoke, both sultry and cruel.

Prattle on. Saying even a word to her was the hardest thing he'd done for a long time. He wanted so badly to tell her everything, and

when a chance finally came to speak to her without those others around, she was wasted. Absently, he pushed a hand up into Mina's fiery hair. The corner of his mouth pulled into a mockery of a smile. Never before had he been so aware of how little control he had over his own movements when close to Mina. Her hair felt like warm water between his fingers, and he bent his face toward hers.

A sharp thump-click sounded through the icy silent night, and he leant back into the shadow of a tree, pulling Mina in closer to him. She nuzzled into his shoulder and he turned to watch the thief boy slinking out of the room at the inn. Roen brought a large flagon up just away from his lips and held it there for a few moments as though stopped in time, then tossed it angrily aside. Clear liquid spilled through the air and fell like rain, and the bottle thumped into nearby bushes.

The thief looked carefully around, and slipped into the shadows himself.

Standing next to Mina, the savage breathed deep through his nose. "He smells of her." Even from this far away, he could smell him, and her on him. And even in the dark, as well as the thief moved, it was easy to see where he went. His time spent with Mina and the other fae had its benefits. He was no longer what he once was, no longer weak.

"Enough about *Her!*" Mina's eyes glittered like sparking flint and her nails dug into his chest. Like the sun passing out from behind a cloud, her face shone with a smile again, but her nails remained clawed in his skin. "My sweet little boy. Who saved you when you were too lost and hungry to survive?"

"You did," he said, dropping his forehead onto hers.

"Who has shown you wonders greater than you could have ever imagined?"

He knew these words, knew the answers he had to give, but they hurt now, as they came through his mouth, more than they ever had

before. "You."

"Who is the most beautiful thing you've ever seen?"

"You."

"Who do you love above all else, even your short mortal life?"

He looked across to the inn. The window to the small back room was now dark, and the thief boy worked his way into someone else's. Through the chilled night air, the familiar scent of cheap packet hair dye, blood and crushed flowers drifted to him. She still smelled just the way he remembered, the way she did back before they both came to this world. He breathed the fragrance deeply, holding it in his chest. His lips pressed hard against Mina's forehead and when he whispered they moved against her skin.

"You."

"You took your time. I started to think you had perished in the waters after all."

"I was just dreaming about this weird guy on a roof, telling me things about soul mates or music or something. It's all fuzzed up and skippy." Memory talked to herself. She was nothingness, floating in a thick, comforting dark. Shapes were forming all around. A horse skeleton of rusted metal and chains swam past. Sprites fizzled like fireworks. Streams of golden light flowed in the distance.

"Sometimes we confuse dream for waking, and real for dream." The voice came from everywhere and nowhere, from inside herself, deep, sad and forceful.

"Am I asleep now, or awake?" Memory grew a hand, followed by

the rest of her body, and reached out to pull a silk tasseled cord. It caused a ribbon of silver to fall which became a road paved in glass. She walked along it.

"You've only just begun dreaming, but I am real. We share this space as we did the dream yesterday morning. I mistook it as only a dream myself until I met you while waking." A tall figure strode out from amongst the condensing shapes.

"You?" Memory said, marching onwards. "I don't want you here."

"You have no choice. I was told we would remain connected, by time and space forever, but never thought I'd see you again for it to matter." Thayl drew a black velvet and ebony throne from the shadows and sat in front of Memory. He shimmered, his eyes less tired than in the real world, but still haunted. "Don't fret. I'm not here to harm you, and don't know if I could here, regardless. This is your mind, not mine."

She kept walking away from him but he remained right beside her in his throne. "That chair isn't mine."

"Well, it is somewhat sparsely furnished here." Thayl gestured to the black. "Where are you going?"

Memory stopped on the path. "It's all empty."

Thayl tilted his head toward a grey alleyway in the distance.

"I don't want to go there."

"Why?" His voice teased.

"Don't remember." Glass cobblestones rearranged under her motionless feet. They lifted and flew, a flock of invisible squares floating around her.

"You don't remember anything."

"I remember you said I was a devil."

"My mistake. Forgive that I startled you. I was simply shocked to see you after the dream we shared. I mistook you to have come alive

from my nightmare. That is all. I think it must have scared you too."

"I'm not a devil?" She couldn't help sounding hopeful.

"Of course not. That first dream we shared was... just a mix of strange visions."

"But..." *Your hand,* she thought.

Thayl cut her off. "But I do know what is real. I even know who you really are and where you are from."

Memory floated, her path entirely gone from beneath her. Her stomach dropped away but she didn't fall.

"But..."

"But," he interrupted again, "you have something I want in return. The girl you were with at Palace de Montredeur."

"Ugh! Typical." Memory hissed and a swarm of tiny dancing gowns nearby caught on fire. "It's always about precious Eloryn! I'm so over it already!"

"Then let me have her and have all your problems solved," Thayl said, his voice as dark and velvet as his throne.

She wanted that. Wanted it so much.

"What will you do with her?" That wasn't what she meant to say.

"No wrong."

"What isn't wrong to a man who killed the woman he loved?"

A flame lit in Thayl's eyes and he arose in fury. He stormed toward her and Memory stumbled backwards.

Flashing shadows passed between them and when they cleared, the anger in Thayl had gone, replaced with simmering grief.

"Daring to say such things when you know nothing at all! I did not kill her. Never would have, never could have." His voice sounded too hurt to be a lie.

Memory fought the urge to back away further as Thayl glared down at her. "But everyone says."

"It's what everyone chooses to believe, that I am the evil to hate. Everyone can believe as they want, let them fear me more. But I want you to know the truth. I want you to see I'm not the one to distrust."

Thayl drew another, simpler chair from the black, offering it to Memory. His face had grown still, carved from wax and too cold to melt. "Sit; I will show you the truth. Once you have some knowledge in this empty head then you can make your judgment."

Thayl returned to his throne, and Memory took the second chair, lowering herself in with hesitation as though it might bite.

"Loredanna and I were in love..." Thayl began.

"You were a stalker," Memory interrupted with a whisper.

"We were in love, together," Thayl said, the corner of his lips turning down in irritation.

A scene lit in front of them. A woman in the finest of gowns with coifed cream hair sobbed uncontrollably, heartbreakingly, into the shoulder of a man; Thayl, when he was younger, straighter. The frown on his face was now fresh and not yet set in permanence.

"She looks just like Eloryn," Memory said.

"This is Loredanna, her mother."

"What did you do to her?"

Thayl raised an eyebrow. "You truly think me a monster? This is my memory, of when she was given news from the Wizards' Council that they had not allowed me to be her husband. My magical talent was considered too weak for the royal bloodline, so she was chosen another partner. She cried for weeks, and was never happy again, from that time till her death. I swore then that those who forced our love apart would hurt even more than she."

"So you killed the King and all those wizards?"

"I've never denied this. It was as they deserved, and I will continue until I see revenge on every wizard of the council who took her from me."

Alward, Memory thought, but it sounded louder than if she'd yelled, echoing through the black around them.

"*Pellaine.* Him most of all. He is mine now, and when I no longer need him I will see justice paid for his crime. He is the one who killed the most perfect being of this world." Thayl's voice dropped into a growling whisper, hissing through bared teeth.

Memory opened her mouth, needing the answer to a million questions.

"Just watch," Thayl murmured.

A new scene flashed by and Memory turned to it. Like a silent movie it played.

The beautiful Queen sat sad and alone, full with child in an unlit room. Through the open frame of a window she watched the moon fading into the sky around it, burnt to red by the earth's shadow. A sound startled her and a smile of hope lit her face when she saw it was Thayl who approached. He held her, and pleaded with her, and through tears she nodded agreement. Reaching up to her neck, she unclasped a chain and removed a heavy amulet, the same crested one Eloryn had owned. She flung it onto the table with a look of disgust and triumph, then took Thayl's hand and not a single other thing and they left.

The vision flickered, cut and jumped, to a forest of grim trees and shadows. Thayl and Loredanna fled into the woods with a look of anxious, terrified hope.

Another jump, and Memory watched Loredanna, wet from the exhaustion of labor, being supported by Thayl. She reached out, crying for her child. A lanky blond man held a newborn baby, taking it away. "Pellaine," Thayl hissed.

The scene flickered, and Alward now held a scroll instead. A baby

lay on the ground of the forest among dead bodies and dead leaves. Reading from the scroll, Alward shot a blast of red light from his hand which hit the young Queen fully where she stood just in front of Thayl, still reaching for her child.

The vision skipped again. Loredanna lay still and limp, held by Thayl. He knelt on the ground and screamed wrath and vengeance. Across the scene, Alward vanished like a ghost into smoke with the baby in his arms. The scene jumped, but did not change. A hooded figure flickered in and out of vision. Loredanna fell alone to the ground, the scene shifted, then she was again held in Thayl's arms.

Memory squinted through her tears. She wiped them quickly, but Thayl had already seen them. A shallow smile formed on his lips.

"These are my memories. Do you trust me yet that I will help return you yours?" His voice was clouded, his eyes unreadable and cold.

"Why would he do that? It didn't make sense!" Memory shook with outrage.

"You are like me, we are strong in emotion. The wizards know only logic and tradition. Loredanna and I broke those traditions when she fled to be with me. Both our lives meant nothing to them from that point on. They only needed her child to continue their ways."

The scene of Loredanna's death still flickered. Thayl watched the younger version of himself with his jaw clenched. The scene spluttered; again a faceless figure was silhouetted in the forest. Memory blinked and the vision had faded away.

"But Alward didn't, Eloryn doesn't..." Memory couldn't get her thoughts straight, something didn't add up, but a noise kept distracting her, breaking up thoughts she tried to form.

Someone was singing.

"Will you bring me the child of the woman I loved?" Thayl asked

urgently.

Three voices roared in unison, another laughed.

"I don't... there are still things... don't make sense, but..." It became hard for Memory to focus. All her surroundings, even her own body, were crumbling away like wet cake. Only the rowdy song remained.

Losing sight of Thayl, she called out in a panic, "You really know who I am?"

Memory woke to the white light of early morning. Too early. *Ugh, my head.* She rubbed seedy eyes to get them working.

Singing floated into the room. Memory heard it as she did in her dream.

"When you catch 'em sneaking round,
You give their hide a tanning,
A kicking or a whipping, or a beating good and sound,
Cause thieves are only good for hanging!"

Visions from her dream washed over her. Her heart started up quickly but she couldn't tell if it was from guilt or exhilaration. If it could be; if only it were all true... She could hardly bear the hope. She remembered most of it, more clearly than she did the parts of the night before she fell asleep. Did her jungle man really come and talk to her? Why the hell did she drink so much? As soothing as it was to purge her thoughts of whether she was a demon, she cursed herself for it now. And Roen for keeping her cup so full.

She sat up gingerly and Eloryn continued to sleep beside her.

Roen wasn't there. Did he really stay out all night? *Wow. Either very chivalrous, or he found Miss Frisky Fingers again.*

Memory wanted badly to go back to sleep, but the singers continued.

"Thieves are thieves and that they'll always be,

No matter what you name 'em,

Cutpurse, dipper, footpad or a booter-free,

A thief's still only good for hanging!"

Fumbling out of bed she woke Eloryn, who winced and looked around the room.

"Where's Roen?" she asked.

"Good morning to you too."

Eloryn's face reddened and she mumbled in embarrassment.

"Hopefully Roen's getting us breakfast," Memory said and poked at her hanging gown. Only a few hot coals remained from the roaring fire of the night before. The morning air was crisp against her skin under the flimsy petticoat.

"Is someone singing?" Eloryn rubbed her eyes and cringed.

Memory chuckled, just a little pleased that Eloryn seemed to be suffering more than her.

"These are dry," she said, tossing the gold dress to Eloryn. She

took a moment to analyze the black gown and realized it had a simpler under-dress she could probably get on herself. The grander skirt, ruined now anyway, was left behind. And frankly she didn't care if the remaining dress was an undergarment or not. The fine sleeves were all but gone, so apart from having Eloryn help with her corset she was dressed and warmer in no time.

Helping Eloryn clasp the back of her dress, she wondered what Thayl, real or dream, would actually do with her. He loved her mother, so maybe he was going to let her be an actual Princess, as she should be, as if she was his own daughter? Memory shook her head to herself. Way too optimistic for her normal taste. She wiggled her toes, feeling them cold and bare, missing her shoes. Noticing her knife where it had fallen on the floor the night before, she slipped it back into her corset when Eloryn looked the other way.

Memory peeked through tattered curtains to see what the noise outside was all about. The daylight stabbed her tender eyes. Outside, a group of men lifted bottles and flasks, singing around a dirty bundle on the ground. During a rousing chorus, one of them threw his foot hard into the lump, which cried out and twisted out of the way, revealing a face.

Memory dropped the curtains back with a gasp.

"What is it?" Eloryn asked, moving toward the window.

Memory blocked her way. "How is your magic feeling this morning, any better yet?"

"Better, but perhaps not reliably so. Mem, what is it?"

"It's Roen. Some men have him all tied up, hurting him. Lory, he doesn't look very good." Memory wanted to look outside again, to find out more, but was too scared. All she could make out before were ropes, blood, and Roen's face.

"What do we do?" Eloryn squeaked a panicked whisper and the

blood visibly drained from her complexion.

Memory felt the hard metal knife, a comforting presence against her skin. She had that, at least. Eloryn had her magic, maybe. That didn't feel like enough.

She held her breath and looked out the window again. The men were gone; Roen too. She could still hear singing, somewhere close. She swore. "Whatever we do, we have to hurry."

CHAPTER SEVENTEEN

"We'll sneak up, see what we can see and go from there." Peering out the doorway, Memory found the area empty. Dirty red painted a patch of ground behind the inn, and more blood marked the path where Roen had been dragged.

"That's your plan?"

"You have a better one?"

Eloryn shut her mouth and followed Memory out the door.

"Maybe they're done with him, and he'll be OK?" The sight of blood made Memory dizzy, made her want to run the other way.

"We have to help him. He has the token for contacting the Wizards' Council." Eloryn half sobbed. "We can't leave him behind too."

In her head Memory rattled through every swear word she knew.

She could hear the singing again behind a thicket of trees.

"Is it the hunters who know us?" Eloryn whispered.

"Didn't get a good look, but there were no uniforms." Memory's mouth felt dry and her head ached out through her eyes. She tried to shake it off and concentrate as they crept toward the boisterous choir. The rough ground hurt her bare feet, already sore from river crawling the night before. Her eyes felt full of sand, no matter how much they watered to compensate, blurring her vision. She winced away from the bushes she pushed through and stumbled forward too quickly-

And she was suddenly being stared at by four large men. One was positively a giant.

Eloryn stumbled into her back.

Having already used all her others, Memory tried to invent a new swear word. *Frotz.*

The men gaped, sneered and laughed at their sudden appearance. Roen lay on the ground behind them, face down, his caramel hair matted with blood and dirt. He struggled to look up and see why the singing had ended mid chorus, and his expression filled with heartbreak and horror. He screamed for them to run, but only a rasping breath came out, mouthing the word.

A long rope hung over a branch above a man wearing a worn top hat. He paused, half way through tying a rough noose.

Another man wobbled forward, sloshing ale from his flask and smiling around protruding teeth. "Mornin' m'ladies, come for the show?"

"Look, they all shocked and proper." The man with the rope smirked and went back to tying the noose.

"If this isn't their flavor we could give them a different sort of show after," a handsome but greasy man slurred.

A couple of the men roared with laughter and clinked flasks.

Giant, Buck-tooth, Greasy and Top-hat; nope, they definitely weren't with the wizard hunters.

Eloryn stepped forward, setting her shaking shoulders square. "Sirs, show your respect. You address ladies of the court. What is happening here?"

Her voice was so formal and firm the men's laughter cut short. Memory also straightened up, desperately attempting to follow her example.

"Just dealing with a vermin problem milady, what we caught a-sneaking round."

"And we gave his hide a tanning!" Greasy sang, causing the others to break back into laughter.

"You are wrong. He's our friend." Eloryn shook her head at them, but her influence over them clearly waned. The girls' dirty and torn dresses didn't help their cause, and the men eyed them suspiciously.

"Then friends with a thief you are, 'cause we caught him right with his nose in our belongings."

"Did he actually take anything?" Memory asked.

"No doubt would have if we didn't catch him; tends to be how these things work, little girl." Greasy winked at her.

"It wasn't his fault, it was mine," Memory said before she could let herself decide against it. Roen shook his head into the ground. Memory licked rough lips and continued, looking to her side for the fragment of an idea that had come to her. "It was just a prank, a dare we made last night after we drank too much. I told him to steal something for me, from the toughest looking men at the inn, in return for..." Memory's imagination ran dry, but the men took her hesitation to have a different meaning, breaking into cheers again.

"I understand that well enough," said Greasy, running his gaze up and down the girls.

"Good. Let him go then." Memory tried to sound commanding but it came out too high pitched.

"Well, m'ladies." Top-hat swung the finished noose about in one hand. "Seems if he's worth something to your fine selves, then he's worth something to us as well."

"A thief like this would fetch a fine bounty I'm sure, should we take him into town," said Buck-tooth. Giant grunted agreement. Memory wondered if they'd bothered teaching the mammoth to talk.

"Oh no, we won't hurt him no more, but maybe you could offer us some compensation for our troubles, if the boy here's worth it to you."

"He is. If it's money you want, we'll pay." Memory could see Eloryn trying to catch her attention from the corner of her eye, and realized too late what she wanted to say. They had no money. They had nothing.

"Money will do just fine, being as you're both too little for my appetites anyhow," Top-hat said.

"Speak for yourself," Greasy said, and laughed when the girls squirmed in response.

"I speak for all of us. We have a deal, for a taste of gold." Top-hat dropped the noose, waiting. Memory hesitated, lost for what to do next.

"We have to check first you haven't beaten him past his use to us," Eloryn said, stepping forward.

"We've got all day, haven't we, boys?"

The men stepped back a respectful distance, letting the girls through.

Memory and Eloryn rushed over and knelt by Roen. He had been left lying on his stomach, arms bound behind his back. Memory rolled him onto his side with care. His face was split and torn in a few places and he groaned when she moved him. Most of the blood on him came

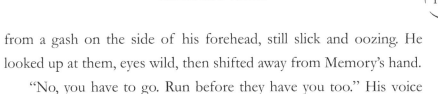

from a gash on the side of his forehead, still slick and oozing. He looked up at them, eyes wild, then shifted away from Memory's hand.

"No, you have to go. Run before they have you too." His voice caught as he whispered. "The token is in my pocket. Take it and go."

"What the hell were you doing?" Memory whispered into his ear.

He turned his face from them. "Wanted to take the flute, have the dragon ourselves."

"It is not even them, thanks be. Just braggarts, pretending to be great with tales and lies." Eloryn reached out her hand, but withdrew it when Roen shifted away with a grunt.

"You idiot, why would you even try that?" Memory stared at her shaking hand, covered in his blood. She wanted to slap him, but figured he'd already had enough. She struggled to keep her voice low, out of hearing of the men who stood nearby, despite how she wanted to yell.

"Because it's what I do!" Roen closed his eyes, letting his forehead fall back onto the ground.

Eloryn's voice trembled. "I don't understand."

"There was no other thief than myself when I returned your bag that day we met. I only returned it because I... I don't even know why." His voice shook as he whispered into the ground, his shoulders tensed beneath a bloodstained shirt. "Just leave me."

Memory shook her head, confused. No other thief...? If he was a thief, what was that to her? Nothing but another lie, in any case. A thief pretending to be noble. A demon pretending to be human. She could guess what would be considered worse.

Eloryn choked out a few confused words before finding a sentence. "But they would kill you."

Memory pushed his shoulder again, forcing him to roll over and face them. "Stop sulking. Can you walk?"

He squinted away from her, but nodded.

"Lory, can you magic up so they think we paid them?"

Buck-tooth kicked a rock across the clearing, skimming it close by them. "Come on! When he said all day, you weren't supposed to take it!"

Eloryn scooped some pebbles into her hand, and bent forward as though speaking to Roen again but spoke to the rocks instead. She opened her hand again and gold coins shimmered. One faded back into a pebble, leaving only four.

"Quick as possible," she whispered and stood up.

Memory dug her small fingers into the knotted rope.

"This is all we have." Eloryn held out her hand. The men gathered forward to look and smirked at her. Giant grunted out a laugh from the back.

"It's just enough. A little less than value, but I guess we feel kindly today. Lucky lad," said Top-hat.

Memory had Roen out of his ropes and helped him up. She couldn't stand the smell of the blood, and staggered from it almost as much as Roen did from his injuries. Once on his feet, he let go of her and stood on his own. He looked at the ground, breathing roughly. Memory turned back and nodded to Eloryn, who handed over the money and the three of them hobbled as fast as they could toward the road.

They were just steps away when the thugs yelled in outrage.

"What is this? Think you can give us fairy gold?" Buck-tooth cried.

"Run?" Memory whispered.

"Can't," said Roen.

"Frotz," Memory said. She glanced back.

Top-hat squinted at her, his chin raised. "Get them. This is unauthorized magic. We'll have a bounty after all. Get them!"

Memory turned to Roen. He turned to Eloryn. Wavering on his

feet, he begged her to run as he twisted the upper hem of his pants.

Eloryn stumbled back a few steps, slow and unsure. Top-hat caught up to her, grabbing her from behind. She shrieked and wriggled as he dragged her back. Roen went after them.

Giant came bearing down on Memory like a wall of flesh.

The sound of pounding feet came from behind her, and she turned, lifting her arms to protect herself from whatever approached. Her savage guardian angel ran toward her. His body blurred past and hit the mammoth man, knocking him down. They rolled out of sight behind bushes.

Greasy and Buck-tooth paused on their way to Roen, blinking, turning from Memory to their leader. He called back to them, "Get the skinny witch before she summons another beast. I've got the blonde, and the boy won't be any trouble."

Turning to approach Memory, Greasy smiled crookedly and her skin jumped.

A flash of light reflected into her eyes. Beside her, Roen drew a thin blade of flexible pale gold from the seam of his trousers. It snapped straight and sharp in his hands. He struck it against Top-hat's face. It was a clumsy movement, his arm visibly stiff and sore, but the shock made the man release his grip on Eloryn, and his top hat fall from his head.

Blood dripped around his mouth. He laughed and spat.

Eloryn ran to Roen's side. He stepped between her and the man, who drew a large bronze sword from his belt, spinning it in his hands. Roen rolled his shoulder, grimacing. He whispered to Eloryn behind his back.

Memory could read the words on his lips. "Just go."

A hand swiped the air in front of Memory and she dodged back, just out of Buck-tooth's reach. Greasy's fist flew in from her side,

hitting her in the face. Her cheek split between his knuckles and her teeth. Her vision darkened and she fell onto her side.

Memory lifted herself on one wobbly hand, trying to will her pain away. She fumbled with her other hand down the front of her corset, grasping for the body-warmed knife.

A calloused hand grabbed her arm, bruising skin and making the handle slip from her fingers. Her eyes bulged. The crush of the man's hand made her faint with terror. She screamed with all her chest.

A flurry of feathers and claws descended from the branches above them. Ravens swooped through the clearing. The thugs swatted back at them. The birds tore at their hands and faces. Memory ducked back down to the ground, covering her head, but the birds left her alone. She could hear Eloryn's voice through the beat of wings, calling the birds to them. Memory reached again for her folded knife.

Top-hat sliced a raven out of the air with his sword. It fell bloody to the ground.

Eloryn cried out in matched pain. She called out more magical words, but a moment later the flock had cleared. Memory heard the sword swing again, and this time Roen grunted sharply.

Still on her stomach, Memory could see boots in front of her. She rolled up onto her feet, flicked her knife open and slashed it at Buck-tooth. He stepped back just out of the blade's arc. Grinning, he pulled a yellow hunting knife from his own belt, waggling it at her. It was two times larger than her flick blade.

He swung. She blocked with a cry, her eyes closed. The metals clashed. Her hand stung from the contact, but she held on.

His blade snapped an inch above the hilt. He cried out in honest shock and dropped the broken weapon.

Greasy laughed, right behind Memory. She tried to swing back at the man, but he slammed her in the shoulder, spinning her the other way. He locked his hands around her wrists, lifting her off the ground. She kicked at him with bare feet.

He squeezed his hand around her wrist holding the knife. She squeezed harder, refusing to let go. She squealed and growled, twisted and wrenched but Greasy held tight. He pulled her toward him, running his nose up her neck. She pumped her legs uselessly in the air.

"Let me go! Don't touch me! Let me go or I'll hurt you!" she cried with a shredded voice.

Greasy threw her onto the ground, knocking the air from her lungs. He gripped both her wrists under one hand and knelt over her, crushing her hips.

He grinned hideously. "Got you."

A deep, primal terror took over, like a nightmare she couldn't remember but that still left her sick and scared. She screamed, and the fire in her lit, pulsing outwards.

The man's weight flew off her, blasted away.

Memory opened wincing eyes, and saw the greasy, horrible man lying bloody against a tree across the clearing. He was all the way over there, not moving, but she could still feel his hands on her. Still feel the force of his weight like a sickness inside her. She screamed again in fury, twitching on the ground where she lay, back arching. All sound left the world and her ears hummed.

She rolled onto her side, heaving air into a mouth that tasted of blood. Her head lolled up and she looked out through drunken eyes.

Buck-tooth stood next to her, fear and anger twisting his lips away from disfigured teeth. He ran the other way.

Roen knelt on the other side of the clearing, slouched forward. Fresh blood made the front of his shirt shine. Top-hat had Eloryn on the ground, a foot on her stomach, but he stared at Memory, angry and shocked.

Leaving Eloryn, the man ran at Memory, his sword held firm and angled straight at her, his eyes fixed and dangerous.

Clinging to her knife in one hand, Memory reached out with the other. Drawing power from the magical fire within her, she threw it at the man with a feral cry.

He skidded across the ground and fell to one knee. He coughed blood.

Through the ringing in her ears Memory heard sobbing, and distantly realized it was her own. The world spun like a mad-man's nightmare. Her skin still crawled. She wanted to tear it off. She put her feet under her and stood, bent and slumped, stumbling toward Top-hat. She swiped at him again, her magic flinging out from her fingertips like an invisible whip, striking him. He fell onto his stomach. Still, still she could feel hands on her. She cried out, and beat the man over and over, bloodying him with the unseen, powerful force.

His grunts of pain were muffled. A movie with the sound too low. Screaming all around her grew louder as her hearing cleared.

"Mem, Memory, please stop."

She barely heard through her own fury. *There are! There are hands on me!* She spun around and swung her knife blindly behind her, meeting flesh.

The voice that gasped was a girl's. Her sight waved back into focus.

Eloryn stood in front of her. A thin scarlet line ran across the width of her chest below her collar bones. She drew short, hard breaths that shook her body.

"What are you doing?" Memory screamed.

"You were going to kill him," Eloryn whispered. Her lips and nose wrinkled as though she were about to cry.

"And he was going to kill me!" Memory yelled into Eloryn's face. Nervous energy filled her, running berserk through her body. Her grip around her knife left her knuckles white and aching.

Eloryn shook her head. Her mouth opened and closed without letting the words out.

"No? No what? What am I not supposed to do Eloryn?" Memory hissed. "How am I supposed to know? I'm not some perfect little princess that gets told what to do her whole life, with all these people around to look after me!" Memory jabbed her knife toward Roen who stumbled their way. "I don't know why I feel like this. I don't know what's wrong with me. Probably because I'm some sort of monster from Hell right? I know that's what you think! You don't even think I'm human!"

"Mem..." Eloryn breathed in anguish.

"Memory, that's enough!" Roen roared, setting himself between Eloryn and Memory's knife. He lifted his thin blade. Its tip was pointed down and defensive, but it sent a clear message.

Memory bellowed wordlessly at them. Her vision darkened, blocked by something. Confusion slapped the anger from her. She coughed out a breath she'd gasped in too quickly and gave her eyes a moment to work. Her vision was blocked by a body. The savage stood between her and Roen, his back to her. His knuckles were covered in blood. He growled.

Roen cried out in shock and Memory heard him stumble backwards.

Adrenaline still tingled in her fingertips. Reality rattled around in her skull, pounding into focus as her pulse steadied. She stepped to the side of the savage's back, unable to see past his wide shoulders. Roen lifted his blade at the animal man, who growled and coiled to pounce.

"Stop! Stop. I'm sorry." Memory's voice went from cry to whisper. She let her knife roll out of her numb fingers onto the ground. "Roen, stop, please."

Roen shook his head, his gaze fixed on the looming savage. Eloryn wrapped her fingers around his arm, making him lower his sword.

The savage stepped toward them again, growling.

"No! Please." Memory grabbed his bloodied hand in both of hers and pulled him back. She could feel his arm tense at her touch. Her chest contracted again into unwilling sobs. "I know you're trying to protect me, but I don't know why. Please don't hurt them."

Twisted strands of dark hair fell over his face but she could still see an expression of pain on it. He opened his mouth and his eyes shifted from her to the others. His lip twitched and he dropped his head away, struggling with something.

"You're not a monster," he whispered.

Memory felt his hand shaking in hers, and for a second, he squeezed her hands back then let go.

He glanced around the clearing at the fallen men. "One more." With one final growl at Roen, soft but no less threatening, he turned away and disappeared into the trees.

Memory fell on the ground and wept.

CHAPTER EIGHTEEN

Roen shifted on his feet in an attempt to steady himself. He breathed out and silently counted to ten.

The pain didn't ease.

Fair enough, it was the least he deserved, but he wished the wooziness would pass. His skull felt as if it swam slowly under his scalp. He struggled for clear thought. This mess was his fault, and the knowledge of that hurt more than the beating. He needed to sort it out and make sure the Princess was safe again. Above all else, they had to get away from here as fast as possible. Two thugs still lay unconscious nearby, but Roen had lost track of the other two and the commotion was surely heard from the inn. There could be more trouble at any moment.

And that savage man, what is his connection to Memory? Is he still nearby? Roen's hands shook. Roen just reached average in height and that savage dwarfed him and had the look of a predator. Even if he was hale he wouldn't have a chance against that beast. Somehow Memory trusted the animal, but after this he didn't know what that meant. Memory had barely blinked at his own confession, which he didn't take as a sign of best judgment of character. She had also hurt Eloryn.

Roen's squeezed his eyes shut. There was too much mess to deal with now, too many questions he didn't want to face. *Later, just start moving.*

"We have to go, now." Roen's voice cracked.

Eloryn jolted but didn't turn to him. She stared at Memory, still crumpled on the ground. Memory's body shuddered, but if she cried it was silent. Eloryn knelt beside her, putting a hand on her shoulder. Memory twitched and pushed away.

"I'm so sorry. I never truly believed it, never believed you could be a monster. I was scared, and admit you scared me too, but I know you are a good person. A good friend," Eloryn said.

Memory mumbled into the dirt. "How could I not be a monster? Look at what I did to them, to you!"

"You didn't mean it. You were just scared and confused. That man, that came to protect you, is he the one who's been following you?"

Memory rolled her head in a vague nod.

"He seemed to know what... who you are. He said you're not a monster, and I believe him," Eloryn said.

Memory's chest convulsed in a final loud sob, then stilled. She rose to her knees, red eyes averted to the ground. A scowl twisted her mouth. "Whatever I am, something made me this way, even if I can't remember what. I'm... I can't help... I didn't..." Memory's jaw tensed. "Roen's right. We need to go."

Memory stood up, stepped to where she'd been staring and snatched her knife from the ground. She folded it closed and tucked it into her corset.

Eloryn's face changed when Memory picked up the knife. Roen couldn't imagine how scared she must have been, being cut like that. The thought of it made his breath shallow. But what he saw now wasn't fear, it was something else; the sort of intelligent confusion he often saw in her face that made him want to smile.

He had no smile in him now.

"Into the thick of the forest, and hope none follow. Go." Roen stood, pointing, and waited for them to walk past. He hesitated to move, his body ached so much. Eloryn stopped and turned back after taking a few steps that he didn't follow.

"Keep going, that way," he said. He made an effort to move casually after them. It hurt. He waited until Eloryn had turned away again before he let his teeth grit and eyes water. Blood still oozed from where the man had jabbed the short sword into his shoulder. It had only just broken skin before he managed to turn away from it, but it still pounded and burned.

They know who I am. They know what I am. The words repeated through his head to the beat of his pain. He'd only told them so they would hate him, so they would leave, be out of danger. They were supposed to leave him to what he deserved. *My secret to the grave. But they know what I am, and I'm still here.*

He'd lived alone with this shame for so long, finding comfort for himself and his crimes in other ways that made him more ashamed. He'd only ever begun stealing out of necessity. No one would hire a seventh son of a seventh son. "Cursed and blessed," the saying told, but Roen so far only knew the curse. He did it for his parents, at

the same time knowing it would kill them to discover the criminal their only remaining son had become in the common world they were forced into. What he did, how he did it had even helped the Princess. He would continue to do anything he could to protect her. But now he could never be anything more.

Roen ground his teeth. What more did he ever hope for? He was a thief and a fool, and from this point on his life was only here to protect the Princess.

A root clung to Roen's foot, sending him stumbling forward. Hands grabbed his arm and steadied him. He was further gone than he'd realized, not even noticing that Memory walked by his side.

Her mouth pulled tight, more a wince than a smile. "You're a mess," she said.

"Thanks. You too."

"Hmm," she nodded.

"You can let me go now."

"Nope. You need the help."

Against all odds, Roen found his mouth twitch into a smile. The strange girl never failed to surprise him. *They were supposed to hate me.* "Why?"

Memory stuck her chin toward Eloryn, walking ahead of them. "She's better than both of us combined. Us losers got to stick together if we're going to have any chance of helping her out."

"Hmm," he nodded.

They walked quietly for a moment.

"Don't ever tell her I said that."

Roen watched Eloryn's back, layered with her flowing blonde hair which had begun to show signs of the wear and danger it had seen these last days. She walked more slowly than a casual stroll, even in this time of flight. They were all moving too slowly. If anyone followed they'd be caught up in no time, but he pushed himself as fast as his abused body could go. Eloryn should be running, but instead, she kept a carefully slow pace. Could she really be waiting for him, even now she knew his secret?

Memory cursed and hopped a few steps on one bare foot. Eloryn waited for the both of them.

The trees around them thinned, and Roen pushed harder to pick up his pace, breaking away from Memory's support. There were signs of a road ahead of them. *This isn't right,* he argued in his head, *there should be no road here.* He charged through a screen of wild hedge and saw it was true.

He collapsed onto one knee, a sheen of sweat dewing him. He could almost cry.

He'd sent them the wrong way.

Roen put his fist into the ground. The plan had been simple; if you can't run, you hide. He couldn't run, and he'd led them straight out into the open, to a main road, on which early morning travelers already moved about. Farmers on carts passed, and women with massive baskets balanced on hips walking produce into town. They couldn't go back; there might be people chasing after them. He wasn't even sure he could stand up again. He couldn't do it. He couldn't protect the Princess, not even that.

"Where are we?" Eloryn asked, walking toward the carved dirt road.

"Stay back in the forest, someone might see!" said Roen, struggling to control his emotions.

Roen licked broken lips, the tangy taste of blood focusing his mind as he got his bearings. He'd gone too far west, taking them straight back to the road and open woods instead of through the thick, concealing forest. Small consolation being it was the right road.

Eloryn and Memory remained waiting under the trees. Roen walked back to them, the pain from the decision he made engulfing the pain from his beating.

"This road will lead to Kenth, where you'll meet with the Wizards' Council. Take the token and run until you can no longer, then keep going as fast as you can. Watch the road for direction but keep hidden from it. Any help I can provide you is outweighed by the risk of my slowing your down. I'll stay, and if we're followed I'll do what I can to stop them reaching you." Roen pulled the silver disc from a concealed pocket and held it out to Eloryn.

"I can heal you," Eloryn said, without trying to take the coin.

"It will take too long."

"I'm not much faster being shoeless," Memory added.

"Try to be. She needs someone with her." Roen moved forward and pressed the coin into Eloryn's hand. The softness of her skin stung him. He pulled away as soon as she held the token.

"Screw that for a plan," Memory said, marching out onto the roadway.

"Mem?" called Eloryn.

"No, stop!" Roen saw what Memory had seen just a moment after her. A horse and covered wagon were being driven up the road from the south, and Memory jogged straight for it, arm waving. It was too late, the wagon pulled to a stop beside Memory.

When Roen caught up to her she already pleaded with the lady in the high driver's seat.

"…were attacked. They took all our money, but if you can give us a ride, anywhere close to Kenth, you can have his sword. It's made of gold or something."

"Can I see it?" The gaunt woman peered down, tucking bushy grey hair behind one ear. A second pair of big eyes and small hands

poked out through a half closed window behind her.

"Sorry Roen, it's all we've got."

Roen frowned and slid the thin knife from his boot where he'd tucked it after the fight. She was right, it was the only thing of worth he had, but this blade was almost like a part of him, and indeed valuable; not just for what it was made of, but also for the quality in which it had been forged. It was the only thing of value he'd ever taken for himself.

He held it up to be seen.

"Electrum, nice, nice. All you have, hey? Look, I can see you're a fine type of folk, and can see you've had trouble. You put that away. No payment needed. We're heading past there regardless. Come in, be our guests," said the woman. Her face, more sun-worn than old, crinkled when she smiled at Memory. She knocked at the shutters behind her and they opened. "Let them in, Bonny. My daughter," she told them. A girl of seven or eight years old poked her head out and grinned through a set of lost front teeth. She disappeared again into the dark of the wagon only to pop back out eagerly at the larger back door.

"Lory, come on!" Memory called out.

"This is dangerous, for them as well as us," Roen whispered.

"Yeah and I don't like the alternatives, so let's go."

The wagon creaked as they climbed up onto the high first step and through the door.

It seemed bigger on the inside, awash with drifting fabrics. Bookshelf balanced over mantel which balanced over stove. Plush cushions made mountains on lounges upholstered on top of shelves and drawers. Everything impossibly stacked into the round roofed space. A bed of velveteen covers stood waist height at the end, beneath the peephole window to the driver's bench up front. Perched on top, Bonny grinned at them, bouncing on the mattress. Her patchwork

dress was the perfect camouflage within the gaudy room.

Roen climbed in last. Memory squeezed up onto the bed next to the brown eyed child. Eloryn sat on a padded seat not quite big enough for two. He stayed standing and Bonny knocked on the wood between her and her mother. The wagon lurched forward. Roen swayed with the movement and thumped his shoulder against a bookshelf. He breathed through the moan of re-awakened pain.

"Please sit down." Eloryn shifted as far as she could to one side of the upholstered bench.

Bonny stuck her tongue between her missing teeth. "I love it when we get visitors. It's always so much fun."

The wagon knocked from side to side and Roen's legs refused to keep him up. He lowered himself next to Eloryn. His shoulder pressed against her no matter how he tried to shift his position. Eloryn pulled her arms into herself, and stared at the floor. The hair tumbling around her face didn't hide the red on her cheeks.

I can't believe I let myself kiss her. After purposely getting her drunk no less. They were just meant to have enough to stay asleep in the room while I got the flute. I wanted to make things better, and I only made them worse. She's not just some tavern wench I can have my way with, no matter how I feel. Roen dug his fingers into his thighs.

"By the Winter King, you look bad. Not very good at keeping yourself safe, huh?" Bonny's eyes glinted as she stared at Roen.

Roen opened his mouth, but Memory was already talking.

"Hey, how about I show you a trick?" Memory reached to the girl's ear and seamlessly pulled out a leaf. Roen wondered for a moment where she'd gotten it from, remembering the leaves on the ground behind his home that felt so far away. Then, through his pain bleary eyes he realized Memory still had dead leaves caught throughout her hair and dress from her tussle on the forest floor.

Bonny snorted. "Oh, come on! You know, you smell bad."

A knock on the window shutters had the girl sighing. The mother's shrill voice called through, making Roen wince. "Bonny, come out here and leave our guests in peace."

"Fine." She gave Memory a skeptical look, and then slipped through the window on her belly, closing it behind her.

"Fun kid," said Memory, eyebrows raised. "But not a bad way to travel is it?"

"I still don't like this," said Roen.

"Better than leaving you behind. I just don't think we should leave anyone behind, for whatever reason." Memory pulled her legs up and wedged her back amongst the cushions, turning her face away.

"We have time, now," Eloryn said to Roen in a quiet voice.

"Time?"

"I can heal the damage those brutes did to you."

"No, don't. I'm all right." The wagon shook and Roen winced. Eloryn's eyes flicked up to his face, clear sympathy filling them.

"If you only don't wish me to because-"

"Too much risk of our hosts seeing," Roen whispered.

"I'll keep watch," Memory volunteered from amongst the pillows.

Beset, Roen gritted his teeth.

Eloryn's voice was quiet but firm. "If you're worried for my safety, then worry that without you well I would suffer more."

He didn't want her to have to do this for him. He was supposed to be helping her, not the other way around. But she was right. How he was now, he was useless to her. But it still hurt to hear her say it, to know that was the only reason she bore his company. "Very well, what do I do?"

"Just be still and relax," Eloryn said. She raised a hand to his forehead and his chest and placed them feather soft on his skin. Roen

saw the color rise through her face and his body tensed.

Eloryn snatched her hands away, then looked at him with a pained expression before starting again. "Please try and relax."

"Is this what you did for me?" Memory asked sitting forward to watch.

Eloryn nodded, and began whispering magical words to Roen's body. Roen felt the air rush out of him and his eyes glazed.

A clattering bump bounced Roen's chin against his chest and he opened his eyes. He wondered why his body was numb, then realized it was just the absence of pain. Eloryn watched him from close at his side. Her skin looked paler than normal, showing soft purple shadows under jade irises. The sympathy in her expression remained. His own eyes dropped away from hers, running down her neck and resting on the thin red line across her chest. The deep slash cut by Memory's knife had closed, but the blood it spilt still stained the gold front of Eloryn's dress. Eloryn shifted in her seat, and Roen looked back up to see her staring, mouth slightly open in a confused look. Roen cursed internally, realizing where he'd just been staring, and turned his gaze away into the rest of the cabin.

"Have I been asleep? How long?" Roen looked around, re-gathering information into a no longer woozy mind. The wagon interior was as he remembered, but now no light showed through the gaps around the wooden door.

"It took some hours. We weren't interrupted. Do you feel better?"

Roen rolled his shoulder, stretched out his back and nodded. He felt great, at least his body did, anyway. His clothing and mind were still in ruins. Roen looked to Memory, sleeping fitfully on the bed, woken when they hit another large bump in the road.

"Thank you. I'm glad you took a moment to heal yourself also." Roen's voice sounded rough even to his own ears. He tried to cover it by continuing to talk. "Can't be much farther till we're there if it's night already." Roen stood up, steadying himself with a hand on the ceiling. He opened the smaller window in the back door of the wagon and peered out.

It was past dusk. A blacker air surrounded them, helped by mammoth trees growing up on either side of the rough trail they rode. This wasn't the main road to Kenth. A wagon shouldn't even be driven on a track like this.

Roen took three stalking steps to the front of the wagon, pots and pans clattering on shelves beside him. He climbed up past Memory and opened the front window.

"How's the driving?" he asked in a cheery voice.

"Just taking a short cut. Not long now." The woman and her daughter sat side by side on the bench in front of him. The girl absently carved into the wood of the bench with a sharp fingernail. Roen smiled and nodded and closed the window again.

He swore under his breath.

"Mem, Eloryn, I think our ride should end here. I don't think they are taking us where we asked," he whispered.

Memory shrugged, groggy from sleep, but nodded to his suggestion as though she expected trouble as the norm. Eloryn looked drained but stood up right away.

Roen lifted his finger to his lips and silently unlatched and swung the back door. It opened to the darkness of the track growing smaller behind them. The wagon moved slowly, hindered by tree roots and rubble. He pointed out, and took Memory's hand as she stepped off.

She dropped out the moving doorway onto the ground and tumbled over herself. The sound of the wagon creaking and rattling covered her swearing. Roen lifted Eloryn down next, trying to judge the movement better this time. Eloryn wobbled when her feet hit the

dirt, but didn't fall. Roen stepped off easily, took them each by a hand and started sneaking them back down the path in the woods.

The wagon came to an abrupt stop. Roen turned back, and saw Bonny perched like a grotesque on the rounded rooftop.

Her brown eyes had turned black to the edges. Her skin now gray; it darkened toward her mouth, now a gaping hole of sharp teeth.

"Don't go. We don't get our prize if you go," she howled in a disturbing imitation of the child's voice.

"Banshee?" Eloryn gasped to Roen.

"Unseelie fae, one way or another," he nodded. "Keep running."

The mother figure appeared in front of them. The magical glamour that hid her true form was gone as well. She seemed bonier than before, taller than any of them. Her eyes were also black, teeth menacing, and bushy hair knotted with tiny bones.

"Just stay back," Roen warned, drawing his pale golden blade against them. "You're not in your rights to hurt us. You would be breaking the Pact."

"Pact, ha! You agreed to come with us, agreed to be ours!" the woman sang at them with a thirsty smile, unworried by the sharp weapon aimed at her.

Roen knew electrum wasn't much use against the fae, that if he made a move before them, he'd be at fault under the Pact, at risk of being Branded, but he held the blade steady regardless. The banshee tricked and manipulated just like all the Unseelie, finding loopholes in the Pact that governed their behavior so that they could satisfy their dark cravings.

"We spoke no agreement." Eloryn stepped forward. "I will Brand you if I must."

"Can't Brand if we don't touch. Come with us! She just wants the magic ones. We're not going to bite, we're going to get a prize!" Bonny,

or whatever her name truly was, bounced on the wagon's roof.

"Who?" Roen grunted, confused.

Bonny laughed in a tinkling, ear-piercing crescendo.

Roen heard the flick of Memory's knife opening and she moved beside him.

The mother leapt back.

"What is that? How do you have that?" she spat.

The knife shook in Memory's hand.

"Cold dead iron. I told you she smelled of it. But I'm not scared, I'm not scared!" The girl-like dark fae leapt from the wagon roof, imitating flight, and landed between Memory and banshee mother. Bonny thrust a grey-skinned hand at Memory, as though she meant to swat the blade from her hand. Yelping, Memory slashed the knife, tracing the smallest line across the girl's arm.

Bonny's eyes bulged. She howled. The point where the blade had touched her arm steamed and hissed and she threw herself onto the ground in fits, screaming vicious curses. The mother hunched over her.

"Pact? Pact! You are the ones who break the Pact!" she screamed wildly. She lunged at them, but the thrashing girl cried out and she stepped back beside her, baring her teeth.

Roen grabbed Memory and Eloryn again by the hands. Mournful howling filled the night as he dragged them away through the moonlit trees.

CHAPTER NINETEEN

They hobbled into Kenth under a cover of dismal clouds. A light wind lifted dry leaves in a dance around their feet. Eloryn had spoken with trees and earth in the forest to find their way, and they walked through the whole night. The effects of the poison in Eloryn had long passed, but pushing herself to heal Roen and lack of sleep left her spark of connection barely alight.

Her feet ached in her torn satin slippers. She wondered how Memory's, completely bare, must be feeling.

The small town huddled like a flock of sheep at the base of wooded hills. The houses were all half crumbled walls built of a dark stone from the nearby mountains, and thatched in patchy straw when they still had roofs. It was secluded, ghostly, and completely deserted.

"Sure this is the place?" Memory asked.

"Where better to hide than a dead town?" said Roen.

"Dead? Creepy much?"

"Dead of the fae. There are none here anymore."

"Isn't that a good thing? They seem sort of nasty," said Memory.

"Good or bad, the fae are what bring prosperity to the world. They leave, and you end up with land like this." Roen tilted his head to the cracked, empty fields and wilted trees. "We'll know soon if this is the right place."

Roen walked forward again, leaving the girls a few steps behind. Tension strung his shoulders tight. Eloryn had traced over the strain there in her healing, feeling it like a weight he'd carried too long, one she couldn't heal but a burden she'd added to immeasurably.

He'd been silent almost the entire night.

Eloryn sighed and followed. They headed down the main street of the ghost town toward a well in the centre of a small square at the other end. Dark woods backed the view like an image from one of her fairytale books.

"What are we meant to do here?" Memory asked when Roen stopped at the well. She circled the ancient structure of moss covered stone and aged bronze woven in floral motifs.

"We make a wish. May I have your knife?" Roen held out his hand and pulled out the coin token with the other. Eloryn had given it back to him during the night, a gesture of her trust, but it didn't seem to please him at all. He took it like a further weight to carry.

Memory passed her knife over. "As long as I get it back."

Roen pulled it open and brought it up in front of his eyes, turning it around. Flicking the blade with his thumb, he glanced at Memory but said nothing, just started scratching into the back of the coin. The knife carved easily through the silver surface.

"Lanval's contact told me to write a message on the coin," Eloryn said, "and drop it in this well. Then the Council should come to us. It's a special coin made by the resistance, showing the Maellan crest, but minted after Thayl came to rule." She wondered what exact wording Roen used in the message, but didn't dare question him.

Memory sat down on the wide rim of the well with an odd look of satisfaction. Eloryn joined her.

"Mmm. Sitting," Memory said.

Roen tossed the coin down the well's mouth and they watched with held breaths. No sound came to tell them it had reached a bottom.

Eloryn smiled a little at the setup. "A magical interception. Coins dropped here must go straight to the Council."

"Wow, communication system and form of income in one. These guys are smart."

"Now you wait." Roen wiped off the blade and handed it back to Memory. She kept it in her hand, flicking and fidgeting with it.

He began walking away.

"Roen?" Eloryn stood up faster than she meant to.

"I won't be far," he called without looking back. She sat down again and watched him go. He reached a mostly intact building half way down the road and sat against the shadowed wall, knees against his chest.

If this worked, he could go back to his parents, and no longer feel the responsibility of my presence. Eloryn remembered seeing a similar look of affliction in Alward's face growing up. Wherever he was now, it was her fault. If anyone else was hurt because of her...

"May I see your knife for a moment?" she asked Memory, looking for a distraction.

"Sure." Memory flicked it closed again and passed it to her.

As the knife came into her hands, Eloryn felt her spark of

connection grow strong and a strange warmth in the metal. It wasn't silver, as she'd first thought. It was something harder. "Could this really be iron?"

"I don't know. Stainless steel or something." Memory shrugged.

"No, it's... this metal is poison to the fae. I don't know how you could have this. There should be no iron in Avall. It was all removed during the Purge, at the forming of the Pact."

"Is there anything that isn't to do with whatever this Pact thing is?"

Eloryn frowned. She often had to remind herself how little Memory knew. Things even a child of Avall knew. "The Pact was a deal made over 1500 years ago between the fae and humans, to benefit both sides. It brought magic and prosperity to the people of Avall, and Avall became a safe haven for the fae in return. Part of the pact is the peace treaty. If a fae hurts a human they can be magically Branded, and vice versa, unless under certain conditions. The Brand is a death sentence. I'm sorry. I should have told you these things before now. If you hadn't been acting in self defense when the banshee attacked, you could have been Branded. The iron itself isn't a crime as such. It simply shouldn't exist here any more."

"You don't think it means I could be from somewhere else, like Hell?" Memory asked, quiet and high pitched.

"I don't think you're a bad person Mem, or a demon." If only she knew more, if Alward had let her study the Veil with him. He had been obsessed with its research, even travelling into the woods where he could perform spells and experiments unnoticed. But he never shared that research with her, never explained why. She had stolen peeks into his work, but not enough for this.

"There are always other answers. I just don't have them for you, I'm sorry." Eloryn had always felt so clever in her home with Alward,

able to answer any question. Now she was just lost. Her eyes turned back down the street, searching for something, and found Roen gone. She looked to Memory, concerned.

"I saw him wander off just now. I'm sure he'll be back. Don't worry," Memory said, despite looking worried herself.

Eloryn lifted her bottom lip in the semblance of a smile and handed Memory her knife. Memory slid down to the ground so she could lean against the well, and closed her eyes. They sat in silence, and Eloryn held her hands tightly in her lap to keep them still. She stared at the sky, her mind racing in circles after any trace of calm she could catch.

Hours passed before Roen returned. He carried a scrap of hessian folded into a bundle. He handed Eloryn a small apple he held in his hand, blushed red only on one side, small and perfect.

"Found one tree still fruiting. They're small, but edible." He propped the makeshift bag against the well, showing a feast of green apples. "Sorry for taking so long."

"No apology needed when you bring food." Memory smiled and bit into one apple, already holding a second in her other hand.

Eloryn stared at the apple, but had trouble bringing herself to eat it.

"You need to eat," Roen told her in dull tone. "You're losing a lot of weight."

He turned back toward the road.

The world suddenly blinked out of Eloryn's eyes. Light and vision vanished, leaving only formless black. She shrieked, echoed by Memory.

"What's happening? I can't see!" Memory cried.

"Nor I!" Roen's voice.

Eloryn whispered a behest to let her eyes see again, and found

they were surrounded by five old men in faded black and purple suits. They held knives in one hand, and scrolls in the other, held up ready to be read. When she looked them in the eye, no longer blinded, they turned to the youngest man for guidance.

"She can still see?"

"Look at her..." another muttered, dumbstruck.

The younger man with a narrow face and hooked nose unrolled his scroll. "It's a trick! Finish this."

"No! Stop please, we called for you!" Eloryn said, folding her fingers into the latticework triangle symbol of the Wizards' Council.

Another age-stooped man hesitated. "They're just children."

"You think they wouldn't appear in any way they could to trap us? Remember how many died the last time we received a message from 'the heir'! Hesitate and how many will die this time?"

"Princess, what's happening?" Roen stood statue still, taut with distress. Memory sat frozen, gripping her knife behind her back with white fingers.

"I can prove it's who I am, let me prove it!" Eloryn cried.

This time four lowered their weapons.

The younger man, vocal against her already, sneered. "How?"

"She has the Maellan crested medallion," Roen said, turning blindly to the voices around him.

"No, it's still at Duke de Montredeur's," said Eloryn.

The man huffed at her.

"But I have the bloodline. I am Maellan!" Eloryn flicked through possibilities in her mind, looking down at the dead, bare ground around them. She spoke her words, a long string of pleading words, spoken loudly for the men to hear how she used them.

From the barren dirt, a meadow of grasses forced through, like green living hair. Wildflowers unfolded. Sprays of grass seeds and dander spread. The old men gasped audibly.

"No book, no scroll? She is Maellan! You cannot dispute that power, Hayes!" a bald, wide-bellied man said.

"You can see the Lady Loredanna clear in her behind the grime she wears," said another.

"Seems so. In which case we all need to be out of sight. We've been exposed too long already. Apologies, Highness." His lips twitched under his hooked nose, still skeptical. "You understand we must be cautious. These two are with you?" Hayes asked.

Eloryn nodded.

Hayes snapped his fingers to the aged man on his left, who began speaking words of annulment to the spell on Roen and Memory's eyes. As he did so, Hayes unrolled his scroll and began reading words that must have been intended to follow the blindness on them. The patch of ground Eloryn had brought to life blazed and shriveled into grey ash.

Eloryn cried out in alarm.

"It had to be done. Your proof was not exactly discreet," said Hayes.

The bald man tilted his head. "Common folk would just have thought it was the fae returned."

"It's not the common folk I'm worried about."

Memory already didn't like them. They were old. Really old. The kind of old that's misshapen with bitterness and arrogance. Hayes was the youngest – forties or fifties, Memory couldn't tell – but managed

to be the nastiest of the lot. How she thought King Thayl would have been, the way people talked about him. She liked him way better than these guys.

The bald man, Waylan, wasn't so bad. Still old, but more friendly than the others. To her at least, anyway. They were all eager to be friendly with Eloryn. Memory itched and squirmed in her corset. If she'd known she would be wearing this dress for so long, she would have picked something more comfortable. She doubted this group of old men would have any clothes for her, even if they cared.

They marched under the cover of a spell to one of the houses they'd passed on the street, which now appeared much larger, and more solid than it had looked before.

Inside the building, the furnishing reminded Memory of Roen's home, with rich items in a small space, but these had not been well cared for. Dust lingered and mixed with a sweet smell of mildew.

They came to a room on the second floor laid out for meetings with mismatched chairs surrounding a wide square table.

"Summon Lucan," Hayes told Waylan.

"The others too?"

"Not yet, better not all be in the same place too soon." Hayes turned his gaze onto Memory.

Eloryn had walked with him through the house, telling him as much as she could of how she'd gotten here. He had no news for her of Alward, or any interest, as far as Memory could see. What little Eloryn had told him about Memory made Hayes's bottom eyelid twitch.

Lucan arrived. His back had the hunch of someone who tried not to be too tall and he clutched a thick tome with loose pages to his chest. He was younger than the others, more comparable to Thayl's age, but not at all comparable in looks.

"The heir, truly we've found her?" he asked, his voice friendly and eager.

"Almost entirely certain," Hayes said, indicating Eloryn. "Leave the minutes book, we'll call council shortly."

Lucan stood motionless, staring at the Princess.

Hayes cleared his throat. "And bring us some refreshments. The heir has had a hard journey."

Lucan nodded, pushed the tome onto the table and slipped back out of the room.

Hayes, Waylan, and three more even older men, matching grey and bearded, sat across the table from Eloryn, Roen and Memory. Memory shifted in her seat.

"Thank you for coming to us," Waylan started with a sincere smile.

"Although you should have come much earlier. You may have saved yourself some hardship from Pellaine's follies," Hayes said. "We had heard from him, once or twice through the years. We suspected he had the heir with him, but he kept his location secret from us for some reason."

I wonder why, Memory thought. She shuddered to think what Eloryn would have been like if raised by these men.

Eloryn only nodded to them, politely stunned.

"Regardless, she's here now. This will mean big changes. Something to rouse the resistance. Finally, a return to rightful rule!" Waylan pounded the table enthusiastically.

Eloryn stuttered. "I'm sorry. I didn't come here for that. I only hoped you could help re-unite me with Alward. If anyone had the power to save him from his imprisonment, I hoped it would be the Wizards' Council."

Hayes shook his head and furrowed his brow, but the sympathy looked insincere. "Your Highness, I apologize, but we cannot risk

ourselves for just one man. Not when your presence has given us some hope for the future. You must put him out of your mind. He's no longer your concern or ours."

"But he is my family."

"Are you the child born of Queen Loredanna and King Edmund Maellan, or do you deceive us? You have a responsibility to Avall and its people that is greater than Pellaine's fate."

Eloryn nodded, her eyes glossy. Memory snorted air through her nose, anger in her rising. She glared down the table at Roen who stared blankly at the wall opposite, the thinness of his lips showing the tension otherwise kept hidden.

Waylan spoke more kindly. "Thayl is like poison to this land. Since his rule we've seen the fae leaving or causing more trouble across Avall. They were never such trouble with Maellan blood on the throne. Maellan blood signed the Pact. The fae honor that."

Hayes locked his gaze on Eloryn like a hawk onto a mouse. "Your Highness, for the sake of Avall, will you forget Pellaine and begin work toward your rightful path?"

Eloryn bowed her head.

Memory bolted to her feet. "Quit it already! Can't you see she's been through enough?"

"Ah yes." Hayes looked at her like he would a smudge on the wall that he was too arrogant to clean. "You're not needed here. You should leave."

Eloryn rose to her feet next to Memory. "Memory is with me. I had hoped someone here could help her with her problem."

"Her problem is not ours, or yours. Respectfully, Highness, you need to grow up and start dealing with issues of greater importance," Hayes said, moving calmly to his feet, his voice rising only a little, but still threatening.

"Fine. Let's start talking about whose problems are whose, shall we?" Memory snapped back. "Like who caused all your issues with Thayl in the first place? Wasn't it you wizards who made the Queen marry someone other than him? They were in love, and you knew it."

"Of course we did," said Hayes. "Thayl had no talent for magic when we chose the Queen's partner and was never right for the kingdom, I think that is clear. If you had a thought in your head, girl, you'd know marriages for the Maellan line have always been arranged, to preserve a strong magic ability."

"They were in love, and you destroyed them with that choice," Memory whispered, the realization hitting her hard. It was true, what Thayl had shown her in her dream. And if it was true, what about everything else?

Eloryn's face drained to white. "What? How did you-?"

"Just gossip, at the ball," Memory cut in, looking away.

"So, what of it?" Hayes moved his words slowly, fixing Eloryn in a stare. "You know this is the way of the royal bloodline, your Highness. It is not our fault, but Thayl's for bearing such villainous vengeance. Calm your guard dog here and show some pretence of your royal heritage, so we can do what is needed for the Kingdom."

Hayes sat back down. Eloryn looked at Memory, stricken, then nodded and sat down too.

Memory wanted to leap across the table, claw Hayes' tongue out and ram-

Lucan interrupted her thought, returning to the room carrying a tray of fine silver implements and pots for tea. Probably for the best. Hayes was a bastard, but she needed to start locking down her violent tendencies. If that was who she was before, she wasn't sure it was who she wanted to be now. She sat down again and satisfied herself with glaring.

Lucan placed the tray on the table in front of Hayes. He began arranging cups and Hayes put his hand out to stop him.

"Call the rest of the council. It's time we start making some serious plans."

Lucan straightened back up, as tall as his hunch allowed.

"Actually, I'll do it. You find the children somewhere to wait, outside the meeting room."

Memory threw one final glare at Hayes as they left.

Lucan let them into a room across the hall. It was someone's study, a table piled with parchment lit by a lonely, grimy window. With a shy smile and bow, Lucan left them alone.

"So much for getting some refreshments," Memory muttered.

Roen's face hung, pale and unreadable. His hair and shirt still stained with dry blood, he hardly looked alive. "Princess, I'm sorry for bringing you here."

"It's my fault, not yours," said Eloryn. "For not going to Alward right away, for trying to let others do it for me. A fault it's time I righted."

Roen shook his head. "Too dangerous."

"I have to try. No one else will."

"Lory, how well do you really know Alward? I mean, how much do you really trust about him?" Memory asked. *Do you know it was him who killed your mother? Would you still want to go to him?*

"What? He is all I ever had!" Eloryn gasped. "I will go to him. Alone, if I have to."

Memory and Roen shared glances of matching disapproval, then both agreed to go with her.

"Then we leave here now, and head back to Maerranton, where we last know he was held."

Eloryn eased the door open and led them out, tiptoeing down the

empty hallway. At the top of the stairs they were stopped by a voice.

"Don't leave, please," Lucan said.

"We were just going outside for some air. It's stuffy in here," said Memory.

"I was listening to what you said. I'm sorry." He shuffled closer to them. His eyes were pale and watery blue. Kind, if somewhat sad.

"Then you'll have to let us go, because we won't stay," said Eloryn.

"Please, just listen. I know Hayes can be harsh, but you do have friends here. I'm a friend. It's a miracle you're still alive, and I'm just happy to keep you that way, not force you into leadership. I could even help you be with Alward again, if you like."

Memory edged in front of Eloryn and looked the man up and down. "Why?"

"Pellaine... Alward was my friend too. We were invested into the council at the same time, same ages, only months before everything was destroyed. I was not even with the council when the Queen and King were married. All of this trouble, it's not mine. The council, they're old, they forget what is real and haven't much of a life left to change. And no one here takes me seriously."

"How could you help us?" Roen asked.

Lucan gave a weak, hopeful smile. "They give me all the tasks of book keeping and communications. I keep the Council's Speaking Mirror. I am in touch with leaders of the resistance in all regions. I know of some within Thayl's ranks, within his castle, even within his prisons."

CHAPTER TWENTY

Lucan hurried them down the street to another building that had appeared derelict before, but now revealed itself as solid and lived in. The council were using some very powerful glamour behests to keep themselves hidden.

Fumbling with his keys, Lucan opened the door and invited them into his home.

"Shouldn't we leave right away? If the rest of the council realize our intentions, they might make us stay." Eloryn asked.

Lucan replied with a crooked smile. "I'm sorry, Your Highness, but I doubt they'll even notice you missing for a while. They've called council. They'll be so wrapped up in debating plans they wouldn't notice if the house fell in around them. It could be days before they

come to anything close to agreement or are likely to call on you again."

Lucan's house had been kept cleaner than the building Hayes had taken them to. An aroma of mulling spices awoke Eloryn's stomach. Lucan sat them in a windowless room he'd made both library and sleeping quarters- the only place with seating enough for all of them. "Just stay here while I speak with my contact, but you are free to leave at any time. If we can find out first where you..." Lucan kept talking as he left the room, his voice trailing down the hall.

Vibrating with nervous energy, Lucan buzzed back in again, bringing them a meal of wild grain porridge and herbal tea. "...exciting. You don't know what an honor it is that I could aid you in any way. The Maellan heir! Not to mention a chance of being free of those other men. I'm sure you can imagine it hasn't been fun living in hiding with no one but them..."

"Lucan, please," Eloryn called to him, stopping him floating out of the room again.

He stood still and blinked a couple of times before smiling with wobbly lips. "Sorry, sorry, I get a bit caught up sometimes. I'm going to try now and contact the resistance member I know who might have had a chance of seeing Alward. I regret, I sincerely apologize, Highness, but please stay here. I must contact him privately or he won't respond to my summons behest."

Eloryn nodded and tried to smooth the pace of her heartbeat. The hope she felt was almost too much to bear. Lucan fluttered at the door, hesitating, then closed it behind him.

Left alone in the full but neatly kept library, Eloryn took a deep breath and settled into a leather armchair.

Memory tried to get Roen talking to her. Her mutterings, out of hearing to Eloryn, managed to get the occasional coughed chuckle or bemused half smile from him, but nothing more. It was still more than

Eloryn was able.

Roen met her eyes suddenly, and she looked away, embarrassed to have been staring. The atmosphere in this room made her chest tight. It was so much, too much, like Alward's library at home. Alward, like Lucan, had lovingly filled every space with books for them and their students. From ancient illuminated tomes to newer press printed collections and Alward's own studies, hand bound and hand written.

The monastery had an extensive library even before Alward arrived. She only had the faintest recollections of the people of the old religion who hid her in her earliest days. Their order valued secrecy on certain subjects, like that of men arriving with motherless children. The old men and women were faded memories by the time she was reading their books.

Eloryn closed her eyes. Leaning back into the armchair, she wondered if those books were still there. After the last of the priests passed away, it was only ever her, Alward, and the books. Often all three together, when she was still small enough to curl up in a chair with Alward and be read to.

I miss him. I miss those books. I even miss the high stone walls. Eloryn wished she had some token, some belonging of his. It didn't matter. Soon they would be together again, she just knew it. Maybe then, she could apologize for her error that brought the hunters to them, and hope he forgave her.

"Lory, wake up."

"No, shush, let her sleep."

Eloryn opened her eyes to see Memory and Lucan looking down at her.

He grinned, shivering. "Oh, she is awake! Good news, Your Highness, oh better than you could have hoped. Alward is already freed, already on his way here for you!"

Eloryn blinked, worried she really had fallen asleep and was dreaming. "How?"

"The greatest luck. Our man in the resistance was assigned to Alward's guard after Thayl met with him in Maerranton. He recognized Alward right away and helped him escape first chance he had."

Eloryn's head buzzed and her pulse built. She pulled herself up straight in the chair. "He's coming here, you said? Why would he come here? We were to go to another home on Rhynn island."

Lucan hesitated just a second. "He knows you're clever, and that with him gone you would seek us out. He's coming here for you. I'll watch for signal of when he arrives. It should be soon. Then we'll go to meet with him and we can all leave."

Eloryn's confusion washed away, and a smile broke across her face, aching unused muscles. She knew Alward would come for her, knew he would escape. He would be there for her again, to look after her.

Next to her, Memory chewed on her fingernails with intense concentration.

"He'll help you too Mem, don't worry. He's so kind, he'll do whatever he can for you." Eloryn smiled in divine happiness. "How long, do you think?"

Lucan's face turned blank. "Oh, well I say I hope soon, but I'm only guessing from the time of his escape. It could be any moment I'm sure, but be comfortable, it may be some wait yet."

Eloryn nodded, but still got to her feet and began pacing. Anxious joy spread through her.

Memory stole her plush armchair. She curled her legs up into herself and stared at a spot on the wall. Eloryn tried to avoid looking at Roen where he sat across the room on a solid wood bench. A sudden, tangible memory of his lips on hers made her trip in her pacing. Her first and only kiss. She had no idea what it meant or why it happened,

and didn't have the voice to ask. Since then, Roen barely seemed inclined to be within the same room as her. Owain came to her mind, followed by the children she taught. She wondered if they were still there in the village, still safe, or if her very presence in their lives had brought trouble to them as well.

Lucan brought in biscuits and mulled wine, and left them alone again, gone to wait for sign of Alward's arrival. None of them ate.

Eloryn moved from pacing, to sitting on the bed, to staring at books, to pacing. The others remained still and quiet. In the windowless room it was hard to tell how much time passed. Rain had been pattering against the roof for a while when Lucan's footsteps thumped up the hall again. She met him at the door.

"He's here," he said, wide eyed.

Memory and Roen got quickly to their feet behind Eloryn.

"No no, please, you two should wait. Alward won't know you. Only the Princess and I should go so he's not alarmed by strangers."

"Nah ah, we're coming too. He'll see we're with Lory and know it's OK," said Memory.

"No! You don't understand; he's careful, he'll be on guard. We need to explain to him alone first or he might think it's a trap. He could leave, or attack you. It must only be faces he knows," said Lucan.

"We won't be long," said Eloryn, not wanting anything to risk her chance of reuniting with Alward. "We'll be back for you right away, and we'll all leave together."

Eloryn nodded to Lucan, who bowed her exit in front of him. She looked back and smiled, to see Memory open-mouthed, and Roen frowning.

Lucan strode out of the building with her and down the street toward the square with the wishing well. His steps were long, and she trotted to keep up with him. She didn't think she could have walked anyway, she was about to burst. She hardly felt the icy rain that fell on her.

Her smile faded as they got closer. She couldn't see Alward. She'd expected he would stay out of sight, and yet apprehension crept in. The ground was uneven, more footprints than could be explained by their own movements marking the mud. A horse whinnied in the distance. Her excitement curdled.

She slowed her pace, and Lucan turned to see why.

"Something's not right," she said.

"Nonsense, come on, don't you want to see Alward?" Lucan grabbed her elbow and pulled her forward. His hand shook.

"Stop it, please. What are you doing?" Eloryn stumbled. She blinked raindrops from her eyes. He kept his grip tight around her arm, dragging her forward, hurting her. She cried out and tried to pull away. He put his other hand around her mouth, half carrying her into the town square.

Two streaks whistled through the air at them. Her arm stung. She clutched at it, tearing out the tiny metal dart. Lucan reached for his neck, grunting in surprise and dropped her. She fell on her hands and knees.

Eloryn felt the spark inside connecting her to magic close down as it had once before. Her head spun and she fought to stay conscious.

A league of men approached from behind the buildings around them, led by one man, devastatingly handsome with bitter eyes.

"My King, I did it, this is her," Lucan stuttered.

Thayl bent down, offering Eloryn a hand to help her up. The sadness in his face brought tears to her eyes. "Yes, I can see. It is her daughter. She is like Loredanna reborn."

CHAPTER TWENTY-ONE

No way, Memory thought. *No way was Eloryn going to leave me here after all we've been through.*

But she had. Alward was here now and she just left her and Roen behind. Sure she said she'd be back, but Memory didn't own the luxury of trust. She had to find out who she was, know that she wasn't some sort of devil. She had to find her family and get back home.

"I'm going after them. Are you coming?" she asked Roen.

Roen dropped his head in an unenthusiastic shake. "Don't want to ruin it for her."

"You're not worried they'll up and go without us?"

Roen huffed out a laugh.

"Fine. Sulk. I'm going to see what's happening." Memory marched

out the room and Roen tried to call her back. By the time she reached the front door, he was walking with her.

"We better not be seen," he said.

"Good thing you're coming with me then."

Memory peeked out, seeing Eloryn and Lucan just within sight, nearing the square. They ducked out the door and behind the crumbling wall of the next house along.

Roen took the lead, dashing down the street behind low walls and unkempt shrubs, avoiding the growing puddles.

They were still far from the square when Roen stopped mid run, skidding on the wet ground before he reached cover. He stood in open sight, staring down into the square.

A shrill cry broke through the patter of rain and Memory followed his gaze.

"Mem, hide," Roen grunted and broke into a direct run.

Memory hesitated, wiping rain from her face. She watched Thayl walk out from behind a building, followed by a group of armed men. Her brain whirred. Maybe this wasn't as bad as it looked. Maybe she could make it not as bad, if she just got a chance to talk to Thayl.

She ran after Roen.

Lucan tugged Eloryn back to her feet. Roen raced for her, leaving Memory behind.

A group of men uniformed in leather military jackets blocked his way. Their leader with his mane of hair and scarred face lunged. Roen twisted past him, sliding low along the ground, and continued to bolt toward Eloryn and Lucan.

Thayl lifted his arm and flicked his rune-covered hand. Light flashed, and Roen was flung the length of the town square. He hit the stone wall of a building with the sound of gravel crunching under boots. He lay still where he fell.

Memory and Eloryn both screamed for him. Memory wobbled to a stop at the edge of the town square, shocked out of movement.

"If your boy's alive, he will stay that way as long as you both stay calm," Thayl said, looking to her and then Eloryn. He nodded to the wizard hunters moving toward Memory and they broke away, circling wide around her instead, blocking off her escape.

Eloryn whimpered, "Where's Alward?"

"*Alward,*" Thayl said, a strange softness in his voice. "Alward was put to death for the crime of murdering Queen Loredanna."

"No. It was you who killed her. He can't be dead. You lie!" Eloryn sobbed out her words.

"I do not. I'm sorry for your loss, and your confusion. The help of Lucan here meant I no longer needed him or his knowledge to locate the rest of the council, and was able finally to see vengeance paid for his crime. He did kill your mother. If you don't believe me, ask her." Thayl pointed straight armed at Memory.

Memory stuttered as Eloryn looked at her with more pain than she could bear to see. "Thayl, he... he showed me things in a dream, showed me his memories of Alward killing Loredanna. I don't know what's true, but that's what I saw."

"It is true. Alward only ever took you in, kept you to himself because of the guilt he felt over what he had done. If he hadn't interfered Loredanna would still be alive. I would never have hurt her," Thayl bellowed.

Eloryn hung limp like a puppet in Lucan's unkind grasp.

"Where are the rest of the Wizards' Council?" Lucan asked.

Thayl smiled rigidly. "Already taken. You've nothing to fear of reprisals from them for your fine betrayal. After all this time, it was almost a shame there was not more of a fight. They were entirely unguarded and unaware, so wrapped up in their meeting. They are

already under guarded escort on their way for formal execution, thanks to you."

Memory's throat grew tight. She didn't like the old wizards, but she just wanted to be away from them, not to have them executed. In her mind she remembered them as being so frail and grey.

Lucan looked about, an unsure smile on his face. "You said I would be rewarded, that you wouldn't hunt me any more if I did this."

"I did, and I honor my word. I will not hunt you any longer. Let the child go," Thayl said.

Lucan released Eloryn, and shockingly she did not fall. She stared blankly, all life leached from her, the rain soaking her through. She hardly blinked when Thayl put his hand on Lucan's shoulder, and Lucan dropped dead beside her.

Memory cried out loudly enough for the both of them. Her feet felt glued into the mud around her, her body tingling but unresponsive.

"Not one member of the Council can be allowed to live," Thayl said. He stared at the body on the ground, lips curling between a smile and a snarl.

Thayl pointed to Eloryn, and a man behind him moved forward with ropes to bind her. Eloryn's eyes snapped wide and she turned to Memory. "Mem, run, RUN!"

Eloryn struggled against the man, but was small in his hands, easy to hold.

Memory's eyes flickered between Eloryn, Lucan's body, and Roen, fallen loosely against the side of a wall, his shoulder pushed out at a horrifying angle. From this distance, she couldn't tell what blood on him might be new. Her own body was as still as his.

"You said you wouldn't hurt her. You said you would tell me who I am," she whispered.

Thayl chuckled without humor. Approaching her, he dropped his

voice to a tone meant only for her. "You still don't know? Interesting you could spend so long with her and not realize you are sisters, but maybe not so surprising. I'm sorry I left you this way, barely human," he said. He really did look sorry.

Eloryn... my sister? Memory's chest hammered like a mallet on a mattress.

He stopped an arm's reach from her and began pulling the fingers of his glove, loosening it, slipping it off his scarred hand. "I don't know how you've found your way back here from Hell, but it is fortunate. The ritual to steal your power was interrupted, leaving you like this, this shell. But I can end your suffering. I can finish taking the rest of your soul."

Memory jolted into movement. Her whole body screamed for flight and she spun to run away. The leader of the wizard hunters stood right behind her. He grabbed her by the throat, turning her face back to Thayl, pinning her against his body in an unyielding grip.

Thayl lifted his bare hand, twisted with carved runes. It began to glow.

He had done it, stolen all her life, her memories, her *soul*. Left her like this. She tore breaths through her crushed throat, her eyes wild. The fire inside her lit, burning her inside and out. A blazing pulse burst from her chest, ached down her limbs and tingled in the tips of her fingers and toes. She wouldn't let him take whatever she had left. She would use whatever magic she had to stop him. She screamed, expending all the air from her lungs, bellowing the force out with everything she had.

Silence followed. Dust and leaves lifted from the ground, floating upwards. Rain hung suspended in the air.

The world pounded and lit around her like a golden supernova.

All Memory could tell was that she was no longer held, and hoped

the same for Eloryn. She screamed for her to run. Acrid smoke filled the air, and she choked on it. She lay on her stomach in the mud, falling again when she tried to get up, her body quivering. She could hear movement around her, men coughing and calling out in shock and pain. The slow rain barely swayed the blinding cloud around them.

Thayl bellowed from nearby, "Catch the girls. Don't let them get away!"

Memory heard fumbling behind her, and a shrill note whistled. Unable to lift herself up, she crawled along the ground. A hand grabbed her ankle with vicious strength, dragging her back, then pulling her up to her feet by a fistful of her hair.

Massive wings beat above them, clearing away the smoke cloud. Men were sprawled throughout the square, dazed and muddy. Memory saw Eloryn on her feet, no one else around her, heading toward Memory instead of running the other way.

A pale shimmer of shadow in the dusk passed over Eloryn, and she froze. In a rush of movement she disappeared under a mountain of black scales and leathery skin. A sickly wet scraping sound could be heard through the square, and the dragon rose from its crumpled position, beating its wings and lifting from the ground. Inside a crushing claw it held Eloryn, talons slid deep into her flesh.

When its feet left the ground, it sprang its claw open and she dropped onto the dirt like a bloody, broken, porcelain doll. The dragon casually lifted back into the sky to circle above.

Eloryn lay still on the ground. Blood pooled around her, mixing with the mud.

"No!"

Memory's mouth hadn't moved, as much as she'd felt the cry tear through her chest.

It had been Thayl who screamed. "Loredanna, no!"

Thayl turned fiercely on the hunter with the scarred face who still held Memory. "You! What did you do?"

Oh God, Eloryn. Memory's eyes watered, her face pulled taut by the fist in her hair. She felt too weak to move, the rain freezing her skin. Thayl's fury terrified her. She twisted limply, trying to see Eloryn over the hunter's shoulder. He squeezed her tighter, and wincing at him, she noticed a thin silver chain running around his neck, and the glint of white bone.

The scarred hunter yelled back at Thayl, hurting her ears. "Only what you told me to!"

"I should never have allowed you to keep that beast. I said to catch them, not kill her!"

Wrenching her body around, Memory spat in the hunter's face, clawing vainly against him with her black nails. He turned to her in shock.

"Stupid bitch, this is your fault." He let her go and brought his hand down over the base of her neck. The blow chattered her teeth, and threw sparks of light into her eyes. She squeezed her hand closed. *Just a bit of a distraction and a flick of the wrist.*

The man grabbed her by the hair again, pulling her back up. She looked him in the eye with a smile soaked in tears. Holding up her hand, she revealed the delicate finger sized flute.

"No!" the scarred man bellowed as though she'd ripped out his heart.

Every man in the square turned to stare at her, uncommon fear in their eyes. In the distance, she saw Roen stirring.

Time slowed.

The scarred hunter snatched for the flute.

Thayl blasted a bolt of violent magic at her.

She clenched her hand with a force that drew blood with her

fingernails. The old, rigid bone within it broke into pieces.

The dragon roared.

And Memory waited to die.

Somehow, she felt nothing. The force of Thayl's magic flew at her, went straight through and killed the scarred wizard hunter behind her instantly. He fell forward, on top of Memory, pushing her down into the mud. His hand was still tangled in her hair. She cried out, pinned on her back beneath the dead hunter, staring up into the falling rain.

High above, little more than a spot in the sky, the dragon sang a deep, mournful cry that would be heard throughout Avall. Then it fell like a stone. It took down three men before the others knew what had happened.

Memory pushed at the dead weight on her with one arm, her other twisted beneath her. She pushed her feet at the ground and they slid in the mud.

Bloodcurdling terror screamed out all around. Roen moved toward her. She cried out for him but it was lost amongst the wailing of the dragon and men.

Roen stopped before he reached her, bending down to something she couldn't see. He bared his teeth, bent forward and scooped up Eloryn's body. He almost fell as he lifted her with one arm, the other hanging limp. He turned, stumbling, running, through the chaos around him, away from Memory, into the surrounding trees.

"Roen? Roen, no, I'm here!" Memory screamed. Her sanity tearing away in strips, she writhed like the possessed. Her consciousness faded out then in. Her insides boiled. The knife kept in her corset scorched her chest, heated to burning. She found herself free, the dead body of the scarred hunter face down beside her.

She rolled onto all fours, panting. The dragon threw itself over and over at the men running through the square as they tried to find cover,

help injured friends, make their escape. Blood covered the ground as though it were the rain that fell. A man in leather armor lay next to her, staring with dead, black-brown eyes. Perceval.

Illness overtook her like a knife in the stomach. Memory vomited wretchedly. She coughed it out, eyes and nose stinging raw. She wobbled and stood up on shaking feet, taking a step to follow Roen. A gust of wind from the dragon's wings threw her back on the ground.

She tried to stand again, and as she reached her feet, there were arms around her. They lifted her, cradling her, wrapping her chest, pulling her off her feet. She wrestled against them but the arms were like a vice around her, pushing her against a wild, scarred body as it ran. Taking her away from the slaughter of the men. Away into the forest. Away from Roen and Eloryn.

CHAPTER TWENTY-TWO

Under the cover of the trees the light rain barely penetrated through. Only the odd, heavy drop fell between the changing leaves, hitting him as he ran.

Memory swore and screamed in his arms, blending with the tortured howls of the men behind them. He hadn't been there to keep her safe. Mina had kept him away, kept him even though he wanted to go to Memory. He'd let her be hurt again.

Memory slammed her knee into his gut so suddenly he fell out of his run, dropping her.

She slipped forward, trying to run back toward the danger. He pounced, tackling her down. They skidded across slimy leaves. The ground opened up beneath them. He twisted around, pulling her on

top of him, wrapping his body around hers. They tumbled down the slope of a gully in an avalanche of red and gold.

He landed hard on his back, and darkness took him.

Gasping, sobbing breaths woke him. His arms were still protectively wrapped around the small weight of her, her dark hair falling in his face.

She thrashed in his arms. "Let me go!" she squealed. "Don't touch me!"

I broke the rules again. But I had to, to save you. His arms went loose with guilt and she pushed out, bursting from their blanket of leaves and scrambling across the ground away from him. She hit the water-carved earth of the steep gully wall and clawed against it.

He pulled himself up slowly, shaky from the fall.

"I need to get back to Lory and Roen," she said, not at all to him. She tried to climb the slope. Too weak. She tore her hands at the rocks and exposed roots, shrieking at them.

He reached out to her.

She beat his hand back, staring at him with ferocious red-rimmed eyes. "I said, don't touch me!"

She forced her back into the dripping dirt wall, cowering from him. "Who are you? Why are you following me? Was it you who hurt me?"

She didn't know him at all - he already knew this - but that she could think he was the one who hurt her like that opened him raw. He frowned, looking back toward the solace of the surrounding forest. Too hard to find the right words.

"What do you want from me?" she sobbed.

He knelt in front of her. What did he want? There'd only been one dream for so long.

"Hope," he said, shrugging as he forced his words to work, "just to find you again. Keep you safe, like I couldn't before."

An angry fire spread in him to say it. He knew what that man on the children's home staff did to her, and he could never do anything to stop it. He was too young, too weak back then. Perfect bully bait, a smaller than average boy who studied hard and had a talent for music. It was her that saved him from beatings from the older boys. He swore to her that he'd protect her one day. She had laughed at him in response. Kindly.

"How do you know me?" Tears still streamed down her face, but her sobbing lessened.

He nodded. "From the other world. You don't remember."

"Other world?" She buckled forward, clutching her stomach as though in pain. "I don't remember anything. Thayl took everything from me, my memories, my... everything."

"I know. I was there."

It was after she'd come back with that knife, shoplifted from somewhere. She looked at it like it was a thing of salvation. But when the man at the children's home had come for her again, the knife mustn't have helped, just as he had never helped. He didn't know what happened. She came back bloody, badly beaten, blind with panic. She'd never been beaten before.

"You ran away from the home. I followed you. When I caught up, that man, Thayl, had you. Don't even know what he was doing to you, but it looked bad and I... just pushed him."

"Oh God, I saw that in my dream. But it wasn't you. It was just a kid, some little boy."

He pulled his lips inward. *She does remember me. Just some little boy.* "It was me. Years ago, don't know how many. I don't get it how you look the same still, but things are different here, all magic and stuff. There was no magic there, only stories of it."

She shook her head at him, "I don't remember anything else before waking up here a few days ago. We were somewhere different? A different world? What does that even mean? It wasn't... hell?"

"Not hell. Just... our world." He shifted his legs, moving back away from her into a crouch. His throat felt tight. She asked so many questions, and he struggled to make his words work. Mina wasn't much for conversation. "I don't know. We were there, then I was here. They're different. The man grabbed me when I pushed him, pulled me back through his weird portal. You tried to catch me and we both fell. I lost my grip on you and you disappeared in the smoke." He swallowed and licked his lips. Sometimes he used to worry that she had never come through at all, that he would never find her. "Then I was in that forest, with all these dead people all around. Thayl tried to use his hand on me, but some woman started yelling at him like he'd done something wrong and I ran off. Been in the forest since."

"If you hadn't followed me, hadn't stopped Thayl..." Her voice broke.

"You ran off without your wallet. I was just taking it to you." He reached into the folded leathers at the side of his hip and pulled the wallet out, worn and tattered, and handed it to her.

She peeled it open, running shivering fingers over the contents. "Oh. Is that my name?"

He nodded. "Sorry it's dirty."

"I- I don't know yours."

"Will."

She reached out timidly for his arm and turned it over to show the wrist, holding hers up against it. Their wrists matched. Rough inked tattoos of the symbol for eternity with a swirl through the centre.

"Did them ourselves."

"Weren't you like, eight or something?"

"You were my best friend." Will's face heated. "And, kind of a bully."

"I'm sorry I don't remember you. I must be such a disappointment."

Will shook his head, but couldn't say what he wanted to; that she was the only thing from that world that he missed, after a while. Except maybe the internet. After he'd lost his parents, everything in that world seemed cruel except for her, no matter how tough she pretended to be. He knew she thought of him as a weedy younger brother, but he didn't care as long as she let him hang out with her. He always figured he'd make it up to her one day.

"Was I happy there?" she asked.

A frown chilled his face, and he looked away with a vague shrug.

She pried herself off the muddy wall, rivulets of water streaming down into the space she left. "Will, I need to find Eloryn and Roen. Can you help me?"

Will stilled himself and listened. No more screams, no more gusting of dragon wings. The smell of blood still lingered, reaching them on a gentle wind. Mina had left with the other sprites, back through the Veil to their homeland as they often did. There was no way to say how long they would be.

Until then, he could look after Memory.

He nodded, took her by the arms and swung her around onto his back. Memory's muscles jumped and tensed when he took hold of her and he cursed internally. In his time spent with Mina and the fae, touching was so natural that he kept forgetting the rules of his and Memory's once-upon-a-time friendship. He pursed his lips, waiting for retaliation, but she remained holding on.

He reached up for the strongest exposed tree roots, and began pulling himself up out of the gully with her holding tightly around his neck.

Roen slipped again. The increasing rain made the ground slick and his body burned.

His arm around Eloryn grew numb, his fingers locked in their grasp around her. His muscles screamed. He wasn't strong enough to carry her, not like this, but he had to get farther away. The trees in the direction he'd taken were thin and leafless, not providing enough cover from the deadly creature if it flew above. His other arm was useless, dislocated, possibly with bones broken. He wished it was numb too.

He floundered further into the woods. Sweat mixed with the dripping rain, running down his hair into his eyes. It stung, blinding him. Barely able to move, he saw a darker shadow, a thicker trunk. He gritted his teeth and dropped down to his knees. Lowering his shoulder, he let Eloryn slip down onto a bed of fallen leaves. He looked the other way.

Roen half walked, half fell into the wide trunk of the oak that covered them, its leaves not yet dropped. His shoulder muscles spasmed and he held back a moan, pulling his knife from his belt and biting down on it. He placed his shoulder up against the lichen encrusted bark and breathed out through his teeth. Then he pushed.

He couldn't believe it had been only a fortnight ago that he'd done this for the first time. He had become too complacent, too sure of his skills, too damn arrogant. The house guards at the estate he'd made a business call to heard him. They gathered secretly, silently, and surrounded him, cutting him off on the second floor. He'd jumped from a window, farther than he'd normally dare, before any of them could see his face. His shoulder tore then for the first time.

He'd relocated it himself before heading home. Somehow, his mother still knew, still saw the way he nursed it, and he had to lie to her even more. He remembered thinking that night that he could never live if anyone found out what he was, what he did. Now he knew there were worse things to lose.

If he'd never injured his shoulder, he would have picked a more challenging mark in Maerranton markets that day. He would never have met Eloryn. Lucky, his mother always told him; that was his blessing. If his *luck* hadn't brought him to her, would she have fallen into the care of someone more capable? Someone who could have saved her from this?

Tears ran into his mouth, mixing with the taste of metal. He pushed harder, and heard the pop as his joint was forced back into place. His knees withered and he bit hard into the knife, knowing he couldn't risk crying out, as much as he wanted to. He breathed through the pain.

Done, he pulled the knife from his mouth, absently noting the teeth marks, and forced himself to go back to Eloryn. He didn't want to know, didn't want to see, but some fool hope in him said there might still be time. Maybe he could save her.

Kneeling back beside her, Roen gently moved Eloryn's limp arms off her chest. Seeing her now clearly, he choked.

He ran his fingers over her neck, feeling for a pulse. His hands hammered to the beat of his own heart: useless. He bent in close over her face. Her normally alabaster skin was icy white. The warmth of a weak breath met his cheek.

"El." He frantically pulled his tattered shirt off his arms. Bundling the cloth, he held it against the torn flesh on her torso, trying to hold in her life. Blood welled up through the fabric, staining his hands. He

tore strips off her skirt and tied them around her waist to pull closed the largest holes in her body.

Eloryn's mouth opened as though in pain, and spluttering a deep breath, she opened her eyes. They were dim and moved slowly, taking in her surroundings. Her eyes flickered over his shirtless chest and a trace of color made it to her cheeks.

"By the... Don't blush now, you haven't enough blood."

"Roen. Are you hurt? Where's Mem?" Eloryn's voice was the softest rasp of whisper.

Roen's emotions caught in his throat. Memory. He saw her fragile body fall under Thayl's deadly magic. No one could survive that. The Wizards' Council members were captured, awaiting execution. Alward was dead too. They were alone, and there was no comfort he could give her but more lies. Before he could answer she began to fade again. Roen squeezed her gently.

"Please, stay awake," he begged her. "Can you heal yourself, with your magic?"

Eloryn's eyelids fluttered. Roen knew it was no use.

"I'm sorry I can't... Is there nothing else I can do? Tell me what to do." He brushed his hand over her forehead, under her hair, feeling it cold under his flushed skin.

"Please don't leave me again," Eloryn murmured.

"Never, Princess. Just don't leave me."

Eloryn stilled. Roen lifted her shoulders, pulling her up into his lap.

Roen cradled Eloryn's body. He stared at her face, as still and silent as she, in too much pain to let tears fall. Hearing the sound of soft footsteps approaching he wrapped his hand around the hilt of his thin knife. His other arm remained around Eloryn. He barely looked up to see who approached.

"Roen! Oh God." Memory came to a stop just in front of him. "Oh God, oh God, oh God."

Roen tightened his hand around the knife hilt. "Spirit."

"It's me," she said, fighting the whine in her voice.

"It can't be. I saw you fall," he said.

"I'm fine. Tell me she's not dead, please." Memory moved closer, and he jumped in shock when she touched him, finally looking at her properly. He twitched again when he saw the tall shape of Will shadowing them. He pulled Eloryn's body closer to him and looked to Memory with a skeptical frown.

"He helped me find you," Memory said. "Roen, please, is she still alive?"

Roen's head dropped. He laid Eloryn flat on the ground so Memory could see.

Memory suppressed a dry heave. The dragon had messed Eloryn up badly. It took her three times to build the courage to feel for a pulse, but when she did, she found one, slow and fading.

Memory looked up into Roen's eyes. Red-rimmed, bloodshot, a question read in them clear for her to see. She nodded in slow motion.

"Do you think you can?" he asked.

No. "Yes. I summoned a dragon. I can do the goddamned impossible."

I can do this, Memory told herself. *God, I hope I can do this.*

Memory took her mind back, remembering how she felt the morning after Eloryn healed her, going over what happened between Eloryn and Roen in the wagon. The way Eloryn described the process. *There is magic in everything, an energy of life that can be spoken to. Our bodies remember what it is to be whole and healthy, and they want to be that way. The magic just gives the body the power to right itself. Reminding it how to be whole. Visiting the broken areas and helping to put them back together.*

Eloryn had spent hours putting Roen back together from just a bruising. Why the hell did she think she could do this? No magic she'd tried worked the way she expected. She was more likely to blast Eloryn away than to help her. Numbly, she realized at this point Eloryn couldn't be much worse off. Beneath thin bandaging, Eloryn still bled. Thayl's words to her repeated in her head, and she cast them away. If this didn't work, she didn't want to think about what she could be losing.

Memory put a shaking palm onto Eloryn's chest, tacky with blood, and one onto her forehead.

She took a deep breath. "Move back a bit, just in case."

Roen stayed and held Eloryn's hand.

This has to work. I hope you trust me, Lory.

She reached out to Eloryn with the furnace of magic within her.

It came faster and easier than she expected. The shock of the connection almost made her break away. Warmth, pulse, blood, muscle and bone. Pain. Surreal and abstract she sensed them. They engulfed her. She focused on the pain, feeling it herself, almost overwhelming. Willing it gone made it so. She imagined Eloryn's pale skin flawless and whole. She mended what she felt torn with a giddy omnipotence, spending energy without guard. She gave her own blood to replenish what Eloryn had lost. At the fringes of her perception, she could taste consciousness. A dreaming mind thick with emotions, memories and an ocean of painful guilt.

Memory gasped back into herself, needing a world worth of air.

She pulled her hands to her aching chest, pressing them against her burning skin. She struggled away from her body's demand to faint. Passing out could come later. She needed to know if it worked, first. The forest was still dusk lit and no one had moved. How long did that take? Did she do enough?

Roen stared, mouth opened, and Memory feebly clawed away the bandaging he'd done. She dug her hands underneath, feeling for skin, finding it smooth and unbroken.

Roen squeezed Eloryn's hand, and Memory shook her gently, then harder, then roughly, calling her name.

Eloryn didn't move.

"I don't know, I thought I did something. Maybe I didn't do it right. Maybe I didn't get in far enough, like she couldn't with me?" Memory rocked on her knees.

Roen's head shook as if he was drunk. Knuckles cracked in a tightening fist.

"I can try again." Memory moved flimsy arms back toward Eloryn, but Roen lifted them away.

"You can't see yourself. You can't try again." Roen held her arms,

and Memory found they were too weak to take from him.

Memory fell onto his bare chest, bridging Eloryn's body beneath them. She let out in long, painful breaths what she couldn't in tears. Roen brought his arms up around her, shaking from the cold, or something else.

"Mem?"

Memory and Roen jerked apart.

Eloryn stared up at Memory wide eyed. Fear, comprehension, and loss played across her face, taking her from relief to pain in seconds.

Eloryn flung herself around Memory, arms tight around her chest, face buried in her shoulder. Memory sat limp, arms hanging awkwardly, and Eloryn bawled.

"He's dead, Mem, he's dead. Alward's dead."

As Eloryn's sobbing quaked through Memory's body, empathy built like acid in her eyes. She wrapped her arms in a returned embrace and held as tightly as the weakness in her body allowed.

Eloryn wept wretchedly, and with the shared wetness of their faces, shared pain, and shuddering sobs shaking them both, Memory wasn't sure whether she wept as well.

"Thayl said such horrible things. They couldn't be true. I can't believe his words about Alward," Eloryn squeaked between gulping teary breaths.

Twice Memory had dreamt of Thayl. Twice she'd met him. Each time there had been things he'd said she also didn't want to believe, and others she hoped weren't lies. She could hardly tell which she wanted most. For now, for Eloryn, she would believe that he lied.

CHAPTER TWENTY-THREE

Eloryn felt more pain in her now than when the dragon had sunk its claws deep into her stomach.

A fury she had never known before overtook her pain. It burnt her tears away. It was her fault. Alward died because of her. If only she'd told him the mistake she made, instead of trying to hide it. Too scared of disappointing him, instead she'd got him killed when he'd done everything to keep her safe, had been everything to her.

Alward only ever took you in, kept you to himself because of the guilt he felt over what he had done. Liar. Why would Alward kill her mother? And if that wasn't true, could he have lied more? Could Alward still be alive?

Desperation ran riot through her with that small spark of hope. She had to know the truth.

"I have to see his body," Eloryn said, pulling away from Memory. "I have to know he is dead, and if he is I need to bury him. No matter what happened, I still love him. I can't just leave his body to whatever Thayl has planned."

"We don't even know where he is," Memory said.

Eloryn screwed up her face. Her body felt too healthy to be holding these dark feelings. The smell of wet leaves and her own blood on her dress were like the aftertaste of death. "If he is dead, he is only a body and no longer has will. He can be brought."

"No way. Lory, you can't be serious?"

Eloryn ignored Memory. Instead, she pleaded with the earth in timeless words of magic, trying to get it to listen, wishing for it. She spoke of Alward, the man who cared for her, taught her, kept her safe. She described every part of his face, his kind smile and ink stained fingers, and how she loved him like a father. She ended with the words she had not long ago taught to Memory. "Beirsinn fair nalldomh."

She felt no connection to the magic within or around her, that vile poison still blocking her. "Beirsinn fair nalldomh!"

Nothing. She screamed, digging her hands into the earth. "Bring him to me!"

She crumpled forwards, her forehead to the ground. "Bring him to me!"

"Magic may not hear you child, but we can. Screeching such vulgar pain." The voice held a regal level of distaste.

Finding herself surrounded by fae, Eloryn jumped to her feet.

At the same time, Memory's savage guardian dropped to his knees. "Yvainne, Mina."

Her body quivering from a whirlwind of emotion, Eloryn stared at him and the fae he knelt to. She couldn't remember anything from when the dragon sheathed its talons into her chest until she woke up and grief consumed her. She floundered, trying to regroup her thoughts. Memory must have healed her, and done it incredibly well. Impossibly so. A shot of panic turned Eloryn around to find Roen. He stood behind her, bloody but alive. Eloryn blinked a double take, wondering where his shirt had gone.

Memory stood up next to Eloryn and spoke to the savage. "Will, do you know them?"

Will nodded.

Eloryn hadn't even noticed his presence before, while anger and tears blurred her eyes. Had he come here for Memory again, or come with the fae? Up from his knees, he moved to stand with the sprites. A red-headed fairy with a young face leant into him and tangled a long fingered hand in his hair.

The gathered fae reflected the twilight tones in a shimmering silver glow. More than she could count, the wild gathering ranged in size and shape, from lithe seven-foot statures to tiny sparkling lights. A bizarre and twisted mix; some had animal eyes, some had antlers or claws, and more, with rough bark skin, glowing glitter, hooves or gossamer veins. Although clothing and hair billowed with its own life, they did not move. They stood unthreatening, and some even nodded respectful bows as Eloryn passed her eyes over them. Seelie fae.

The only threatening movements were the glares and whispers directed toward Memory, who wobbled on her feet and looked more grey and ill than she had after calling the dragon through the Veil. Guilt edged in amongst Eloryn's other emotions.

"I'm sorry to have disturbed you," Eloryn said with downcast eyes. Seelie they may be, but no less dangerous to anger.

"Your call was loud, but not futile. We are pleased to know you have want. It means we can bargain. You may call me Yvainne. I know who you are." The tallest of the fae, waif thin, took an elegant step

forward through a cloud of wafting silver hair.

"Bargain, for what do you wish to bargain with me?" Eloryn's voice wavered. There were lots of stories regarding fairy bargains. Few of them ended well for the human side.

"We will bring you the body of your Alward." Yvainne spoke like sweet chimes in a breeze.

So he is dead. Eloryn's heart shuddered. "And what in return?"

"You will take Thayl's place on the throne, and renew the failing Pact with Maellan blood."

"But if-" Memory started.

Yvainne cut Memory off, her voice turning hard. "Not you. Daring to carry cold iron." If she was the type to spit, Yvainne looked as though she would now. "No matter what you may think, you do not belong in Avall. You. A vessel too full. Liable to spill and spoil all around."

The fae hissed in unison.

Memory simply gaped.

Yvainne turned back to Eloryn. "That is our offer, Maellan. Do you take it?"

"No." Eloryn swore she heard audible sighs from Roen and Memory, but she focused on Yvainne. Pain and fury inside had been startled into submission, but still smoldered throughout. The word she sought came to her. Revenge. That is what she wanted, never having imagined before she could want it. Thayl had killed Alward, and she wanted it paid back. If she could do that, then it was a small step to take the throne after emptying it. "No, not as the offer stands. I will make a bargain though, for one more thing in return."

Yvainne smiled pleasantly, sending a tremor through Eloryn.

"Mem, you said Thayl showed you his memories of how my mother was killed?" Eloryn spoke over her shoulder, keeping her eyes

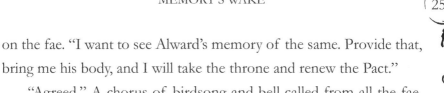

on the fae. "I want to see Alward's memory of the same. Provide that, bring me his body, and I will take the throne and renew the Pact."

"Agreed." A chorus of birdsong and bell called from all the fae, covering the protests of the friends at her back.

"This is our binding deal." Yvainne suddenly stood with her hand on Eloryn's chest. Eloryn gasped to feel the spark of connection relight within her.

"We must go, and let the Summer Court know what has passed. The body will be brought." Yvainne turned, and sprites all around began blinking out of sight. Some sparkled away into tiny lights, and some skipped into the Veil.

Yvainne flicked her eyes to Will. "You stay. Keep watching that one."

"Keep watching?" Memory whispered.

The red headed fairy at Will's side glared hardest at Memory, and passed the glare briefly to Yvainne before vanishing.

"Wait, how is the memory shown?" Eloryn cried.

"With your blood on your hand, and the body of the man, know what you want in your heart and plunge that sinful blade into his." Yvainne pointed to Memory and faded away.

Eloryn's bones turned to wet rope. Binding deal made, she slumped back to the ground, waiting on what that would entail.

"What the hell, Lory?"

"Princess, you should not have."

Only Will did not yell at her. The strange young man crouched beside the ancient oak's trunk, blending into the shadows, watching with hurt eyes.

"It is done," she said. The biggest decision she'd ever made. Maybe the only one she had ever made, that wasn't just to follow another's. She hoped she would not regret it too much.

Memory put a hand on her shoulder, squatting down next to her. When she spoke, her voice was devastatingly tired. "Is this going to be worth it? I get the revenge thing. I so do. Thayl, he told me..."

Memory's words ended as Veil mist spread in curls below them, across the ground, leaving behind a man's body as it passed.

Eloryn's nose twitched, and her tears came again.

She found comfort that, in death, Alward looked at peace. Wavy graying blond hair he never managed to brush if she didn't remind him, a thin face with kind eyes, the face she knew better than any other. No outward signs of injury. No torture. No expression of pain carried with him to death. He seemed to be asleep, but was no less dead for that.

She gripped the shirt at his chest in both hands with tearing strength and wept into it.

"You died for me. And lived for me," she whispered into his cold body. "I'm sorry, I'm so sorry. What I am, my useless title that causes all this damage... I will make it mean something. I will own it. I will never, ever forget you."

Eloryn knew she was watched, knew they all listened to her and waited for her. She still let herself cry some more.

Sitting up, she looked down into her hands. Plenty of her blood on them still. They shook visibly.

"Memory, I need your knife."

"Are you sure you want to do this? Maybe sometimes it's better not to know," Memory stammered.

"Please, Mem."

Memory placed the folded iron blade into her hands.

Eloryn delicately, slowly, pulled it open and held it point down above Alward's no longer beating heart.

A silent snarl bared her teeth, and she rattled with erratic nerves,

but could not push the blade.

Not only was her body stubborn, but her mind was in turmoil.

Roen knelt on her other side. "Are you sure?"

Eloryn nodded without really knowing.

From one side, Roen placed his hand onto hers. From the other, Memory did the same. And they pushed.

Eloryn cried out as though the blade pierced her own heart.

The three of them became ghosts; misty forms in a forest. Not this one, but another that they knew. The very place Eloryn and Memory had first met. Eloryn knew the trees well, having spoken to them, though here they were smaller, the brush thinner, making a small clearing. Alward ran toward them, more solid than them, or his dead body on the ground. He was young and fresh with the look of courageous purpose.

Wisp light filled the woods. A dozen men and women bearing weapons followed Alward through the dense trees.

He stopped and stared straight past Eloryn, Memory and Roen with a look of horror. All three followed his gaze.

A gruesome scene like an illustration from the books of blackest magic stood behind them.

Dark hooded figures circled Loredanna, turning on the forest floor in fits of hard labor. Young Thayl assisted anxiously as the baby came.

Behind them, blackest swirls of Veil mist tore the air, outlining a hooded shape that held aloft another newborn. Screaming and wet from birth, blood spilled from the baby's chest, a rune freshly carved into it.

"Stop. Stop this evil!" Alward yelled.

The leading figure loosed a disturbing chuckle from beneath the hood, and rolled the crying baby off long finger tips, letting it fall

alone through the tumultuous Veil door.

Figures clashed around them, through them. Guards and chambermaids fought fiercely with those in hoods and cloaks, fighting for their Queen, and giving their lives.

Insubstantial as air, Eloryn, Roen and Memory stood back to back, watching the vision around them. Each swung sword or club made them flinch, only to pass harmlessly through.

Alward stood next to them, scroll in hand, reading words of power. As more fighters fell, between individual battles, glimpses could be seen.

Thayl pulled Loredanna to her feet. No longer torn by labor, blonde hair stuck to her cheeks with sweat. Another newborn lay on the forest floor, lying silent as bodies fell around it.

Thayl scooped Loredanna up into his arms, turning his back on the battleground and the newborn. Loredanna struggled, weak with exhaustion. She cried out, reaching desperately for her baby that was left behind.

She flailed. "No! Let me go. My babies, I won't leave them!"

Fingernails tore his cheek, and she ripped free of his hold, pushing past him, switching their places in the most fateful of moments.

Then she froze, arms still reaching toward her child, struck by a red bolt of magic. Thayl cried out, catching her falling body.

Next to them Alward also stood frozen, one arm outstretched. The scroll drifted to the ground, dropped from his other hand. Horror dawned on his face as the last of Loredanna's protectors were dispatched around him.

"Loredanna. No, no, no. Loredanna!" Thayl cried as her body gave in, piece by piece in his arms.

She only had eyes for Alward, arm pointing to her child, as she breathed out words. "Save them. Keep her safe."

Watching through time and death, Eloryn could feel the tangible power of her words; words imbued with a force stronger than any behest.

Alward moved in an instant, snatching up the newborn, tucking her into his cloak.

Thayl dropped Loredanna to the ground, roaring into a charge at Alward who backed away with the tiny, precious bundle.

Behind Thayl, Loredanna's last breath passed through her lips, bringing with it final words of magic. Alward faded into the Veil, taking with him the newborn, just now starting to cry.

The vision faded away. Eloryn whispered some words, and watched Alward's body sink away into the earth. As the body sank, a pure white stone as large as Eloryn rose in its place. The knife, rejected, glinted on the freshly turned soil.

Eloryn placed her hand on the stone tenderly. A few more words and she dropped her hand away, but the impression of it remained, permanent in the smooth facing of marble.

"Goodbye."

CHAPTER TWENTY-FOUR

"That was-?" Eloryn began saying, turning away from Alward's grave.

"That was me." Memory bent down gingerly and reclaimed her knife. She wiped it on her already filthy skirt and put it away. "Look, I don't get all of it, not by half, but the baby with the cut chest; that was me. That was this," she said, tapping the front of the corset where it covered her disfiguring scar. "Thayl told me, just before the dragon got you; he said we were sisters. I didn't know then whether it was true, how it could have been true."

"Twins." Roen coughed a weak laugh. "To think we were worried that you looked so much like Eloryn. The resemblance is even clearer now the Princess has lost weight."

Memory fixed a glare on Roen. "You better not start calling me Princess."

"Alward never said a thing, nothing at all about a twin. But, there was always something he searched for, something he said was lost. His research into the Veil, his experiments in the woods... Are you sure it was you?" Eloryn asked.

Memory gave a wry laugh. "How the hell could I be sure? I'm just trying to add up what I've found out so far, and that's what it seems to come to."

Eloryn took a step forward, raising a hand. "May I see how you appear without the dye in your hair?"

"Uh, I guess?"

Eloryn whispered a few words, and Memory felt no change.

Roen however blew a soft whistle. "There's no question. Identical."

Memory reached and twirled a lock of hair in front of her eyes, finding it the same ivory blonde as Eloryn's. She wished for a mirror, to see if she really did look just like the beautiful, delicate creature Eloryn, whom she'd spent unconfessed time envying. It made sense, more than any other explanation had so far, but it just seemed surreal not only to now have a sister, but an identical twin. Whenever she imagined finding her family, she imagined happy smiles and hugs all around. Now, she stared at her twin, too awkward to move. Eloryn stared back mutely. Memory waited for some overwhelming joy or familial love to wash over her. It didn't come. She felt for Eloryn, undeniably, but was it the way a sister feels? Maybe she was in shock. Maybe the unanswered questions still blocked her.

She pounded her forehead with her palm. "But, but, but... We saw when we were born, but what happened next?"

A quiet voice came from the shadows nearby. "You always said you were found as a baby, right near the orphanage. All cut up with

that wicked scar you like showing people."

Will, oh God, I completely forgot he was here. Still watching me from hiding, Memory thought, unsettled by the idea. Will told her he wanted to protect her, but his fairy friends didn't seem to have the same intent. She couldn't help wondering whose purpose he served first.

"And I grew up there? In some other world? How could there be another world?"

"There were other lands, once," Eloryn said. "Before the Pact. But the fae foresaw the end of days, which is why the Pact was made. Avall was separated into the Veil, to save the fae and the people of Avall from the hell that would swallow the rest of the world. Maybe, maybe some human life has survived beyond Avall?"

"Our world wasn't Hell." Will shifted in the shadows, his voice quiet and hard.

"I didn't mean..." Eloryn dropped her head, then looked back up at Memory. "I'm just saying what I know of Avall's history. To travel across the Veil into other lands simply isn't done. The fae used to, to bring back imports to trade, but even they haven't for centuries."

Memory paced short, shaky steps, putting together the pieces of her lost life. Her body felt weak and wasted, but her mind ran on overdrive. "Thayl travelled through, Will saw him. Thayl came after me, to steal the magic from me, when I was like this, same age and everything. He took my memories, my powers, and all three of us fell back through."

She faintly saw Will nod in the darkness of the oak's shadow.

"You got there at the same time as Thayl. Dead bodies all around, you said, so it was before he took over, just after we were born? Oh God, that was sixteen years ago."

Memory ran out of direction for her mind and her feet. He'd waited for her, lost in the forest for sixteen years? How could she

possibly have been a good enough friend to have deserved that? Her current record didn't feel up to scratch. She turned away, suddenly finding it hard to look at Will. Her next question came out in a whisper. "But I didn't get through. I was what, just gone all that time?"

"The place we first met, where you appeared in my Veil door, it was the very same clearing we were born," Eloryn told her. "It makes sense. If that is where you left this world from, that is where you would return into it. If you were lost in the Veil, time within it does not behave the same. You did not change, age, even think for all the years you were held by it. In magic, like calls to like. When I stumbled through, a troubled Veil door already, it pulled us both out there. It is all I can guess."

"Same DNA definitely falls in the alike category. And if you hadn't? I'd still be what? Nowhere? Forever?"

Eloryn bit her lower lip and shrugged.

"Uh, but I still don't get it! Thayl had no magic, right, only got it from me? The magic he used to kill the King-" *My father?* "and the wizards right after we were born, but he took it from me when I was this age? Thayl said we were connected, in space and time. Could he have travelled forward in time into the other world to find me even though it was right after we were born here?"

Roen cleared his throat. He stood next to Will, looking grave. "Memory, I know you still have questions but we've tarried here too long. I'm told by your tracker here we were far too easy to find," he said, tilting his head to Will. "We need to start moving again, now, before the trail of blood leads more to us. Most of Thayl's men were killed, but he lives. He could be anywhere."

"You're right. I'm sorry. Which way do we go?" Memory said, dragging her wandering mind back to her current problems, away from those of her past. She felt half dead from the magic she'd used

to heal Eloryn, and she hoped they wouldn't have to go far this time. She was so tired of running.

"Wherever we can hide."

"No," Eloryn said, more firmness in her voice than Memory had ever heard.

"Princess?" Roen turned back, having already taken a few steps.

"I can't keep running. There is only one place for me to go now. To Thayl, to do what must be done."

Memory had heard Eloryn use this tone before, times she pulled her shoulders back and acted the noble part. But in the past it never sounded true, as some wisp of doubt, some whine always tinged its color. Not any more. This was the voice of royalty, royalty with a purpose.

"There is nothing that must be done but keep you safe. Both of you, now more than ever, both equal as heirs and in Thayl's want of you," Roen said, his voice gruff and low.

"There is an unbreakable oath to the seelie fae. There is revenge."

"Revenge?" Roen lifted his hands, still red from her blood. His voice rose and he yelled, right at Eloryn. "You think of revenge when less than an hour ago you were lying bloody and dying? How do you think you can beat this man who's killed so many who tried? What could you possibly do?"

Eloryn blinked as though she would cry. Roen's words echoed in the tangible silence, but when Eloryn spoke again, her voice did not waver. "We know more about Thayl and his magic than anyone ever has. I can take his power from him. Take back all he stole from Memory, and take back my throne. Our throne. I will see revenge for the death of our father, for the Wizards' Council, for Alward and for our mother. And I know how I will do it all."

Silence again. Everyone stared at Eloryn.

Memory forced her tense shoulders down. "So what's the plan, Princess? As much as the idea of seeing Thayl again makes me want to barf out my happy thoughts, I'm with you. I want back what's mine." *I want back my soul. I don't want to feel like THIS any more. Without my soul, I might as well be a demon.*

Eloryn smiled in straight mouthed relief. "I do have a plan. Mostly," she admitted. "There is a clear connection between you and Thayl. Your rune scars, his runed hand, and his magic. Thayl is simply using magic he stole from you. If we can separate him from that, he will be nothing more than a normal man. My hope is, given the nature of magic, that once freed the power and memories should also return where they belong."

"And his guards, his army, his wizard hunters and anti-magic poisons?" Roen growled.

"They will be suffering other distractions, and won't stop me reaching Thayl," Eloryn countered. "All I need is a way to get us into the castle."

Roen turned away, tearing a hand through his hair. Memory grabbed him by the shoulder and pulled him back. He winced at her, his eyes pleading.

"I can't do this, I can't keep you safe if you take this path," he said.

"It's not your responsibility to keep us safe, Roen," Memory said. "You don't even need to be here if you don't want to. We all look after each other, even if that's when facing our problems instead of hiding from them."

Roen shook his head, looking away into the black of silhouetted trees.

"You needn't stay any longer Roen. I will look after myself now, and I'd rather not see more trouble for you on my behalf," Eloryn said, a quiver finally breaking into her voice.

Roen stalked straight up to Eloryn with such ferocity it seemed he could hit her. Eloryn flinched but stood her ground.

He breathed deeply three times before he spoke, with each word separate and low. "I won't leave you again."

In the pause that followed, a gust of wind like a cool night breeze was their only warning.

Then the air rushed, blowing down so strong it knocked them off their feet, throwing them onto the forest floor. The strongest branches of the ancient oak that sheltered them screeched and split, a massive weight bending them down.

Memory gasped away from the wet dirt in front of her face. She spun onto her back, confused, and looked up to see that the sky had fallen. Pitch black and sparkling in stars, it draped over the tree above, and slithered off it, down around the branches to the ground in front of her. It snapped huge emerald cat eyes at her, sniffing then snorting hot air. Her now blonde hair gusted and fell.

Memory screamed. Eloryn next to her sat motionless in terror. Memory dragged her into a protective embrace, Roen backing in front of them. Will appeared by their side, growling like an animal. A clutch of cornered mice awaiting the cat.

The dragon took a step forward with a claw still slick in Eloryn's blood, washed under that of many others.

"Quiet small ones." The creature lowered its glittering head down to their level. He spoke without movement, in a low growl that reverberated through their bodies. "I am not here to destroy."

They remained huddled together. The beast made no other action, just waited and watched.

"You won't hurt us?" Memory asked, confused.

"Indeed no." Words came slowly, an earthquake of sound. "I come to grant a boon for my release from imprisonment, in the last

time I shall ever be in service to a human." Its last word held such distaste it made Memory squeeze Eloryn tighter.

"Thank you," Memory said in a squeak, feeling even more a mouse. "For not killing us."

The dragon's head gave a shallow nod. "What else would you have from me?"

"What the hell's a boon?" Memory hissed into Eloryn's ear.

"Anything I can offer that is within my power," the dragon answered through unmoving mouth, the sound growling through their bodies.

Memory gaped, wide eyed. "And what is within your power?"

A sound like autumn leaves, crumbling stones and crashing tides. The dragon laughing?

"We'll have no more debts with fae creatures," said Roen.

"This is no debt. You will be rid of me forever once my boon is given. Now think well on what you would have."

Eloryn stammered, still clinging to Memory. "Could you-?"

Huge green eyes fastened on hers. "Let the one to whom I'm indebted ask." The dragon raised its voice, enough for them to feel it like an ache inside.

Memory shivered under the weight of its gaze. What did she want most? "Can you bring back my memories?"

"Not while they are held by another."

Her mouth moved uselessly. She rolled her eyes, looking for inspiration. She needed her memories back. Without them how could she even know what she wanted? Thayl stole them from her and she had to find a way to get them back. "We need to get to the castle and deal with Thayl. Can you get us to Thayl? Fly us there?"

The dragon huffed. "I am no beast of burden. You think like those hunters, seeing me only as a predator and animal, never even considering my true power. So be it. You want to travel, then for your boon I will teach you how. I have seen how you fold the world and move across it. You have the power already, but random, limited, human."

"The Veil doors?" Eloryn breathed.

"Only that one will learn," the dragon boomed, pointing with a reaching claw at Memory. "Defying nature's laws as she does, yet it is still she that I owe."

With a lash of its tail, the dragon took Memory and vanished with her into the Veil.

CHAPTER TWENTY-FIVE

Within the Veil, time meant nothing. Neither did space, or self. Memory could see panic within her like watching from a distance, but a strange sense of calm kept it smothered. The very sensation, although disconcerting, made her grateful. It meant she could still think, still feel. She still existed. This time, unlike the last time she had spent within the Veil, she was aware. Even if it still felt only like a faded dream as she lived it.

In the presence of the dragon, the raging winds she remembered of the Veil were also calmed. Hollowness and pure power surrounded them. She could almost see it moving, a force of nature and life within the gusts and ribbons of wind that flowed out like a golden tide. It swarmed like particles around her chest, warming the fire within her.

The dragon whispered to her, its voice worming its way deep into her subconscious. The long pages of magical words any other person in Avall would need to behest a Veil door were distilled into basic theory. A concept rather than a contract, a way of understanding that Memory could use. The idea of using it horrified her. *What if I could be lost again?*

After a length of time that felt both instant and eternal, the dragon brought Memory back to her friends and the forest. The looks of outrage and horror she had seen on their faces when she was snatched away were still there. Not a moment had passed for them.

Memory breathed deeply, enjoying real air in her lungs until Eloryn latched onto her in a shaking embrace, squeezing the air back out again. Over Eloryn's shoulder, Memory smiled to Roen and Will. Will flinched and turned away. Looking faint, he leaned suddenly against the trunk of the closest tree. *I could have been lost again.*

Eloryn let go, backed away and looked at her with a face full of questions. The dragon spoke as though in answer, all its focus on Memory. "You've been taught, now you must be tested, to know you can control what has been bestowed."

"Right now?" Memory gulped, filled with stage fright.

"I will watch over your first journey through the Veil. You will be safe."

Memory turned to Eloryn and Roen. "Where do we go from here? To Thayl?"

"Somewhere safe," said Roen. His jaw moved as though he had to force the words through. "If Eloryn has a plan, we will hear it, but we will hear it somewhere safe."

"I know where." Eloryn nodded, and took a long moment before she turned her eyes from Roen back to Memory. She spoke her words of magic that formed images of illustrations and maps.

Eyes closed, Memory filled her mind with the place Eloryn shared with her. The fire within her burned and she could feel the Veil all around her, how it hovered over and connected to the physical world like a shimmering net. She reached with her hands but touched nothing. She moved as though conducting an orchestra, pinching the Veil, bringing it together by two points of the world like folding a map, and tore it at that point. She opened her eyes to see the dark wisps of Veil door standing in front of them.

The fire inside her cooled and with the chill that followed she felt a rush of disappointment that she'd succeeded. Memory shook pins and needles out of her hands. It would have been better if she couldn't do it. She never wanted to step through a portal like that again. Just seeing this magical doorway - like the one from her very first memory, the one she summoned the dragon through, the one she was thrown through as a baby - made her chest ache as though it had been carved again.

The dragon waited.

Under his intimidating gaze, Eloryn stepped up to the doorway first. She nodded to Memory confidently, but the next step, the one that would take her into the Veil, didn't come.

"Do you not trust your sister, or do you not trust me?" the dragon rumbled. It almost sounded amused.

Eloryn paled. Memory didn't find it particularly funny either. She and Roen took their place on either side of Eloryn, and took a step.

Eloryn and Roen vanished, but a hand grabbed onto Memory, pulling her back. She looked up into Will's eyes.

Will shook his head in a brisk movement, his mouth formed "No" but no sound came out.

The dragon's shape loomed behind Will like a mound of black diamonds. Impatience oozed from him. Roen and Eloryn were already

on the other side of Avall. "I have to go through. Come with me?"

Will slumped forward as if in pain. He reached a hand toward the smoky tendrils, then looked into her eyes. "This time I won't let go."

Memory crushed his hand in hers. She tried to be brave, for him, but still released a tiny, crying scream as she stepped through.

They arrived at a small cottage. It overlooked a sea that ended in a horizon of mist, lit by a near full moon. Lonely on a rocky bluff made barren by salty winds, a grove of malformed grey trees skirted the cottage, making it more sinister than cozy. Will vanished again into those trees the moment they arrived.

The dragon did not travel with them, and Memory knew she wasn't the only one to hope they wouldn't meet again.

Slowly, they shuffled indoors. Their grand scheme to stay up planning was laid to waste when they all passed out from exhaustion.

"That's it," Eloryn said.

"That's the plan?" asked Memory.

"That is the plan."

"Huh," Memory said. She sat on the very edge of a plush armchair, knees bouncing, chewing her lips. Blood red rays of the setting sun cast over waves below and through the wide open windows, dragging in the smell of rotting seaweed and sea foam. They had slept like the dead, and woken late. In the remaining hours of sunlight, Eloryn reviewed every last piece of information they had, every angle and advantage, until she finally explained her plan.

"It isn't any good?" Eloryn stood in front of the windows, backlit almost too brightly to look at, lips pulled into her mouth and frown forming.

"No, I mean, it's sort of brilliant. Free the Wizards' Council as a distraction, then some identical twin shenanigans to cat and mouse Thayl off on his own. Having the resistance help once Thayl is beaten is good. I reckon there'll be some unhappy people around."

"I won't ask the resistance to act until we've done our part, so they aren't exposed. I think they will agree to that. Alward has a Speaking Mirror here that he used to contact suppliers when setting up this home, and I saw that Lanval owns one, so we can send our messages through him." Eloryn drew in a deep breath. "I wasn't sure I could bring it all together, but the dragon giving Memory the knowledge of Veil doors was the final piece."

"Stupid dragon making me the important part," Memory muttered to herself.

Roen's head wobbled, somewhere between a nod and a shake. "I won't say I like it, but it could work, if your theories are right."

Eloryn turned a shade of pink that glowed in the setting sunlight. "All laws of nature and magic say they are. Like calls to like. Energy will channel to where it belongs."

"It still sounds dangerous," said Roen.

"I'll keep Mem and myself moving fast. I can behest our bodies to react quicker, keep us a step ahead of Thayl. He won't know which of us is which. I think we've a good chance of luring him away from the rest of his men with glimpses of us."

Roen leant forward in the matching armchair across from Memory. "And you say your behest can also help me fight better, to hold back any men with him until he's on his own? Will too, if he shows up again?"

Eloryn nodded, moved as if to pace, but instead fidgeted in place.

Memory leaned back into the upholstered comfort, pulling her knees up in an effort to stop their jittering.

This cottage had been set up by Alward, Eloryn had told them when they arrived. A home away from home in case their other was lost, bought and fully stocked with essentials by Alward's guidance from afar. Stocked and furnished but too sparse to be considered cozy. Memory now sat in a simple cotton dress, more grey brown than lilac, taken from a small supply in a room fitted for Eloryn. Inexpressible happiness filled her to be out of the destroyed black ball gown. Clean, dry, fed *and* sitting. All the good things in life. But a dark unease at what lay ahead continued to build.

"I don't know, isn't it risky though? He'll still have his magic the whole time. We know he hit me once and it did nothing, but the two of you... We're going to have to get so close to him. Maybe it should just be me. I can do it, lure him out by myself," Memory said past the fingers in her mouth, having graduated from chewing her lips to chewing on them.

"I can't let you take that risk on your own," Eloryn said firmly. "He could have any number of men with him even with the distractions. You need us there to help. Even if you're immune to his magic again, he could hurt you in other ways."

Roen rested his elbows on his thighs and bent his head down into his hands. "If anyone is to confront Thayl on their own it should be me. He doesn't know me, and I can probably sneak in close enough without being seen. Both your lives are too valuable."

"It needs to be all of us for the plan to work. Thayl needs to see Memory and me. I need to be there, close by, for my behests to work. Memory must be there for the chance to get her memories back."

"Then Roen at least can stay behind then, and Will; he doesn't need to be part of this either," Memory said, volume growing.

Eloryn paused with her mouth open, looking across to Roen.

"Not a chance." Roen's voice was barely below a yell as he stared at the two of them.

"But-" Memory said, her voice rising again to match.

"Mem, Roen, please, if we do this, we have to do it together. I won't let either of you do this without me, so you won't stop me. It is my plan. Now, do we follow it? Together?"

Roen nodded gravely then put his head down into his hands.

Memory tore off her last fingernail between her teeth and chewed on the rough fibers left behind. Her mind whirred, but all she could catch from the thoughts that flew past was a large amount of cursing.

She shrugged and nodded.

Eloryn sighed out enough air that she visibly decreased in size. "Then we do it tonight."

"I figure you heard all of that?" Memory said out loud to the copse of trees, feeling foolish.

With the faintest rustle of leaves, Will dropped down in front of her, landing as easily and quietly as if he'd simply taken a step forward. She squeaked a gasp of shock at his arrival. At this point she could do without such surprises, and punched him in the arm in retribution. She thought she saw him smile in response, but it passed too quick for her to be sure.

Seeing him here now, so close in front of her, she realized she hadn't ever really looked at Will. William? William what? He had just

been "that animal man". But he wasn't that. He was some normal boy whose life she'd ruined, lost in her own insane world of issues. Half the time she forgot he was even there, watching her from a distance. So many questions she hadn't asked him, things she hadn't seen. He seemed several years older than her now. On his bare chest large pale scars showed against the worn skin, silver in the moonlight. Clothing, if it could be called that, covered only parts of him. It was an odd mixture of finely made but worn garments and the furs that added to his animal appearance, all held together by strips of leather. He stood straighter than he normally did, making him even taller than she'd thought. She only just came to his biceps.

"Maybe you shouldn't go," he said.

"Don't you want me to get my memories back? Then, I would remember you too." She smiled, but her lips shook for some reason.

"Maybe. But others, maybe not. Maybe you shouldn't." He seemed uncomfortable, his eyes turning from edge to edge but not toward her.

Memory snorted. "Considering the grand memories I've made for myself so far this time around, really, what could be worse?"

No answer. Will's breath formed a shimmering haze as it shook from his mouth.

Memory lost the wry smile from her face. "I'm not talking about happy endings here. I honestly don't think that this will turn out the way Lory wants it to, but we have to do something."

"Then hide. I can keep you hidden, in the forests…"

"With your fairy friends? Maybe you haven't noticed, but they don't seem to like me at all."

"Somewhere, somehow I'd keep you safe."

He sounded so much like a child at that moment, so touchingly, that Memory breathed out a giggle. She instantly regretted it. He looked at her as though that laugh was something familiar and hurtful.

"I'm going to do this. One way or another," Memory muttered. "What are you going to do?"

"Mina, Yvainne, the other fae... they won't help. But they're close. They're watching to see what happens. If it's done, after that, I don't know. But I will help. I'll follow you. As long as I can." He looked behind him into the trees, then finally brought his eyes onto her face. The corner of his mouth twitched. "I've never seen you without your hair dyed."

"You don't dig the blonde?" Memory folded her arms up into her chest, lifting her eyebrows. This was the one person in all Avall that knew the most of her life. His opinion suddenly seemed to matter a lot.

"Never in a dress either. You're different." The cool blue of his eyes remained fixed on hers, assessing her, making her heart jitter. "Everything is different here."

"I'm sorry. I don't know what I was like before."

Will huffed, mouth lifting slightly more, almost a smile. "You would never say sorry, before."

The faintest flicker of light caught the corner of Memory's eye, and Will turned away from her again.

"I have to go," he said.

"Oh, well, do you want to stay tonight in the house or...?"

Will had already taken three long strides, then stepped up into the trees and disappeared. Memory's words drifted to nothing.

She wished she could do that light spell, to light up the trees and see where he went. She just couldn't get it to work, a simple thing like that. If she couldn't even do that, why did she think she could do what she had to for Eloryn's plan? This wasn't going to work. The blood drained from her to think of what would happen if it didn't.

CHAPTER TWENTY-SIX

Roen watched Eloryn push the study door open and step out, looking grey and empty. She didn't notice him, sitting still and silent in the same armchair as before. He hadn't lit the room, finding no lamps or lighters in a wizard's home, and unable to do it himself any other way. Still just a thief hiding in the shadows.

A tiny wisp followed Eloryn and lit her face. Twin tears ran down and joined under her chin.

Roen cleared his throat.

She wiped frantically at her cheeks. "It's so dark in here. Sorry, you startled me."

"How went the messages?" he asked softly.

"I was able to speak with Duke Lanval. He won't be involved, as

expected, but had information about the Wizards' Council. They still live, and I know where they are held. He also agreed to rush messages to his contacts in the resistance, so they can rally as many men as they can for this morning. He was more agreeable knowing that if we do not achieve our part, there is no risk to them. He said we were foolish, but wished us luck." Eloryn's voice had lost the regal edge it held before. She sounded tired, and more emotional than she wanted to show.

Roen leant forward out of the shadows, rose out of his chair and over to Eloryn's side before he knew why. Once there, he couldn't find reason enough to voice. He spoke awkwardly. "Are you all right?"

Eloryn nodded and smiled. Both looked false. "Where's Mem?"

Roen's hand, half lifted toward Eloryn, dropped and balled into a fist. "Gone outside to see that savage."

"I don't think he means harm, from what I understand happened to him," Eloryn said, her eyes following the line of his arm to his hand. He unclenched it, self conscious in the memory of her fingers wrapping his. Her innocent gesture that he took advantage of.

"Who's to say he's not also struck with vengeance, for his lifetime lost in the woods?" Roen turned and walked back to one of the two armchairs. Nerves jumping too hectically to sit again, he leant into the backrest from behind. One armchair meant for Alward, one for Eloryn, and nothing more. Even now he wore a shirt of Alward's, taken from what would have been his room. Eloryn had given it to him with a trembling smile, and as much as wearing it was necessary it made him uncomfortable. He pulled at the neckline of it, unbuttoning the collar that now felt too tight.

"Memory told me that when she healed me, I was bandaged in your shirt. I don't think I would have lasted, without what you did for me. I wanted to thank you," Eloryn said from across the room.

Thanking me for evidence of what I couldn't do. Bandages instead of behests,
Roen thought, shaking his head. The image of Eloryn's gold dress,
torn to shreds and bloodstained, came to him as a further reminder.
Roen could see her in the new, clean and whole olive dress she now
wore, and how it made her eyes and hair luminous, even though he
didn't turn and look.

A sudden realization almost made Roen buckle over. He dug his
fingers into the dusty upholstery of the armchair. Who Eloryn was,
who he was… even after everything that had happened, everything she
knew about him, some madness in him still clung to hope. The pain of
that hope shredded his insides as he saw clearly. If their plan worked,
restoring the Maellan line and the Wizards' Council to power, then he
and Eloryn wouldn't be allowed together any more than Loredanna
and Thayl were.

Roen covered a groan by clearing his throat again. "We don't have
to do this. You're safe here, you could just… stay."

Eloryn moved to his side. "I know who I am is a burden to
everyone around me. Understand, this is what I have to do to lift that.
But my burden is not yours. You can be free of it at any time."

"I said I wouldn't leave you and I won't. Not until you're safe,"
Roen said through unopened teeth. He glared into the fabric of the
armchair, but still felt her next to him like the warmth of sunlight on
bare skin.

"I don't want you to feel responsible for me. You saw what became
of the last man who did."

"It's not just that."

"Would you still be here with me now, if I was never a princess?"
Eloryn's tone became cold.

Roen's voice came up short, breaking before a word could come
out. He forced the words through. "I didn't know you were a princess

when I returned your bag that day."

Despite the words spoken being true, Roen cursed himself as a liar. He wouldn't have been here, now, if he hadn't seen that medallion, hadn't known with one look. He wouldn't have put himself at risk to hide them from the guards. And if that hadn't ended badly, he simply would have used her, like he did other women, and then forgotten her. That was the reality of who he was; criminal, philanderer, sparkless seventh son of a seventh son. A man who had no place by her side.

Eloryn only saw the lie, one that he'd been starting to believe himself. *It's time we were both reminded of the truth. There is no future here.*

"Thank you, for that also, that you returned me my belongings back then," Eloryn said softly.

Roen coughed a rasping laugh, and she took a step back when he looked up at her in anger. "Thanking me! That I stole the pack in the first place? You're too naïve for your own good. You have no idea who I really am."

Eloryn's lower lip trembled, and she stepped back again. "I'm… I need to get some sleep before we leave."

Roen dropped his head down onto the back of the armchair. After a few quiet moments, he noticed Eloryn hadn't moved.

"I don't regret that you stole from me. There is not one action I've seen you take that hasn't been of noble cause. That is who I know you are." And she left.

"Sweet dreams, El," Roen muttered once she was long gone from the room. He straightened back up, and went to fetch the bottle of fortified wine he had seen in the pantry stores when searching for lighting.

Memory threw an arm up over her head, trying to relieve the stuffy warmth of the feather quilting on top of her. The chill of the night air was even less comfortable and she pulled it into the bed again.

She rolled her tongue around her teeth, counting them, and wiggled her toes. Her eyes, unwilling to close, traced dark shadows on the exposed rafters of the ceiling.

She flung herself onto her side, knocking into Eloryn.

"Please, Mem. You should try to sleep."

Memory breathed deeply through her nose and stretched flat on her back again in her half of a small bed. It lasted a few seconds before she turned on her side facing Eloryn, propped up on an elbow.

"So, sisters huh?" Memory said through half her mouth. "It's kind of weird, right? Really. Very seriously. Weird."

Eloryn muttered under the covers just out of Memory's hearing.

"Did you just swear? No way." Memory poked Eloryn with her bare foot.

"Mem, we only have a few hours left." Eloryn tried to move out of Memory's reach but there was nowhere to go. She turned onto her back and sighed pointedly.

"Come on, you haven't thought about it at all? I mean, we're sisters, twins even. It's got to at least be better than me being some kind of demon doppelganger. Well, maybe not by much," said Memory. "I am already stealing your clothes."

"I don't know yet what to think. I thought I knew my past. I never imagined having a sister. Now please will you sleep, or at the least let me do so?"

"If I'm bothering you too much I could go share Roen's bed instead."

Eloryn's eyes snapped open and turned mechanically toward Memory. "His bed is smaller than this one."

Memory cradled her cheek in her hand, grinning at Eloryn. "But he's cute, huh? Seems like the kind of thing sisters would talk about. Nice body too. I mean, Will is way more built, but I can't say I was unhappy Roen lost his shirt for so long."

"I'm glad my almost being killed by a dragon had such a benefit for you."

"Ooh, she *has* got a sense of humor. Biting too. See, we are sisters after all." Memory could almost hear Eloryn roll her eyes.

"Mem, what is it you really want to talk about?"

Pursing her lips, Memory rolled onto her back, her shoulder up against Eloryn's.

She still felt the remnants of the need to get home she used to feel so devastatingly, but knew now she was as much at home here as anywhere. Any family she had sought was now right here beside her. And her stolen soul? Could she just live without the parts of it that were gone? The way her insides burned themselves away, the way she kept doing things that felt so wrong... No, probably not. Something had to be done. But this?

"I don't know if I can do what I have to do tomorrow," she said.

"I believe you can," Eloryn said with more confidence than Memory could stand.

"I don't know if I want to," she said with barely any sound at all.

Eloryn didn't respond, and Memory started to hope she hadn't heard.

"I know it's going to be difficult. I would trade places with you if I could," Eloryn finally whispered. "I don't know why your magic works how it does, whether it was your time in the other world or your time in the Veil that caused it. I'm sorry that and the dragon's boon mean so much of the plan relies on you. But if it helps, remember what Thayl has stolen from you."

"Yeah, about that…" Memory muttered. How could she tell Eloryn that it wasn't just her memories that were gone, that were at stake, but her very soul?

"He didn't just steal your memories, your magic. He stole your whole life; your throne, your father, your mother, your sister, your world." Eloryn found and squeezed Memory's hand under the covers.

"Yeah. All those things." Memory pulled her hand out of Eloryn's and rolled the covers back, stepping out of her side of the bed. "It's just that I feel like I've been looking for my family for so long, maybe even before I lost my memory. I'm not sure I can risk losing that again so soon."

Memory spoke quickly to cover any reply Eloryn may have formed. "I'll try and get some sleep, I promise. I just need some time."

Eloryn sat up in bed, looking in the moonlight like the Ghost-girl Memory first met. "Finding out you're my sister didn't change anything for me, because you already were in every way that mattered."

"Always with knowing the words." Memory paused at the doorway. "Can I take some of Alward's clothes, for Will? I want to give him something, you know, me not with the words and all."

Eloryn agreed. Memory tried to counteract the force of a shiver playing up her back and walked out. What she was going to do next would be harder than she first thought.

"Thayl? Thayl!"

The calling voice grew closer, and Thayl's eyes drew into small slits, annoyed by the interruption.

"Where the hell are you? Son of a…" A small figure popped onto the verdant horizon, seeming almost as surprised as he.

He smiled in recognition. His heart beat painfully. "Loredanna."

Rising from the wood and copper bench, Thayl strode quickly through the manicured rose garden. He met her with a wrapping embrace.

"Ew, gross, really?" She pushed him away violently.

Thayl froze, head tilted back, eyebrow twitching. "You?"

"Yeah me," the girl said in a defensive mumble.

"Not dead then?"

Thayl thought he saw her hesitate before she spoke again. "Just. Someone saved me, healed me."

"You've also changed." Thayl stared at her rough cropped hair, now a heartbreakingly familiar blonde.

"Not a lot."

Thayl dropped onto the garden bench, suddenly right behind him again. He rubbed his eyes, knowing he was dreaming. *You shouldn't be able to feel so tired in a dream.* He often dreamt of Loredanna amongst these roses. Beautiful, blessed moments of dream. Not tonight though. On every rose vine blossoms turned to ash and fell onto the ground as dust. "What do you want, demon? Why are you here?"

"Don't call me that. You know I'm not," Memory said, frowning at him.

"Tormentor, then."

She folded her arms across her chest and paced in front of him. "I came to make a deal."

"Why would you, now, knowing what I want from you?" Thayl blinked his eyes clear and leaned back, draping both arms along the back of the bench.

"I'm kind of hoping you want other things more, and maybe we

can forget about that whole sucking-my-remaining-soul-out thing?"
Memory peeked from the corner of her eye and made another lap in
front of him. "You've got the Wizards' Council, and with Alward dead
too, I'm out of other options."

Thayl stared, waiting.

She licked her lips, and then blurted her words out under his still
gaze. "Eloryn's alive."

Thayl jumped to his feet. Storm clouds doused rose bushes that
now stood as big as ancient oaks, filling the air with the scent of rain.
The shade of a bloodied dragon swooped overhead, making Memory
flinch.

"You'd better not lie. What do you offer?" Thayl growled.

"Eloryn. I can bring her straight to you. But you have to promise
you won't try and take more soul or memories from me. I don't even
need the other ones back. I know I wasn't happy in that hell I was in."
Memory's pace increased with the rapid flow of her words. "And also,
I want to rule after you. I know you never married, that you have no
heir. I want to be your heir. I should be anyway. I'm older than Eloryn,
but everyone only ever wants her."

Thayl put out an arm, stopping the girl in her tracks. She stood
pouting in front of him, all fire and unshed tears. As full of emotion
as her mother.

"Those are your complete terms?" Thayl asked. "You bring me
Eloryn, I take no more memories from you and make you my heir?"

"Will and Roen, they aren't anything to you. I want them too,
alive," she said, her cheeks colored feverishly and shoulders shaking.
"It has to be a promise."

The child was too terrified to know what she was doing. Thayl
smiled.

"I agree. By the fae, our deal is binding, our oath unbreakable.

Repeat what I just said." He pointed solemnly at her, waiting, and she fumbled out the words.

The garden returned to its original state. Warm sunlight shone from an unclouded sky above a field of thorned beauty. Thayl suppressed a joyous reel of laughter.

He dragged a finger through her hair, and smiled at the look of horror on her face as she shied away from him. "I didn't know you were identical twins. Even when I travelled through the Veil, right after your birth and found you grown, magic matured and ready to steal, you looked not a thing like your mother. Not like now."

"How did you do it? How did you find me when I was sixteen, just after I was born?"

"You think I know?" Thayl's laughter boomed through the garden. "You think I planned it all? Think child, what magic did I have, before I stole yours? I had help."

"The one who dropped baby me through the veil door?"

"How do you know her?" Thayl looked around, alert, then calmed. He hadn't seen the witch in years, since the last time she appeared demanding he repay his debt. A debt he only owed when his revenge was complete. He knew when it was, she'd return, and that would be soon.

"I saw what really happened when I was born, what you didn't show me in our little memory lane excursion," she said.

"And how do you judge me now? What wouldn't you do for the people you love?" Thayl said, watching her expression.

"Probably not carve up their baby and throw it into Hell," she said through a twisted mouth.

"What do you know? You obviously have no people you love," Thayl mocked with a smile, but strain pulled it into a sneer. It didn't matter what this girl thought, he still knew the truth of his part, and

she wouldn't be around much longer to torment him with her words and her face. His smile calmed and he watched her steadily.

"What are you going to do with Lory?" Memory asked. "I know you want her alive. You didn't want the dragon to hurt her."

"You bring her to me. That is our pact. What I do with her after that is whatever I wish. I am not too old yet to take a wife. I'm sure she'll be agreeable when death is her only other option."

Memory wobbled back a short step as though trying not to fall.

"Regretting the terms of our deal already?" he asked with melodramatic sympathy.

"You could say that," she whispered.

"Perhaps you should have considered them more carefully. But we are bound now," Thayl said. "Don't be glum. You get a kingdom and your two boys to play with. There is more I can show you too, about your past, after you've completed your side of the bargain. Which you intend to do, how?"

Memory's face lost all emotion and life. "It's happening soon, early this morning while it's still dark. Eloryn thinks we will be going to free the Wizards' Council, and with them as a distraction, we would come for you, but I'll bring her straight to you instead. I just need to see where to take her."

Thayl shifted the world around them to the castle with a blink. Flying by walls and doors of spectacular wealth, he led her to the main hall with a growing smile.

The room dripped with ivory and gold. Crystal chandeliers spun colored light throughout the room, lighting the blood-red carpet beneath.

This was the very place where the blood of King Edmund and many of the Wizards' Council went cold some sixteen years earlier. This would be the place his final revenge would be had.

"Bring her to me here."

This was the place every last member of the Wizards' Council and this cursed offspring of Loredanna and her forced husband would meet their ends. As the child faded out of his dream, he let laughter of relief and anticipation fill the grand hall.

CHAPTER TWENTY-SEVEN

Memory awoke covered in a thin sheen of sweat, still exhausted, anxious and restless. If it hadn't been for the dream she wouldn't believe she had slept at all. She'd never made it back to bed. Her limbs were locked into a crumpled form fitted to the armchair she slept in. Only moonlight showed through the wide windows of the sitting room. Early morning but still dark, it must almost be time to go.

The front door opened and Roen walked in from outside, covered in a damp layer of dew. He looked pale, his tawny eyes lined in red and smudged grey underneath. His face, still so charming, was marked by a frown that had become far too familiar. Thayl's face, with his tired, bitter eyes played into her mind.

"You shouldn't frown so much. Wind will change and you'll get

stuck that way," Memory said and stood up beside him, groaning when she stretched her back. She paused and frowned as well. "Is that actually true? Is that some magic thing?"

"If it was, I don't think it would apply to me," Roen said, but his face softened.

"Look, I know it's not exactly kittens and circuses right now, but I hate to see you always sad. Isn't there anything that can make you smile?"

Roen looked at her through haphazardly ruffled hair. The golden color of it over his tired eyes made him look like a fallen angel. His eyes searched over her face and his lips turned upwards.

The smile that appeared slid away quickly when Eloryn joined them. They all stared at each other in silence for a few moments, until Eloryn spoke. "Ready?"

Memory nodded. *I should tell them. I should warn them. I shouldn't be doing this at all.* Memory struggled to hold their gaze and excused herself instead, leaving the cottage. *It's too late now.*

Outside, the air was thick and white, as though the Veil mist from the horizon had grown and rolled in like a tide. The mist caught and refracted the moonlight, making the night brighter than it should be, and formed cold droplets on her skin.

Memory knew she could create the Veil door inside, but the idea of it felt weird to her. It was somehow easier to grasp the concept out in the open, and at the moment, anything easier was better.

Her pulse fluttered behind her collar bone, echoing up through her throat like a feeling of sickness. She tried to imagine how this might play out. It felt as though all her other experiences until now hadn't ended very well. She struggled to picture the possibilities before her. If she had more experience, more memories to draw from in general, would she have made different choices? Would she have, if her soul weren't broken?

Roen stepped outside, Eloryn behind him. She smiled thinly. "This will work. We will get your memories back."

Memory chewed her lips, her face flickering between smile and frown. No matter how this ended, she just wanted to get it done.

On the low stone boundary wall, Memory saw the clothing she'd left out for Will the night before, now soggy from dew and sea breeze. He wasn't anywhere in sight. Memory sighed, not sure whether in sadness or relief.

"Mem, it's time," Eloryn said.

Memory caught her breath. The last chance to back down; unbreakable oaths aside. She wasn't sure whether creating this Veil door or what lay beyond it scared her more. She wondered what happened if you broke an unbreakable oath.

Memory tore a hole in the world, ready to lead them all to their fate.

"Ready?" Roen took them each by a trembling hand.

"Wait. Just, I need a moment." Memory pulled away. She flicked her eyes back and forth through the fog, seeking any movement. *It's for the best. He shouldn't have to be part of this.* Memory turned back to the Veil door.

The roof of the cottage creaked, and Will stepped down, standing behind Memory almost as though her small form would hide him from the others.

"You don't have to come," she whispered, staring at the ground.

"I won't lose you again." He held out a hand. She took it and led them all through.

It took a moment for Memory to recover from passing through the Veil. It felt just as it had every time – like being pulled through a bastard hybrid of a vacuum cleaner and a smoke machine while having a bad hangover.

The big castle room wasn't as glowing and pretty as it had been in the dream, despite being brightly lit. A smell of decay filled the hall. The finely decorated walls were dusty and run down.

Memory squinted, her eyes still adjusting to the change in light.

Scores of guards in solemn military uniform didn't help the atmosphere. Between every few guards the old men of the Wizards' Council were held, subdued and shackled. At the end of the hall, Thayl towered, staring down at them from a raised dais.

"What happened? Why are we here?" Eloryn cried.

Memory turned and watched her friends with sad eyes. Guards grabbed them from behind, locking shackles around their wrists. Will threw his fists into one guard's gut, knocking him back three steps. A heavily gauntleted hand hit the back of his neck and he fell to his knees. Shaking off dizziness he tried to stand again. Memory shook her head at him, her expression full of warning.

The look he returned stung, but he stilled.

Memory's teeth clipped against each other, knocked by panicking nerves. No guard came to shackle her.

Comprehension showed on Roen's face first. He spoke slowly, dangerously. "Mem, what are you doing? What have you done?"

Eloryn said nothing, her face shaking with emotion.

I can do this, I can do this, Memory thought, playing the mantra on repeat.

Roen wrenched his hands in the manacles, testing their strength.

Thayl called down the hall to them, his voice echoing in the perfect acoustics. "Don't bother to fight. The shackles are runed to

block any behests. Memory, why don't you come here and take your rightful place to watch the executions?"

Memory, feet still bare, pushed slowly over the carpet toward Thayl. She winced her eyes shut and called back without looking behind her. "I'm sorry, Eloryn. This is the only way I can get what I want."

The gaze of every wizard and guard in the room followed her. The weight of judgment in their eyes rattled her, making each step she took a painful internal struggle. Hayes shook his head in disgust as though this was foreseen.

I can do this, I can do this.

Midway down the long hall she called to Thayl, "You said once I brought you Eloryn, you could tell me more that you knew about me."

Thayl barked a laugh. "Obviously I was lying. I just wanted to make sure you would come, so I could dispose of you."

Memory's stomach acid turned to steam, bubbling up through her body. But she was prepared for the worst. Thayl made no threatening move yet. He stood as confident and smug as she hoped he would, after finding just the loophole in her bargain she knew was there.

She continued toward him, projecting every bit of real pain and fear she felt into her words. "You can't, we made a deal!"

"You people and your deals. I learned long ago that when making a deal, you should be sure exactly what you will be getting. As you have yours, my side of our bargain is honored. You are my heir. Does everyone here understand that?"

A low chorus of agreement sounded through the ranks of guards as she progressed down the room.

"But that doesn't mean I can't kill you." The laughter fled from Thayl's voice. "If I can't have the rest of your power, I can't risk anyone else having it. As much as you look like Loredanna now, you're too damaged to be anything to me. Better to put you out of your misery."

Thayl lifted his rune-scarred hand.

Not yet. Not close enough. Memory's mind found a new height of panic-fuelled overdrive. "There's something you don't know!" she cried out. "Something Alward knew, Eloryn knew, that you didn't. Something you need to know before you do anything to us."

Thayl sniffed, his eyes half shadowed by dark eyebrows. His hand relaxed. "Tell me if you will, but I'll make no more deals with you."

Just steps away, Memory said quietly, as earnestly as possible, "You're our father."

The impact was instant. Thayl's frown deepened, eyes widened, mouth gaped.

Memory stepped right up in front of him. *I can do this.* Eloryn's plan was too risky, putting too many people in Thayl's line of fire: Eloryn, Roen, Will. What she always wanted, since she could first remember. Her family. This way, they might be prisoners, but they were alive. This way, if she screwed up, it was all on her.

"Can it be?" Thayl whispered, his forehead scored with deep lines.

Now. *I can do this.* "Of course it can't. Obviously, I was lying."

Fury screamed from him, shooting through his outstretched hand.

Memory screamed out at the same moment, focusing all her thought on the sharpest sword in the room. "Beirsinn fair nalldomh! Bring it to me!"

Thayl's magic passed harmlessly through her.

The sword now in Memory's hand passed through Thayl's wrist.

The world ended in blinding light.

Thayl's scream echoed down the hall to Eloryn. She saw his hand fall to the floor. It thumped in time with her heartbeat, and then the end of the hall lit as if a sun had been born within the room. She shielded her eyes with shackled hands, the light too painful to look upon.

A sandy-haired man stepped forward, peering into the glow. He turned around and raised an arm high in the air.

Guards loyal to Thayl stood dumbstruck by the violent amputation and explosion of magic. Those not loyal to Thayl were ready, waiting on the opportunity they had been promised. At the signal, they stepped forward and unlocked shackles down the line of wizards.

Eloryn's breath shook and she tried to comprehend what happened. This wasn't her plan, but the result was the same. *She did it. She really did it.* Thayl's rune-scarred hand was cut off, the source, the vessel of his power removed, leaving him powerless, a normal man and returning what he stole to Memory. *But we were supposed to be there with you Mem, helping you.*

The fluttering moment of peace broke. Cries of outrage marked the beginning of the battle when the actions of the resistance were seen and comprehended. Warring bodies scattered the hall and the eerie light show faded.

"Roen, please hurry," Eloryn whispered. The guards behind their back, apparently none on their side, were blinking out of their stupor. Roen forced a click from his shackles with a small strip of copper.

He left them hanging from his wrists and worked at Eloryn's. The fastest guard charged at his turned back. Will struck the man with his shackled hands, knocking him away in a spinning tumble.

Will growled. The guards hesitated, regrouped, drew weapons.

Roen pushed Eloryn's shackles off her wrists in revulsion. He caught her eye for a moment then turned to Will. Her heart felt as

though it would tear out to follow him.

Another guard came running at them. Eloryn breathed out words in a flurry, speaking to the wood of the floorboards under the carpet. They rotted and splintered. The guard fell knee deep into the hole she made, sprawling under Roen's feet. Roen brought a boot down hard onto the base of the guard's neck. His attention turned away from Will's manacles, he couldn't turn back, as two more men charged, four coming behind.

"You need to get out of here. I can't hold back so many." Roen shook off his unlocked bonds and took a sword from the man on the floor.

"You can. I'll help." She knew there would be fighting, one way or another, and this was part of her plan that she could still do. Eloryn spoke more words of magic. Roen guided her behind him, backing her up against the nearest wall, parrying away blows from the men who followed.

"By the fae," Roen wheezed when her behest took effect. His next strike ripped the sword from his opponent's hand with enough force to lodge it into the wall where it flew.

Will smiled, teeth bared like a predator. Her words reached his body too, taking his strengths, making them stronger. He leapt across at the next wave of guards, pulling the first of them into a spinning tackle that tumbled the rest of the row.

The Wizards' Council stood between Eloryn and the chaos of fighting. Unprepared, they used simple magic, anything they had that didn't require being read. Roen and Will fought back those who made it through to threaten Eloryn. She kept a steady stream of words flowing, renewing the energy they spent.

A cacophony of painful cries, clashing weapons and rumbling magic filled the ornate hall, a hall made for dances of a less violent nature. Bodies fell, but the resistance won ground.

"This might actually work. I thought she... I can't believe Memory did that," Roen yelled over his shoulder, the confidence from the power Eloryn gave him clear in his voice. "Just up to the Council and resistance to get everything under control now."

Eloryn took a breath and a moment away from her words of behest. "Can you see her? Is she coming back to us?" The scarring white light that erupted from Thayl's severed wrist had gone, but the roaring battle now obscured that end of the hall.

"Can't see yet." Roen frowned, starting to lose the ease with which he kept more than one man at bay.

Eloryn raced her magic words back out again, keeping him strong. Will broke away from their side. Eloryn's eyes locked onto his back. He forced through a new surge of guards, cracking his still shackled hands against attacking swords.

"Will, come back!" Eloryn yelled between behests. He kept going, moving out of her reach of influence.

He pushed a man down, climbing him like a ladder. Stepping across other men's shoulders, he raced for the other end of the hall, clearing half the room before falling into the crowd again.

Eloryn followed his path with her eyes. Through a gap in the blurred motion of battle she saw a heart-shattering tableau.

Thayl still lived, still stood, wounded but awake. Memory lay beneath him, unmoving, collapsed on the dais.

Thayl tore a silk banner from the wall, pulling it with one hand and wrapping it around the bleeding stump where the other had been. Feral anger showed in every movement, in the twist of his face. He spoke words Eloryn couldn't hear and spat on Memory. Keeping hard eyes on her, he bent and picked up the sword still wet with his own blood.

Eloryn's pulse beat so fast it burned. *There's no one there to help her.* A line of guards held others back from the dais, protecting Thayl as the Wizard Council protected her. The resistance focused on blocking new waves of castle troops that headed toward the clearest enemies in the room – the Council, Roen, the defensive line around Eloryn. Everyone, everyone fought for her and no one fought for Memory.

Thayl examined the sword coldly. He stepped with menacing purpose over Memory's slumped body.

Eloryn's magic words faltered. She saw Will in the crowd, the only one fighting against the tide. He tore bodies out of his way, pushing through toward Memory. None of Eloryn's magic reached him any more. He fought with desperate strength as though it still did. Outnumbered, unarmed, already bleeding, the guards overwhelmed him, bringing him down.

Eloryn watched Roen fighting for her for a heartbreaking moment. *I'm sorry.* She changed the meaning of the ancient words she spoke.

Roen pushed a pair of disarmed men, knocking them back with the last burst of strength she gave him. In the second of time that bought him, he turned to Eloryn. The confusion and concern on his face wrenched her insides. *He knows I've abandoned him.*

Eloryn's knees folded, life seeping out of her. The sound of the battle dimmed.

Through clouded eyes she watched the two thrown down guards get back to their feet, pulling at Roen. He shook them off. He called out to her but she couldn't hear. Feather slow she drifted to the floor, sight flickering out like a finished wick. Four, five more men latched onto Roen and he thrashed to reach her. They forced him down onto his knees, stomach, pushing his face onto the floor, pinning down each limb. His fingertips outstretched in front of her face were the last thing she saw as her eyes closed.

CHAPTER TWENTY-EIGHT

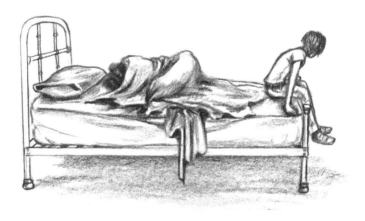

Eloryn found herself in a strange and horrifying world. She tried not to regret her decision as she blinked wide eyes and calmed her breathing.

This was not like a normal healing. Even for being out of her body she didn't expect this. She'd been channeled right into Memory's dreaming consciousness. *Like calls to like.*

A hard grey ground lay beneath her. Machines of grey metal lined the streets and grey buildings towered nightmarishly high up into a grey sky. Even the air tasted grey. A world full of metal and dust, all grey, everything grey.

It pounded like a ravaged heartbeat. The whole world pulsed, crumbled, being torn down and built up again with each beat, shaking

and shifting. Eloryn put a hand to her mouth and fought the urge to be sick. She reminded herself she wasn't even in her physical body.

Images all around twisted and tore like burning paintings, blending the nightmare into a mess of malformed scenes. Streets led out in every direction further than she could see.

She screamed out for Memory.

The movement of people down one street caught Eloryn's eye. She broke into a run toward them. The street became an open park, appearing under her feet and before her eyes. Strange contraptions jutted from the ground that a group of children swung and stood on.

"Memory." Eloryn breathed out in relief.

The dark haired girl didn't react. She had Memory's face, but younger, a different hair cut, half black, half blue. She mouthed off at an older boy backed by a group of his friends. He called her something that almost made Eloryn faint to hear.

Memory broke his nose with her first punch. Then she kept hitting.

They vanished before Eloryn could blink or move.

She spun, disorientated, finding herself alone on the street again. She jogged back for the crossroads, calling out Memory's name every second step. Desperation burned in her.

Her next step brought her into a dark hallway.

A looming shadow stood in front of her. The wide-set man leant on a mop and grinned in a way that twisted Eloryn's insides. He stared right at her and she lost a shaking breath before a sound behind her spun her around. Memory, now with blood red hair, backed into the shadows against the wall and ran away.

Eloryn ran after her. She caught up with her in a new hallway lit with a strange crisp brightness. A different Memory, different age, different hair color. She stood by a door left slightly ajar, sneering and picking her nails. Words floated out from three adults within.

"I'm sorry. We thought we could handle it. But she's..." said a woman on one side of a desk.

"She's too much for us to deal with. She's just too old, too troubled," the man next to her said, holding her hand. An older man across the desk nodded and smiled as if he heard nothing new.

Eloryn reached for Memory. "Mem, please, can you hear me?"

A flash of a storeroom filled with brooms, mops and colored containers jumped in front of Eloryn, snagging the breath in her throat. A large silhouette approached her, making soothing noises.

Then Eloryn was alone in darkness. No, not alone. There was a bed next to her with someone in it. Body curled as tight as any could be. Suppressed whispers of sobbing came from the youngest Memory Eloryn had seen yet. Tiny and blonde, she looked just like Eloryn had when she was ten, except for the hair being cut short around her ears. The scene shifted before her eyes, but remained the same. Only Memory's age, Memory's hair changed. Then again, older still. A small boy with dark hair sat awkward and silent at the end of the bed. He reached a hand out toward the huddled, weeping Memory, but pulled it back without touching her. Staring at his hand, he clenched it into a small fist.

Eloryn pressed both hands against her chest. She struggled a slow breath from the stabbing quick gasps that were overtaking her. The first time she'd tried to heal Memory, she couldn't get in at all, blocked by a barrier of distrust and fear. Now she understood why. These visions made no sense, but sheer grief overflowed from them. *Is this the suffering that made her what she is? We were born just moments apart. If I had been first instead...*

Eloryn's heart beat an erratic shiver through her body. She backed up against a wall, the next fragment of vision taking her completely off guard.

Memory, the Mem she knew. Sixteen years old, black and pink hair, wearing the very same clothes she first appeared to Eloryn in. Her open knife dropped on the floor. The wide-set man yelled and scowled and beat her and beat her and beat her until the world exploded around them.

Eloryn was back on the street.

She rolled forward and heaved terrified sobs. *This is no good. These aren't Memory, they're just visions of her past.* Caught up in these nightmares she wasn't going to reach Memory in time.

Again, a black and pink haired Memory appeared, running down the street with a wild look of glee on her face. Her pockets were filled and heavy. Eloryn didn't chase this time, but young Will did, struggling to keep up. A man came out of the doorway they'd run through, bellowing at them as the stallholder had in the markets where they met Roen.

She followed them with her gaze and saw a flash of strange blackness in an alleyway they passed.

Reaching for hope, she ran into the alley. She saw another Memory, backed into a corner, huddled into herself. Memory in a dress, hair flickering between blonde and black. Eyes achingly wide but lacking awareness. Shivering but not moving.

Eloryn raced to her. The world shook with another heaving beat, building and falling. A void of blackness pushed outwards from Memory. A nothingness, forcing the world away, forcing the visions away, forcing Eloryn away.

"Mem, please," Eloryn cried. "Please hear me, let me help you. You have to wake up. You have to get up or you'll die."

Memory remained unmoved, uncaring.

Eloryn had come looking for something she could heal, some wound she could fix, to wake Memory up and save her; leaving her body behind since she wasn't able to reach her any other way. But there was nothing here she could repair. No wound, no physical blow had caused this.

Eloryn reached for her. The expanding darkness struck her back. Flung against the opposite wall, she slumped into piles of grey refuse. "Mem, I can't lose you too. I don't know what to do. I knew by coming here I couldn't leave again without your help. But I wouldn't leave you anyway, even if I could. Not to this. Not alone."

Memory's mouth opened a crack. Her bottom lip quivered. Eloryn tumbled on top of her and held her, no longer pushed away.

Squeaking, hysterical whispers flowed from Memory's mouth. "It's too much, too much, all at once, everything, it's too much, I can't, everything, I can't."

The memories. A lifetime of memories, all at once. Eloryn cursed herself that she hadn't realized, in all her theories and planning, what that would mean. But how could she have known the nightmare these memories held?

Squeezing Memory in her arms, she tore over options and outcomes, racing through them. She could not slow the intake of these memories, or help Memory accept them in some other way. Neither would be fast enough to save her body as well. Maybe she could force them all away again, but if she did, they might be lost forever.

"I'm so sorry. I promised you I would get your memories back, but more than that I want you to live," Eloryn said. Her tears dripped into her sister's hair.

Memory looked up at her with a shaking mouth. "I don't want to, I can't like this..."

Eloryn hesitated, even while knowing any moment could be their last, unsure how time flowed here or what happened outside. "I'll make it stop. But then you have to wake up, you have to wake up now!"

Something dripped on her face and she tasted the metal of blood. Memory's chest burned, inside and out, the knife she kept stashed there heated to scalding. Deafening sounds of battle smacked into her, thrumming through the floor she lay on and ringing in her ears. Memory's eyes snapped open. Her gaze raced up the wet sword pointed at her chest to an arm that lifted and tensed and a darkly handsome face torn with a gruesome snarl.

She rolled across the floor and the sword stabbed down into the carpet. Thayl roared.

Throwing her legs off the edge of the dais, she stood from a crouch in time to duck again when Thayl swung the sword at her, screaming violently. She stumbled away from him.

"You lost it all. It was better left with me!"

Memory raced to fill confusing blanks in her mind propped between raging panic and anger. She'd cut off Thayl's hand, then only blind pain filled the next gap. *Did I faint? Likely. I did just sever someone's limb.* Blood drained from her so quickly she almost fainted again. *Oh my God I severed someone's limb.* Memory gritted her teeth. She did what she had to do, to stop Thayl, to get her memories and soul back. So where were they?

Something else was happening that she didn't understand. Her mouth spoke of its own accord, a language she didn't even know. She could feel a familiar presence inside her, another consciousness she'd tasted before. *Eloryn. My sister. How?*

"Soulless demon!" Thayl hissed at her. One of his arms ended in

a bound and dripping stump, the other with the sword lunging into attack again. Memory did not step back.

His sword stabbed left and she shifted right, moving smoother and faster than she knew she could. Magic from Eloryn's words, spoken with her own mouth, flowed through her and made her stronger. She took Thayl by his sword hand with one of her own. Twisting the wrist, bones crunched under her fingers. The sword dropped. She forced her other palm up under his chin with teeth shattering strength. Thayl slammed onto his back.

She snarled and picked up the sword.

"Guards, guards to me!" Thayl screamed.

A dozen of his closest men scrambled toward their King. Memory's hand shifted, her mouth still moving rapidly. A solid rush of wind blew the soldiers back into the wreck of battle.

Memory choked on the words. Her own blank hole of pain was being filled, flooded. Eloryn's grief and rage poured in, overwhelming her. Her hand around the sword twitched and lifted mechanically. She stared at it open mouthed, not having willed the action herself. She could feel her face turn feral, fighting with her own emotions and Eloryn's.

"Lory, please stop."

He deserves this. The words screamed inside her, but weren't her own.

She shrieked so madly Thayl froze where he'd fallen, staring at her as though he saw a real demon.

The bronze sword swiped across as if drawn to a magnet within Thayl's neck. The tip pressed into the soft flesh. Thayl gagged, waiting with wild, terrified eyes.

You're not a murderer Lory, not you.

Her body shuddered, battling against a will not hers. She screamed aloud, "ELORYN!"

The sword fell from her hands.

Memory and Thayl stared at each other for a long moment. Thayl brought his bandaged stump up against his chest, grasping it with his hand.

Memory grimaced then forced her face still, staring down at him. "Game over."

His eyes flickered across to the sword that lay on the ground beside him.

"Don't think I can't take you out with this if I need to," Memory hissed, pulling her hand into a fist in front of him. She kicked the sword out of his reach.

Memory turned to the brawling chaos of the hall. Seeing their King lying prone on the dais, more castle guards rushed at her.

"Stop!" she bellowed, in a voice loud enough to crack plaster scrolling from the walls.

Throughout the hall, fighters stumbled in shock. Some turned from their battles and were taken advantage of by those not distracted by the loud interruption.

"I said stop. Now. Everyone!" Words continued to flow from her, from Eloryn, feeding on the fire within her. She crumbled every blade, every piece of armor and metal held by men in the room.

The fighting stopped.

Men stumbled out of motion, confused. Despite wary glances to others around them, all attention turned her way. The small girl, standing over the defeated king, looked out at the sea of blood-spattered faces. She didn't know which side was which. She didn't think half of them knew either.

What now, Lory?

You know.

Memory pulled herself up straight and called out into the hall. "Thayl is finished. The Maellan heir is back. If you're not happy with that you better get the hell out of here now."

A brief moment of stillness passed then a third of the men in the hall turned and fled. They pushed away through the shell shocked crowd, running in blind panic. No one tried to stop them.

The remaining men turned to her with the look of awaiting their next order. A dozen or so pushed to the front, approaching her. She tensed, but they stopped below the dais and made the hand symbol she had seen Eloryn make. The resistance.

All eyes on her, Memory stuttered under the pressure. She pointed to Thayl. "Someone, come tie him up already."

A wiry man with sweat soaked sandy hair came forward, scooping a dropped pair of manacles from the ground on his way. He gave her a short bow. "If you serve the Maellan heir, then I serve you. I am Peirs. I'm what you might call the leader of this mob, if they've ever been enough to lead."

She nodded to the older man, swaying from the after-burn of adrenaline. "Thanks, for helping."

Peirs shackled Thayl's feet, shaking his head with an incredulous smile. "Thanks are all to you. A child who defeated this monster that no man could, and did it..." Peirs paused and his grin widened. "Single handed."

One of Piers' men threw him a tasseled rope from a nearby curtain. He tied it about Thayl's arms. Thayl sat slumped and silent, eyes turned so far down they were almost closed. His body quaked with visible tension. No longer a monster. Just a man now.

"It wasn't just me." Memory looked out into the unfamiliar crowd and stepped off the dais.

Peirs began calling out orders and all guards within the room

looked to him. Faces all around, but no one she knew. The room was thick with people but they cleared a path for her, letting her through.

Through the murmurings and movement she heard Roen's voice, pleading. She picked up her pace. A crowd of wizards huddled in the back corner of the hall. She ran up to them but they didn't move for her as the rest of the room did.

She clawed through between them, pushing through despite their shocked exclamations.

In their midst, Roen knelt over the top of Eloryn. He bent down with his forehead on hers, hands on her shoulders, lifting and shaking her. "El, please," he whispered, his voice strangled.

Hayes knelt beside him, holding Eloryn's wrist, feeling for a pulse. He tried to move Roen out of the way and Roen pushed him back with a grunt, slamming the older man against the wall. He turned back to Eloryn, pulling her up into his arms.

"Stop this madness and let me see to her!" Hayes spat.

Memory knelt next to Roen and caught his eye. She put her hand on his, uncurled his fingers from a tight fist, and gave him a timid smile. His head tilted and he stared, all grief and confusion. He blinked, taking in who she was, and moved away from Eloryn without hesitation.

Hayes tried to take his place and Roen forced him back with his whole body. "Not you."

Eloryn was deathly white. Memory smiled wryly. "I hope you know what you're doing, sleeping beauty."

She lowered herself down. Her blonde hair draped into her sister's and she kissed her on the forehead.

A breathless moment stretched until Memory's chest ached. Eloryn's body gave a terrifying shudder. Green eyes opened. Eloryn blinked and her natural pink returned to her cheeks.

"There she is, back where she should be," Memory said.

"I knew you could do it," Eloryn propped herself onto her elbows. Her head hung weakly but she smiled.

"Smart ass," Memory muttered. She shifted back off her knees and helped Eloryn up. "We did it."

Memory heard a shaking breath pour out of Roen. She smiled at him with a pouting bottom lip. He stared back blankly.

Released by Roen, Hayes dusted his black and purple suit down emphatically and turned his attention to Eloryn.

"Waylan, Bors, Madoc, see to guarding Thayl. The rest of you help Peirs getting this rabble under control," Hayes said, taking Eloryn's hands out of Memory's as though she needed further support.

Eloryn straightened up, nodding to someone across the hall. Memory followed her gaze and saw Yvainne tipping her head in return. Her form already grew transparent. Her eyes turned to Memory in a cold glare like a warning before she disappeared.

The grey flock broke apart, each taking a moment to bow to Eloryn before moving away.

Throughout the room, order became visible again. Men grouped into rows. Some rows moved across the floor, where bodies blended red with the carpet, aiding and clearing as they went.

Memory felt a dull weight form in her as she stared at the bodies. *Did I do right? Would more have died if the fighting began while Thayl still had magic?* A deep exhaustion filled her, every muscle spent and aching. She swallowed away the feeling and searched her gaze over every corner of the room.

"Where's Will?"

Roen's face had locked back into a frown. He lifted a hand to her face, and wiped his thumb gently beside her mouth, fingers lingering on her cheek. When he pulled it away it was red with blood. He spoke quietly. "Lost him for most of the fight, but when everything stopped I saw him drag himself out through a window."

"He didn't stay? Was he OK?" Memory asked in a squeak. Her own hand came up and cupped her cheek involuntarily. It didn't hurt. The blood wasn't hers.

"Injured, but didn't seem too badly. He's a strong one. Shackles gone with the rest of the metal." Roen's lips twisted to the side, not really a smile. "I don't think he likes to be seen by so many people."

Memory nodded unenthusiastically.

Hayes still held Eloryn by a hand, and put another in the middle of her back, leading her away. "It's a miracle you survived, your Highness. Such a reckless plan from that girl. But we finally have success against the tyrant Thayl. Now we can work together on ensuring our future and that of the kingdom."

Eloryn pulled away from him. "Wizard Councilor Hayes, I'm sorry I have left you uninformed, but that girl is my twin sister. Maellan heir as much as I."

Memory smiled at him when he turned to her in shock. She considered poking out her tongue, but decided against it.

"Her appearance; I thought it some magic ploy, a part of her plan. Her interaction with Thayl... Don't play tricks. Tell me how it can be so?"

Eloryn sighed, looking to Memory and Roen as she talked. "Hayes, we thank you for the help you've given us, and have trust in you for the help you'll continue to provide. I know this is only the beginning for what must be done for Avall, but please understand, we've been through more than you can imagine. Indulge us our whims a little longer. There will be time for it all later."

Hayes glowered for a moment, then bowed his head. "And what is it time for now, Your Highness?"

"Highnesses," Eloryn corrected.

"Highnesses."

"Mem, what is it time for now?"

Memory looked across the room to a wide arch window. Warm rays of morning light spilled in, bringing a contentment too overpowering to fight. She smiled at Eloryn. "It's time for bed."

Peirs gave priority to assigning the best of his men to the care of the twins. Ten men led Memory, Eloryn and Roen through the castle to their requested destination.

They walked silently down long corridors lined with suits of armor and tall stained glass windows. Memory gawked openly. She wished she had a camera then reminded herself this was her home now. *Home.* Servants gossiped together at a distance and stared at the passing escort. Some bowed and kneeled. No one gave them any trouble.

They reached wide double doors at the end of a corridor that had been chained closed. The largest guard dispatched the padlock with a sharp blow from the hilt of his sword. This part of the castle had been closed off, but they continued through the uncared for hallways over tattered carpets, up stairs with creaking, dusty banisters.

They stopped at a doorway carved with roses and painted ivory white. Memory ran her hand over the designs, feeling them smooth and glossy under her fingers. The paint here was not cracked or chipped. It smelled fresh. She put her hand around the cold brass handle and turned, clicking the latch.

The guards took up position, flanking either side of the door.

Memory motioned to Eloryn, who stepped through into Loredanna's chambers.

Memory followed her in. No dust settled on the fine pale furniture and silken upholstery. Nothing was torn or blemished. Jewelry and hairbrushes were laid out on the dresser as though their mother had used the room yesterday. It didn't have the appearance of a room recently cleaned, but one that had always been well looked after.

Above a chaise lounge hung a life size portrait of Loredanna in a thick, ornate frame. It showed her not much older than her daughters, dressed for coronation in all finery, including the Maellan crested medallion.

The room smelt of soap and roses, and Memory brushed her hand over the petals of a fresh cut bunch beside the bed.

Memory thought back to how Thayl had held her when she walked into his dream rose-garden, when he thought she was her mother. Although the thought still made her skin crawl she suddenly wished she had reacted in some other, unknown way.

She coughed lightly. "At least it's clean in here."

Eloryn stood in the doorway, staring in only. She nodded, eyebrows pinched as she shared looks with her twin. Roen hadn't crossed the threshold.

Memory drifted back to them.

Roen shifted on his feet. He hadn't said a thing since telling her about Will, and he seemed to be having trouble again now. He leant in closer to them, whispering low, "I worry for trusting your safety to these strangers."

Memory giggled at him, tilting her head. "What would you worry for? We're safe now, we did it. The three of us are unbeatable, and everyone knows it." She raised her voice cheekily at the end.

Roen's mood didn't crack. "I won't be staying."

Memory's head snapped back up straight, and she furrowed her eyebrows deeply as though doing so would let her read his mind.

Eloryn stammered, "But, you said you wouldn't…"

"You're safe now. I'm going back to my parents, back to-" He faltered, and cleared his throat. "Maerranton. I don't belong here."

Roen turned his head down and to the side, caramel hair falling down over his eyes.

Memory opened her mouth in outrage, but Eloryn spoke first. "Of course you have a place here, you and your parents. Their titles will be reinstated. They will be returned to court with the highest honors for all of what they gave." She shook her head at him. "Even if you weren't already a Prince, you'd have earned the title."

Roen's shoulders shuddered, and a tear rolled off his cheek and splashed onto the floor.

Quicker than thought, Memory lashed her arms around him in a crushing bear hug. He put his head down into her shoulder, soaking it silently, and squeezed her back with bruising strength.

Eloryn breathed raggedly next to them. Memory pried an arm off Roen and reached for her. One of Roen's arms loosed too, shaking, reaching out. Eloryn stepped into them and the three wrapped around each other tightly.

They held him until he stilled. And then a little longer.

He pulled away from them, hands lingering in theirs, his eyes red but dry.

"I will go. I want to see my parents returned safely. But I will come back." A small smile softened his face. "Memory. Eloryn." The smile continued to grow. He bowed deeply to both of them then departed.

Memory closed the door behind him. With mirrored movement she and Eloryn pulled back covers on each side of the bed and tucked themselves in. They lay face to face, holding hands between them like children in a fairytale.

Eloryn closed her eyes. "I'm so sorry you didn't get your memories back. They might be lost forever, but I won't stop trying to get them back for you, if you want."

Memory watched her sister's frowning face. "I'm not so worried. I found out my name, where I was, and know who I am. Found all the family and friends I dreamed of. Hell, I even got myself a castle. I'll make a new home, new memories."

Whatever else might still be wrong with me, wherever the lost parts of my broken soul are, for now at least I'm alive, can live, here with my family. She stared over Eloryn's shoulder, where daylight brightened the diamond cut glass window of the balcony doors. Outside a thorny vine grew around the balustrade. The silhouette of a wild young man perched on it in front of the sun. She smiled. "Besides, things never just disappear. They have to go somewhere, right?"

Eloryn's eyes fluttered back open again. She looked both shocked and accusing. "You found out your name? When? What is it? What am I to call you now?"

Memory smiled and closed her eyes. "Memory. Just call me Memory."

ACKNOWLEDGEMENTS

I found an email from 2003 where a fan asked me why I removed all mention of "Memory's Wake" from my website. I replied it was because I didn't think it would ever be finished.

It lay untouched for a long time, poked at here and there, changed through many versions, and was finally completed in 2011. I have a lot of people to thank for helping it get there.

From the very beginning, I'd like to thank my obssession with comics and desire to create my own, for which the first ideas for this story started to form. I have to thank John Noble, who is dearly missed, for introducing me to the magic of fantasy role-playing games (Dungeons and Dragons V.2 to be specific). The adventure, the danger, and the most magical part of role-playing - the story telling.

I want to thank Steven Withrow, who helped my earliest concept form into something more substantial. He also gave Memory her name, and is still a master artist with words.

Dear thanks to my editor Sally Odgers, who provided encouragement along with the technical refinement I needed.

My thanks go to all my friends from the old forums of www.australianfantasyart.com who read through my first, short version of Memory's Wake, and cheered me on despite how rubbish it was. And more recently, to my friends at sff.onlinewritingworkshop.com who read and critiqued my current version, teaching me how to write again. Specifically, Erica Lovell, Lydia Kurnia, Dy Loveday, Phillip Spencer and Ladonna Watkins. I hope to see all of your books in print soon!

My family were always there for me, and in particular my husband, David, who I'm sure I almost drove insane grilling him over every tiny plot point in my story over many versions.

And last, but not least, to all the fans of my artwork, who believed in me when I took the jump from visual art to writing, and encouraged me every step of the way. I wouldn't have done it without you.

ABOUT THE AUTHOR

It's an undeniable truth that Selina Fenech has been lost to fairytales since she first laid hands on books. Even before she could read, the magic shown in the illustrations within those pages had her bewitched. When she could read, she fell into the worlds created by authors, never wanting to re-emerge, wanting them to be real.

Faced with overwhelming heartache that our own world wasn't so full of magic and adventure, Selina did the only thing she could. She began creating her own worlds of magic with her art and her words.

One of the saddest things to happen in her otherwise happy childhood was when other children taught her that books weren't cool. For almost a decade Selina turned away from books and writing and submerged herself in her visual art. During this time she became a successful fantasy illustrator, supporting herself with sales of her art that now have a worldwide following.

But the love of books remained, and once again was embraced. Because they are cool, by the way. Books are very, very cool.

Memory's Wake is Selina's first novel.

Selina lives in Australia with her husband, an unnamed cat, and a lorikeet who's far too clever.

Find out more about Selina at her official website-
www.selinafenech.com

Made in the USA
Coppell, TX
24 April 2020